"BEWARE, BEWARE"

Like a yo-yo from some branch high above him, a red-banded spider the size of a man's fist descended. "Beware, beware," the tiny voice issued from dripping mandibles. Mr. Slippery looked carefully at the spider's banded abdomen. There were many species of deathspider here, and each required a different response if a traveler was to survive. Finally he raised the back of his hand and held it level so that the spider could crawl onto it. The creature raced up the damp fabric of his jacket to the open neck. There it whispered something very quietly.

Mr. Slippery listened, then grabbed the animal before it could repeat the message and threw it to the left, at the same time racing at top speed up the incline that suddenly appeared before him.

He stopped when he reached the crest of the hill. Beyond it, he could see the solemn, massive fortress that was the Coven's haven. The trail leading down to it was much more open than the swamp had been, but the traveler proceeded as slowly as before: the sprites the warlocks set to keep eternal guard here had the nasty—though preprogrammed—habit of changing the rules in new and deadly ways.

To my sister,
Patricia Vinge,
With Love.

VERNOR VINGE
TRUE NAMES
...and Other Dangers

BAEN BOOKS

TRUE NAMES AND OTHER DANGERS

This is a work of fiction. All the characters and events portrayed in this book are fictional, and any resemblance to real people or incidents is purely coincidental.

Copyright © 1987 by Vernor Vinge

All rights reserved, including the right to reproduce this book or portions thereof in any form.

A Baen Books Original

Baen Publishing Enterprises
260 Fifth Avenue
New York, N.Y. 10001

ACKNOWLEDGMENTS: The following stories have appeared previously and are copyright as follows: "Bookworm, Run!" *Analog Science Fiction/Science Fact* March 1966, © 1966 by Vernor Vinge; "True Names," *Dell Binary Star #5*, © 1981 by Vernor Vinge; "The Peddler's Apprentice," *Analog Science Fiction/ Science Fact*, August 1975; © 1975 by Joan D. Vinge and Vernor Vinge; "The Ungoverned," *Far Frontiers*, Fall 1985, © 1985 by Vernor Vinge; "Long Shot," *Analog Science Fiction/Science Fact*, August 1972, © 1972 by Vernor Vinge.

First printing, November 1987

ISBN: 0-671-65363-6

Cover art by Gary Ruddell

Printed in the United States of America

Distributed by
SIMON & SCHUSTER
1230 Avenue of the Americas
New York, N.Y. 10020

CONTENTS

Introductions by Vernor Vinge.

This is about a little boy who grew up in the 1950s. The little boy could talk and write much better than he could think, but he did have a good imagination, and he read everything he could by people much smarter than he. As a result, he saw rather early where things were going, and spent the next thirty years writing about that vision.

I was that little boy, and this story collection revolves around that central vision, and its possible consequences.

I had always wanted to know the future of science, to participate in revolutions to come, and science fiction showed the most optimistic (and the most pessimistic) of futures. Yet, the closer I looked, the more unreadable things became. I wanted interstellar empires (interplanetary ones at the least). I wanted supercomputers and artificial intelligence and effective immortality. All seemed possible, yet there were inescapable consequences of unbridled optimism. Our technological success is ultimately based on human intelligence. If we can use technology to increase (or create) intelligence, then we have made a fundamental change in the rules of the game, as important as our original rise to sentience.

The first story I ever wrote (that sold) was a look at the beginning of this process. Instead of Artificial Intelligence (AI), I wanted Intelligence Amplification (IA). The means seemed at hand: after all (I thought) what is memory but retrieval of information? Why couldn't human reason be augmented by hardware? (Perhaps it's fortunate that at the time I had no technical knowledge of computers. I might have been discouraged, ended up writing really hardcore science-

1

fiction . . . about punch cards and batch processing.)

It was 1963. I was a sophomore at Michigan State, and was planning to write about the first man to have a direct mind-to-computer link. I even thought I might be the first person ever to write of such a thing. (In that, of course, I was wrong—but the theme was rare compared to nowadays.) I worked very hard on the story, applying everything I knew about sf writing. I put together a social background that I thought would make things interesting even where the story sagged: cheap fusion/electricity converters had been invented (that worked at room temperature!), trashing the big power utilities and causing a short-term depression. (In a sense, this was a sequel to Randall Garrett's story, "Damned If You Don't." I admired that story very much; economic depressions were faraway, alien beasts to me.) And of course, there would be experiments with chimpanzees before the IQ amplifier was tried on my human hero.

Having thought things out, I described the plot to my little sister. She suffered through my endless recounting, then remarked, "Except for the part about the chimpanzee, it sounds pretty dull." What a comedown. Still . . . she had a point. The chimpanzee story had an obvious ending. After it made me famous, I could write the important story, the one with the human hero.

John W. Campbell liked the chimpanzee part, too. (And unlike my sister, he got a kick out of the Randall Garrett references.) Eventually, he bought the story for Analog.

So. It's 1984 (as seen by a teenager from the early 60's), and we have a hero with a very serious problem:

2

BOOKWORM, RUN!

They knew what he'd done.

Norman Simmons cringed, his calloused black fingers grasped "Tarzan of the Apes" so tightly that several pages ripped. Seeing what he had done, Norman shut the book and placed it gently on his desk. Then, almost shaking with fear, he tried to roll himself into a ball small enough to escape detection. Gradually he relaxed, panting; Kimball Kinnison would never refuse to face danger. There must be a way out. He knew several routes to the surface. If no one saw him . . .

They'd be hunting for him; and when they caught him, he would die.

He was suddenly anxious to leave the prefab green aluminum walls of his room and school—but what should he take? He pulled the sheet off his bed and spread it on the floor. Norman laid five or six of his favorite books on the sheet, scuttled across the room to his closet, pulled out an extra pair of red and orange Bermuda shorts, and tossed them on top of the books. He paused, then added a blanket, his

3

portable typewriter, his notebook, and a pencil. Now he was equipped for any contingency.

Norman wrapped the sheet tightly about his belongings and dragged the makeshift sack to the door. He opened the door a crack, and peeked out. The passageway was empty. He cautiously opened the door wide and stepped down onto the bedrock floor of the tunnel. Then he dragged the sheet and its contents over the doorsill. The bag dropped the ten inches which separated the aluminum floor of his room from the tunnel. The typewriter landed with a muffled clank. Norman glanced anxiously around the corner of the room, up the tunnel. The lights were off in the Little School. It was Saturday and his teachers' day off. The Lab was closed, too, which was unforeseen good luck, since the aloof Dr. Dunbar was usually there at this time.

He warily circled about a nearby transport vehicle. *Model D-49 Ford Cargo Carrier, Army Transport Mark XIXe. Development Contract D-49f1086-1979. First deliveries, January, 1982 . . . RESTRICTED Unauthorized use of RESTRICTED materials is punishable by up to 10 years imprisonment, $10,000 fine, or both: Maintenance Manual: Chapter I, Description . . . The Mark XIXe is a medium speed transport designed to carry loads of less than fifteen tons through constricted areas, such as mine tunnels or storage depots. The "e" modification of the Mark XIX indicates the substitution of a 500-hp Bender fusion power source for the Wankel engine originally intended for use with the XIX. As the Bender pack needs only the natural water vapor in the air for fuel, it is an immense improvement over any other power source. This economy combined with the tape programmed auto-pilot, make the XIXe one of . . .* Norman shook his head, trying to cut off the endless flow of irrelevant information that came to mind.

With practice, he was sure that he would eventually be able to pick out just the data he needed to solve problems, but in the meantime the situation was often very confusing.

The passage he was looking for was between the 345th and 346th fluorescent tube—counting from his room; it was on the left side of the tunnel. Norman began running, at the same time pulling the sack behind him. This was an awkward position for him and he was soon forced to a walk. He concentrated on counting the lighting tubes that were hung from the roof of the tunnel. Each fluorescent cast harsh white light upon the walls of the tunnel, but between the tubes slight shadows lingered. The walls of the passage were streaky with whorls almost like wood or marble, but much darker and grayish-green. As he walked a slight draft of fresh air from faraway air regenerators ruffled the hair on his back.

Norman finally turned to face the left wall of the passage and stopped—343-344-345. The liquid streaks of pyrobole and feldspar appeared the same here as in any other section of the tunnel. Taking another step, Norman stood at the darkest point between the two lights. He carefully counted five hand-widths from the point where the wall blended into the floor. At this spot he cupped his hands and shouted into the wall: "Why does the goodwife like Dutch Elm disease for tea?"

The wall replied: "I don't know. I just work here."

Norman searched his memory, looking for one piece of information among the billions. "Well, find out before her husband does."

There was no reply. Instead, a massive section of bedrock swung noiselessly out of the wall, revealing another tunnel at right-angles to Norman's.

He hurried into it, then paused and glanced back.

The huge door had already shut. As he continued up the new tunnel, Norman was careful to count the lights. When he came to number 48, he again selected a place on the wall and shouted some opening commands. The new tunnel was slanted steeply upward as were the next three passages which Norman switched to. At last he reached the spot in the sixth tunnel which contained the opening to the surface. He paused, feeling both relief and fear: Relief because there weren't any secret codes and distances to remember after this; fear because he didn't know what or who might be waiting for him on the other side of this last door. What if they were just hiding there to shoot him?

Norman took a deep breath and shouted: "There are only 3,456,628 more shopping days till Christmas."

"So?" came the muffled reply.

Norman thought: *NSA (National Security Agency) cryptographic (code) analysis organization. Report Number 36390.201. MOST SECRET. (Unauthorized use of MOST SECRET materials is punishable by death.): "Mathematical Analysis of Voice and Electronic Pass Codes," by Melvin M. Rosseter, RAND contract 748970-1975. Paragraph 1: Consider L, an m by n matrix (rectangular array—arrangement) of (n times m) elements (items) formed by the Vrevik product . . .* Norman screamed shrilly. In his haste, he had accepted the wrong memories. The torrent of information, cross-references and explanatory notes, was almost as overwhelming as his experience the time he foolishly decided to learn all about plasma physics.

With an effort he choked off the memories. But now he was getting desperate. He had to come up with the pass code, and fast.

Finally, "So avoid the mash. Shop December 263."

* * *

A large section of the ceiling swung down into the tunnel. Through the opening, Norman could see the sky. But it was gray, not blue like the other time! Norman had not realized that a cloudy day could be so dreary. A cold, humid mist oozed into the tunnel from the opening. He shuddered, but scrambled up the inclined plane which the lowered ceiling section formed. The massive trapdoor shut behind him.

The air seemed still, but so cold and wet. Norman looked around. He was standing atop a large stony bluff. Scrub trees and scraggly brush covered most of the ground, but here and there large sections of greenish, glacier-scoured bedrock were visible. Every surface glistened with a thin layer of water. Norman sneezed. It had been so nice and warm the last time. He peered out over the lower land and saw fog. It was just like the description in the "Adventures of the Two and the Three." The fog hung in the lower land like some tenuous sea, filling rocky fjords in the bluff. Trees and bushes and boulders seemed to lurk mysteriously within it.

This mysterious quality of the landscape gave Norman new spirit. He was a bold adventurer setting out to discover new lands.

He was also a hunted animal.

Norman found the small footpath he remembered, and set off across the bluff. The wet grass tickled his feet and his hair was already dripping. His books and typewriter were getting an awful beating as he dragged them over the rough ground.

He came to the edge of the bluff. The grass gave way to a bedrock shelf overlooking a drop of some fifty feet. Over the years, winter ice had done its work. Sections of the face of the cliff had broken off. Now the rubble reached halfway up the cliff, almost like a carelessly strewn avalanche of pebbles except that each rock weighed many tons. The fog worked in and out among the boulders and seemed to foam up the side of the cliff.

Norman crept to the edge of the cliff and peered over. Five feet below was a ledge about ten inches wide. The ledge slanted down. At its lower end it was only seven feet above the rocks. He went over, clinging to the cliff with one hand, and grasping the sack which lay on the ground above him with the other. Norman had not realized how slimy the rocks had become in the wet air. His hand slipped and he fell to the ledge below. The sack was jerked over the edge, but he kept his hold on it. The typewriter in the sack hit the side of the cliff with a loud clang.

He collected his wits and crawled to the lower part of the ledge. Here he again went over, but was very careful to keep a firm grip. He let go and landed feet first on a huge boulder directly below. The sack crashed down an instant later. Norman clambered over the rocks and soon had descended to level ground.

Nearby objects were obscured by the fog. It was even colder and damper than above. The fog seemed to enter his mouth and nose and draw away his warmth. He paused, then started in the direction that he remembered seeing the airplane hangar last time. Soon he was ankle deep in wet grass.

After about one hundred yards, Norman noticed a darkness to his left. He turned and approached it. Gradually the form of a light plane was defined. Soon he could clearly see the Piper Cub. *Four place, single-jet aircraft; maximum cargo weight, 1200 pounds; minimum runway for takeoff with full load, 90 yards; maximum speed, 250 miles per hour.* Its wings and fuselage shone dully in the weak light. Norman ran up to the Cub, clambered over the struts, and pulled himself into the cabin. He settled his sack in the copilot's seat and slammed the door. The key had been left in the ignition: someone had been extremely careless.

Norman inspected the controls of the little aircraft. Somehow his fear had departed, and specific facts now came easily to mind. He saw that there was an autopilot on the right-hand dash, but it was of a simple-minded variety and could handle only cruising flight.

He reached down and felt the rudder pedals with his feet. By bracing his back against the seat he could touch the pedals and at the same time hold the steering wheel. Of course, he would not be able to see out very easily, but there really wasn't very much *to* see.

He had to get across the border fast and this airplane was probably the only way.

He turned the starter and heard the fuel pumps and turbines begin rotating. Norman looked at the dash. What was he supposed to do next? He pushed the button marked FLASH and was rewarded with a loud *ffumpf* as the jet engine above the wing ignited. He twisted the throttle. The Cub crawled across the field, picking up speed. It bounced and jolted over the turf.

. . . Throttle to full, keeping stick forward . . . until you are well over stall speed (35 miles per hour for a 1980 Cub) . . . pull back gently on the stick, being careful to remain over . . . (35 miles per hour) . . .

He craned his neck, trying to get a view ahead. The ride was becoming smooth. The cub was airborne! Still nothing but fog ahead. For an instant the mist parted, revealing a thirty-foot Security fence barely fifty yards away. He had to have altitude!

. . . Under no circumstances should high angle-of-attack (climb) maneuvers be attempted without sufficient air speed . . .

Instructions are rarely the equal of actual experience, and now Norman was going to learn the hard way. He pushed at the throttle and pulled back hard on the stick. The little aircraft nosed sharply upward, its small jet engine screaming. The air speed fell and with it the lifting power of the wings. The Cub seemed to pause for an instant suspended in the air, then fell back. Jet still whining, the nose came down and the plane plunged earthwards.

Imagine a plate of spaghetti—no sauce or meatballs. O.K., now picture an entire room filled with such food. This wormy nightmare gives you some idea of the complexity of the First Security District, otherwise known as the Labyrinth. By analogy each strand of spaghetti is a tunnel segment carved through bedrock. The Labyrinth occupied four cubic miles under the cities of Ishpeming and Negaunee in the Upper Peninsula of Michigan. Without the power of controlled nuclear fusion such a maze could never have been made. Each tunnel was connected to several others by a random system of secret hatches, controlled by voice and electronic codes. Truly the First Security District was the most spy-proof volume in the solar system. The Savannah plant, the CIA, Soviet IKB, and the entire system of GM factories could have co-existed in it without knowledge of each other. As a matter of fact, thirty-one different Security projects, laboratories, and military bases existed in the Labyrinth with their co-ordinates listed in a single filing computer—and there's the rub . . .

"Because he's been getting straight A's," Dr. William Dunbar finished.

Lieutenant General Alvin Pederson, Commander of the First Security District, looked up from the computer console with a harried expression on his face. The two men were alone in the chamber containing the memory bank of United States Government Files Central, usually referred to as Files Central or simply Files. Behind the console were racks of fiber glass, whose orderly columns and rows filled most of the room. At the base of each rack, small lasers emitted modulated and coherent light; as the light passed through the fibers, it was altered and channeled by subtle impurities in the glass. Volume for volume, the computer was ten thousand times better than the best cryogenic models. Files Central contained all the information, secret and otherwise, possessed by the U.S.—including the contents of the Library of Congress, which managed to fill barely ten per cent of Files' capacity. The fact that Pederson kept his office here rather than at Continental Air Defense Headquarters, which occupied another part of the Labyrinth, indicated just how important the functions of Files were.

Pederson frowned. He had better things to do than listen to every overwrought genius that wanted to talk to him, though Dunbar usually spoke out only when he had something important to say. "You'd better start at the beginning, Doctor."

The mathematician began nervously. "Look. Norman has never had any great interest in his schoolwork. We may have given the chimp high intelligence with this brain-computer combination, but he has the emotional maturity of a nine-year-old human. Norman is bright, curious—and *lazy;* he would rather read science fiction than study history. His schoolwork has always been poorly and incompletely done—until six weeks ago. Since then he has spent virtually no time on real studying. At the same time he has shown a complete mastery of the factual information in his courses. It's almost as if he had an eidetic memory of *facts that were never presented to him.* As if . . ."

Dunbar started on a different tack. "General, you know how much trouble we had co-ordinating the chimp's brain with his computer in the first place. On the one hand you have an African chimpanzee, and on the other an advanced optical computer which theoretically is superior even to Files here. We wanted the chimp's brain to co-operate with the computer as closely as the different parts of a human brain work together. This meant that the computer had to be programmed to operate the way the chimp's mind did. We also had to make time-lapse corrections, because the chimp and the computer are not physically together. All in all, it was a terrifically complicated job. It makes the Economic Planning Programs look like setting up Fox and Geese on a kid's Brain Truster kit." Seeing the other's look of impatience, Dunbar hurried on. "Anyway, you remember that we needed to use the Files computer, just to program *our* computer. And the two machines had to be electronically connected."

The scientist came abruptly to the point. "If by some accident or mechanical failure, the link between Files and Norman *were never cut, then* . . . then the chimp would have complete access to U.S. Files."

Pederson's preoccupation with other matters disappeared. "If that's so, we've got one hell of a problem. And it would explain a lot of other things. Look." He shoved a sheet of paper at Dunbar. "As a matter of routine, Files announces how much information it has supplied to queries during every twenty-four-hour period. Actually it's sort of a slick gimmick to impress visitors with how efficient and useful Files is, supplying information to twenty or thirty different agencies at once. Up until six weeks ago the daily reading hung around ten to the tenth bits per day. During the next ten days it climbed to over ten to the twelfth—then to ten to the fourteenth. We couldn't hunt down the source of the queries and most of the techs thought the high readings were due to mechanical error.

"Altogether, Files has supplied almost ten to the fifteenth bits to—someone. And that, Doctor, is equal to the total amount of information contained in Files. It looks as if your monkey has programmed himself with all the information the U.S. possesses."

Pederson turned to the query panel, typed two questions. A tape reel by the desk spun briefly, stopped. Pederson pointed to it. "Those are the coordinates of your lab. I'm sending a couple men down to pick up your simian friend. Then I'm sending some more men to wherever his computer is."

Pederson looked at the tape reel expectantly, then noticed the words gleaming on a readout screen above the console:

The co-ordinates you request are not On File.

Pederson lunged forward and typed the question again, carefully. The message on the screen didn't even flicker:

The co-ordinates you request are not On File.

Dunbar leaned over the panel. "It's true, then," he said hoarsely, for the first time believing his fears. "Probably Norman thought we would punish him if we found out he was using Files."

"We would," Pederson interrupted harshly.

"And since Norman could use information On File, he could also *erase* information there. We hardly ever visit the tunnel where his computer was built, so we haven't noticed until now that he had erased its co-ordinates."

Now that he knew an emergency really existed, Dunbar seemed calm. He continued inexorably, "And if Norman was this fearful of discovery, then he

probably had Files advise him when you tried to find
the location of his computer. My lab is only a couple
hundred feet below the surface—and he surely knows
how to get out."

The general nodded grimly. "This chimp seems to
be one step ahead of us all the way." He switched on
a comm, and spoke into it. "Smith, send a couple
men over to Dunbar's lab . . . Yeah, I've got the
co-ordinates right here." He pressed another switch
and the reel of tape spun, transmitting its magnetic
impressions to a similar reel at the other end of the
hookup. "Have them grab the experimental chimp
and bring him down here to Files Central. Don't
hurt him, but be careful—you know how bright he
is." He cut the circuit and turned back to Dunbar.

"If he's still there, we'll get him; but if he's already
made a break for the surface, there's no way we can
stop him now. This place is just too decentralized."
He thought for a second, then turned back to the
comm and gave more instructions to his aide.

"I've put in a call to Sawyer AFB to send some
airborne infantry over here. Other than that, we can
only watch."

A TV panel brightened, revealing a view from one
of the hidden surface cameras. The scene was misty,
and silent except for an occasional dripping sound.

Several minutes passed; then a superbly camou-
flaged and counter-balanced piece of bedrock in the
center of their view swung down, and a black form in
orange Bermuda shorts struggled out of the ground,
dragging a large white sack. The chimp shivered,
then moved off, disappearing over the crest of the
bluff.

Pederson's hands were pale white, clenched in
frustration about the arms of his chair. Although the
First Security District was built under Ishpeming, its
main entrances were fifteen miles away at Sawyer

Armed Forces Base. There were only three small and barely accessible entrances in the area where Norman had escaped. Fortunately for the chimpanzee, his quarters had been located near one of them. The area which contained these entrances, belonged to the Ore REclamation Service, a government agency charged with finding more efficient methods of low-grade ore refining. (With the present economic situation, it was a rather superfluous job since the current problem was to get *rid* of the ore on hand rather than increase production.) All this indirection was designed to hide the location of the First Security District from the enemy. But at the same time it made direct control of the surface difficult.

A shrill sound came from the speaker by the TV panel. Dunbar puzzled, "Sounds almost like a light jet."

Pederson replied, "It probably is. The ORES people maintain a small office up there for appearances' sake, and they have a Piper Cub . . . *Could that chimp fly one?*"

"I doubt it, but I suppose if he were desperate enough he would try anything."

Smith's voice interrupted them, "General, our local infiltration radar has picked up an aircraft at an altitude of fifteen feet. Its present course will take it into the Security fence." The buzzing became louder. "The pilot is going to stall it out! It's in a steep climb . . . eighty feet, one hundred. It's stalled!"

The buzzing whine continued for a second and then abruptly ceased.

The typewriter departed through the front windshield at great speed. Norman Simmons came to in time to see his dog-eared copy of "Galactic Patrol" disappear into the murky water below. He made a wild grab for the book, missed it, and received a

painful scratch from shards of broken windshield. All
that remained of his belongings was the second volume of the Foundation series and the blanket which
somehow had been draped half in and half out of the
shattered window. The bottom edge of the blanket
swung gently back and forth just a couple of inches
above the water. The books he could do without;
they really had only sentimental value. Since he had
learned the Trick, there was no need to physically
possess any books. But in the cold weather he was
sure to need the blanket; he carefully retrieved it.

Norman pushed open a door, and climbed onto the
struts of the Cub for a look around. The plane had
crashed nose first into a shallow pond. The jet had
been silenced in the impact, and the loudest sound
to be heard now was his own breathing. Norman
peered into the fog. How far was he from "dry" land?
A few yards away he could see swamp vegetation
above the still surface of the water; beyond that,
nothing but mist. A slight air current eased the gloom.
There! For an instant he glimpsed dark trees and
brush about thirty yards away.

Thirty yards, through cold and slimy water. Norman's lips curled back in revulsion as he stared at the
oily liquid. Maybe there was an aerial route, like
Tarzan used. He glanced anxiously up, looking for
some overhanging tree branch or vine. No luck. He
would have to go *through* the water. Norman almost
cried in despair at the thought. Suffocating visions of
death by drowning came to mind. He imagined all
the creatures with pointy teeth and ferocious appe-
tites that might be lurking in the seemingly placid
water: piranhas to strip his bones and—no, they
were tropical fish, but something equally deadly. If
he could only pretend that it were clear, ankle-deep
water.

Dal swam silently toward the moonlit palms and

*palely gleaming sands just five hundred yards away.
Five hundred yards, he thought exultantly, to freedom, to his own kind. The enemy could never penetrate the atoll's camouflage . . . He didn't notice a
slight turbulence, the swift emergence of a leathery
tentacle from the water. But he fought desperately as
he felt it tighten about his leg. Dal's screams were
bubbly gurglings inaudible above the faint drone of
the surf, as he was hauled effortlessly into the depths
and sharp, unseen teeth . . .*

For a second his control lapsed, and the fictional
incident slipped in. In the comfort of his room, the
death of Dal had been no more than the pleasantly
chilling end of a villain; here it was almost unbear-
able. Norman extended one foot gingerly into the
water, and quickly drew it back. He tried again, this
time with both feet. Nothing bit him and he cautiously lowered himself into the clammy water. The
swamp weeds brushed gently against his legs. Soon
he was holding the strut with one hand and was neck
deep in water. The mass of weeds had slowly been
compressed as he descended and now just barely
supported his weight, even though he had not touched
bottom. He released his grip on the strut and began
moving toward shore. With one hand he attempted
to keep his blanket out of the water while with the
other he paddled. Norman glanced about for signs of
some hideous tentacle or fin, saw nothing but weeds.

He could see the trees on the shore quite clearly
now, and the weeds at his feet seemed backed by
solid ground. Just a few more yards—Norman gasped
with relief as he struggled out of the water. He
noticed an itching on his legs and arms. There had
been blood-drinkers in the water after all, but fortunately small ones. He paused to remove the slugs
from his body.

Norman sneezed violently and inspected his blanket. Although the mists had made it quite damp, he wrapped it around himself. Only after he was more or less settled did he notice the intermittent thrumming sound coming through the trees on his left. It sounded like the transport vehicles back in the tunnels, or like the automobiles that he had heard and seen on film.

Norman scrambled through the underbrush in the direction of the noises. Soon he came to a dilapidated four-lane asphalt highway. Every minute or so, a car would appear out of the mist, travel through his narrow range of vision, and disappear into the mist again.

MOST SECRET (*Unauthorized use of MOST SECRET materials is punishable by death.*) He had to get to Canada or they would kill him for sure. He knew millions, *billions* of things labeled MOST SECRET. Nearly all were unintelligible. The rest were usually boring. A very small percentage were interesting, like something out of an adventure story. And some were horrifying bits of nightmare couched in cold, matter-of-fact words. But all were labeled MOST SECRET, and his access to them was certainly unauthorized. If only he had known beforehand the consequences of Memorizing It All. It had been so easy to do, and so useful, but it was also a deadly, clinging gift.

Now that the airplane had crashed, he had to find some other way to get to Canada. Maybe one of these cars could take him some place where he would have better luck in his attempt. For some reason, the idea didn't trigger warning memories. Blissfully unaware that a talking chimpanzee is not a common sight in the United States, Norman started down the embankment to the shoulder of the highway, and in the immortal tradition of the hitchhiker in "Two for the Road," stuck out his thumb.

* * *

Three minutes passed; he clutched the blanket more tightly to himself as his teeth began to chatter. In the distance he heard the thrum of an approaching vehicle. He stared eagerly in the direction of the sound. Within fifteen seconds, a sixty-ton ore carrier emerged from the fog and lumbered toward him. Norman jumped up and down in a frenzy, waving and shouting. The blanket gave him the appearance of a little Amerind doing a particularly violent rain dance. The huge truck rolled by him at about thirty-five miles per hour. Then when it was some forty yards away, the driver slammed on the brakes and the doughy rollagon tires bit into asphalt.

Norman ran joyfully toward the cab, not noticing the uncared-for condition of the starboard ore cranes, the unpainted and dented appearance of the cab, or the wheezy putputting of the Wankel rotary engine— all signs of dilapidation which would have been unthinkable four years before.

He stopped in front of the cab door and was confronted by a pair of cynical, bloodshot eyes peering at him over a three-day growth of beard. "Who . . . Whash are you?" (The condition of the driver would have been unthinkable four years ago, too.)

"My name's Norman—Jones." Norman slyly selected an alias. He resolved to act dull, too, for he knew that most chimps were somewhat stupid, and couldn't speak clearly without the special operations he had had. (In spite of his memory and intelligence, Norman had an artificial block against ever completely realizing his uniqueness.) "I want to go to"—he searched his memory— "Marquette."

The driver squinted and moved his head from side to side as if to get a better view of Norman. "Say, you're a monkey."

"No," Norman stated proudly, forgetting his resolution, "I'm a chimpanzee."

"A talkin' monkey," the driver said almost to himself. "You could be worth plen . . . wherezhu say you wanna go . . . Marquette? Sure, hop in. That's where I'm takin' this ore."

Norman clambered up the entrance ladder into the warm cab. "Oh, thanks a lot."

The ore carrier began to pick up speed. The highway had been blasted through greenish bedrock, but it still made turns and had to climb over steep hills.

The driver was expansive, "Can't wait to finish this trip. This here is my las' run, ya know. No more drivin' ore fer the government an' its 'Public Works Projects.' I know where to get a couple black market fusion packs, see? Start my own trucking line. No one'll ever guess where I get my power." He swerved to avoid a natural abutment of greenish rock that appeared out of the mist, and decided that it was time to turn on his fog lights. His mind wandered back to prospects of future success, but along a different line. "Say, you like to talk, Monkey? You could make me a lot of money, ya know: 'Jim Traly an' His Talkin' Monkey.' Sounds good, eh?"

With a start, Norman realized that he was listening to a drunk. The driver's entire demeanor was almost identical to that of the fiend's henchman in "The Mores of the Morgue." Norman had no desire to be a "talkin' monkey" for the likes of Traly, whose picture he now remembered in Social Security Records. The man was listed as an unstable, low competence type who might become violent if frustrated.

As the ore carrier slowed for a particularly sharp turn, Norman decided that he could endure the cold of the outside for a few more minutes. He edged to the door and began to pull at its handle. "I think I better get off now, Mr. Traly."

The ore carrier slowed still more as the driver lunged across the seat and grabbed Norman by one of the purple suspenders that kept his orange Bermuda shorts up. A full grown chimpanzee is a match for most men, but the driver weighed nearly three hundred pounds and Norman was scared stiff. "You're staying right here, see?" Traly shouted into Norman's face, almost suffocating the chimpanzee in alcohol vapor. The driver transferred his grip to the scruff of Norman's neck as he accelerated the carrier back to cruising speed.

"Crashed in a shallow swamp just beyond the Security fence, sir." The young Army captain held a book up to the viewer. "This copy of Asimov was all that was left in the cabin, but we dredged up some other books and a typewriter from the water. It's only about five feet deep there."

"But where did the chim . . . the pilot go?" Pederson asked.

"The pilot, sir?" The captain knew what the quarry was but was following the general's line. "We have a man here from Special Forces who's a tracker, sir. He says that the pilot left the Cub and waded ashore. From there, he tracked him through the brush to the old Ishpeming-Marquette road. He's pretty sure that the . . . um . . . pilot hitched a ride in the direction of Marquette." The captain did not mention how surprised the lieutenant from Special Forces had been by the pilot's tracks. "He probably left the area about half an hour ago, sir."

"Very well, Captain. Set up a guard around the plane; if anyone gets nosy, tell them that ORES has asked you to salvage their crashed Cub. Fly everything you found in the cabin and swamp back to Sawyer and have it sent down here to Files Central."

"Yes, sir."

Pederson cut the connection and began issuing detailed instructions to his chief aide over another circuit. Finally he turned back to Dunbar. "That chimp is not going to remain one step ahead of us for very much longer. I've alerted all the armed forces in the Upper Peninsula to start a search, with special concentration on Marquette. It's lucky that we have permission to conduct limited maneuvers there or I might have an awful time just getting permission to station airbornes over the city.

"And now we can take a little time to consider ways of catching this Norman Simmons, rather than responding spastically to *his* initiative."

Dunbar said quickly, "In the first place, you can cut whatever connection there is between Files and Norman's computer."

Pederson grinned. "Good enough. That was mixed in with the rest of the instructions I've given Smith. If I remember right, the two computers were connected by a simple copper cable, part of the general cable net that was installed interweaving with the tunnel system. It should be a simple matter to cut the circuit where the cable enters the Files room."

The general thought for a moment. "The object now is to catch the chimp, discover the location of the chimp's computer, or both. Down here we can't do anything directly about the chimp. But the computer has to be in contact with Norman Simmons. Could we trace these emanations?"

Dunbar blinked. "You know that better than I, General. The Signal Corps used our experiment to try a *quote* entirely new concept in communications *unquote*. They supplied all the comm equipment, even the surgical imbeds for Norman. And they are playing it pretty cozy with the technique. Whatever it is, it goes through almost anything, does not travel faster than light, and can handle several billion bits per second. It might even be ESP, if what I've read about telepathy is true."

Pederson looked sheepish. "I do recognize the 'new concept' you mention. I just never connected the neutri . . . this technique with your project. But I should have known; we have only one way to broadcast through solid rock as if it were vacuum. Unfortunately, with the devices we have now, there's no way of getting a directional bearing on such transmissions. With enough time and as a last resort we might be able to jam them, though."

Now it was Dunbar's turn to make a foolish suggestion. "Maybe if a thorough search of the tunnels were made, we could find the—"

Pederson grimaced. "Bill, you've been here almost three years. Haven't you realized how complicated the Labyrinth is? The maze is composed of thousands of tunnel segments spread through several cubic miles of bedrock. It's simply too complex for a blind search—and there's only one set of blueprints," he jerked a thumb at the racks of fiber glass. "Even for routine trips, we have to make out tapes to plug into the transport cars down there. If we hadn't put his quarters close to ground level, so you could take him for walks on the surface, Norman would still be wandering around the Labyrinth, even though he knows what passages to take.

"About twice a day I ride over to Continental Air Defense Headquarters. It takes about half an hour and the trip is more tortuous then a swoopride at a carnival. CAD HQ could be just a hundred yards from where we're sitting, or it could be two miles—in any direction. For that matter, I don't really know where *we* are right now. But then," he added with a sly smile, "neither do the Russki or Han missilemen. I'm sorry, Doctor, but it would take years of random searching to find the computer."

And Dunbar realized that he was right. It was general policy in the First Security District to disperse experiments and other installations as far as possible through the tunnel maze. So it had been with Norman's computer. With its own power source the computer needed no outside assistance to function.

The scientist remembered its strange appearance, resting like a huge jewel in a vacant tunnel—where? It was a far different sight from the appearance of Files. Norman's computer had the facets of a cut gem, although this had been a functional rather than an aesthetic necessity. Dunbar remembered the multicolor glows that appeared near its surface; further in, the infinite reflections and subtle refractions of microcomponent flaws in the glass blended into a mysterious flickering, hinting at the cheerful though immature intelligence that was Norman Simmons. This was the object which had to be found.

Dunbar broke out of his reverie. He started on a different tack. "Really, General, I don't quite see how this situation can be quite as desperate as you say. Norman isn't going to sell secrets to the Reds; he's as loyal as a human child could be—which is a good deal more than most adults, because he can't rationalize disloyalty so easily. Besides, you know that we were eventually going to provide him with large masses of data, anyway. The goal of this whole project is to test the possibility of giving humans an encyclopedic mental grasp. He just saw how much the information could help him, and how much easier it could be obtained than by study, and he pushed the experiment into its next phase. He shouldn't be punished or hurt because of that. This situation is really no one's fault."

Pederson snapped back, "Of course, it's no one's fault; that's just the hell of it. When no one is to blame for something, it means that the situation is fundamentally beyond human control. To me, your

whole project is taking control away from people and
giving it to *others*. Here an experimental animal, a
chimpanzee, has taken the initiative away from the
U.S. Government—don't laugh, or so help me—"
The general made a warning gesture. "Your chimp is
more than a co-ordinator of information; he's also
smarter than he was before. *What're the humans we
try this on going to be like?*"

Pederson calmed himself with a deliberate effort.
"Never mind that now. The important thing is to
find Simmons, since he appears to be the only one
who," Pederson groaned, "knows where his brains
are. So let's get practical. Just what can we expect
from him? How easy is it for him to correlate information in his memory?"

Dunbar considered. "I guess the closest analogy
between his mind and a normal one is to say that he
has an eidetic memory—and a *very* large one. I
imagine that when he first began using the information he was just swamped with data. Everything he
saw stimulated a deluge of related memories. As his
subconscious became practiced, he probably remembered only information that was pertinent to a problem. Say that he saw a car, and wondered what year
and make it was. His subconscious would hunt through
his copy of Files—at very high speed—and within a
tenth of a second Norman would 'remember' the
information he had just wondered about.

"However, if for some reason he suddenly wondered what differential equations were, it would be a
different matter, because he couldn't *understand* the
information presented, and so would have to wade
through the same preliminary material that every
child must in order to arrive at high-school math.
But he could do it very much faster, because of the
ease with which he could pick different explanations
from different texts. I imagine he could get well into

calculus from where he is now in algebra with a couple hours of study."

"In other words, the longer he has this information, the more dangerous he'll be."

"Uh, yes. However, there *are* a couple things on our side. First, it's mighty cold and damp on the surface, for Norman at least. He is likely to be very sick in a few hours. Second, if he travels far enough away from the First Security District, he will become mentally disoriented. Although Norman doesn't know it—unless he has specifically considered the question—he could never get much farther than fifteen miles away and remain sane. Norman's mind is a very delicate balance between his organic brain and the hidden computer. The coordination is just as subtle as that of different nerve paths in the human brain. The information link between the two has to transmit more than a billion bits of information per second. If Norman gets beyond a certain point, the time lapse involved in transmission between him and the computer will upset the coordination. It's something like talking by radio with a spacecraft; beyond a certain distance it is difficult or impossible to maintain a meaningful conversation. When Norman goes beyond a certain point it will be impossible for him to think coherently."

Dunbar was struck by an unrelated idea. He added, "Say, I can see one reason why this could get sticky. What if Norman got picked up by foreign agents? That would be the biggest espionage coup in the history of man."

Pederson smiled briefly. "Ah, the light dawns. Yes, some of the information this Simmons has could mean the death of almost everyone on Earth, if it were known to the wrong people. Other secrets would *merely* destroy the United States.

"Fortunately, we're fairly sure that the Reds' domestic collapse has reduced their overseas enterprises to about nil. As I remember it, there are only one or two agents in all of Michigan. Thank God for small favors."

Boris Kuchenko scratched and was miserable. A few minutes before, he had been happily looking forward to receiving his weekly unemployment check and then spending the afternoon clipping articles out of the *NATO Armed Forces Digest* for transmission back to Moscow. And now this old coot with his imperious manner was trying to upset everything. Kuchenko turned to his antagonist and tried to put on a brave front. "I am sorry, Comrade, but I have my orders. As the ranking Soviet agent in the Upper Peninsu—"

The other snapped back, "Ranking agent, nothing! You were never supposed to know this, Kuchenko, but you are a cipher, a stupid dummy used to convince U.S. Intelligence that the USSR has given up massive espionage. If only I had some decent agents here in Marquette, I wouldn't have to use idiots like you."

Ivan Sliv was an honest-to-God, effective Russian spy. Behind his inconspicuous middle-aged face, lurked a subtle mind. Sliv spoke five languages and had an excellent grasp of engineering, mathematics, geography, and history—*real* history, not State-sponsored fairy tales. He could make brilliantly persuasive conversation at a cocktail party or commit a political murder with equal facility. Sliv was the one really in charge of espionage in the militarily sensitive U.P. area. He and other equally talented agents concentrated on collecting information from Sawyer AFB and from the elusive First Security District.

The introduction of Bender's fusion pack had produced world-wide depression, and the bureaucracies of Russia had responded to this challenge with all the resiliency of a waterlogged pretzel. The Soviet economic collapse had been worse than that of any other major country. While the U.S. was virtually recovered from the economic depression caused by the availability of unlimited power, counter-revolutionary armies were approaching Moscow from the West *and* the East. Only five or ten ICBM bases remained in Party hands. But the Comrades had been smart in one respect. If you can't win by brute force, it is better to be subtle. Thus the planetary spy operations were stepped up, as was a very secret project housed in a system of caves under the Urals. Sliv's mind shied away from that project—he was one of the few to know of it, and that knowledge must never be hinted at.

Sliv glared at Kuchenko. "Listen, you fat slob: I'm going to explain things once more, if possible in words of one syllable. I just got news from Sawyer that some Amie superproject has backfired. An experimental animal has escaped from their tunnel network and half the soldiers in the U.P. are searching for it. They think it's here in Marquette."

Kuchenko paled, "A war virus test? Comrade, this could be—" the fat Soviet agent boggled at the possibilities.

Sliv swore. "No, no, no! The Army's orders are to *capture*, not destroy the thing. We are the only agents that are in Marquette now, or have a chance to get in past the cordon that's sure to be dropped around the city. We'll split up and—" He stopped and took conscious notice of the buzzing sound that had been building up over the last several minutes. He walked quickly across the small room and pushed open a badly cracked window. Cold air seemed to ooze into the room. Below, the lake waters splashed against the pilings of the huge automated pier which incidentally contained this apartment. Sliv pointed into the sky and snapped at the bedraggled Kuchenko. "See? The Amie airbornes have been over the city for the last five minutes, at least. We've got to get going, man!"

But Boris Kuchenko was a man who liked his security. He miserably inspected his dirty finger-nails, and began, "I really don't know if this is the right thing, Comrade. We—"

The fog had disappeared, only to be replaced by a cold drizzle. Jim Traly guided the ore carrier through Marquette to the waterfront. Even though drunk, he maintained a firm grip on Norman's neck. The car-rier turned onto another street, and Norman got his first look at Lake Superior. It was so gray and cold; beyond the breakwater the lake seemed to blend with the sullen hue of the sky. The carrier turned again. They were now moving parallel to the water along a row of loading piers. In spite of the rollagons, the carrier dipped and sagged as they drove over large potholes in the substandard paving material. The rain had collected in these depressions and splashed as they drove along. Traly apparently recog-nized his destination. He slowed the carrier and moved it to the side of the street.

Traly opened his door and stepped down, dragging Norman behind him. With difficulty the chimpanzee kept his balance and did not land on his head. The drunk driver was muttering to himself, "Las' time I drive this trash. They can pick up the inventories themselves. Good riddance." He kicked a rollagon. "Just wait till I get some Bender fusion packs. I'll show 'em. C'mon, you." He gave Norman a jerk, and began walking across the street.

The waterfront was almost deserted. Traly was heading for what appeared to be the only operating establishment in the area: a tavern. The bar had a rundown appearance. The "aluminum" trim around the door had long since begun to rust, and the memory cell for the bar's sky sign suffered from amnesia so that it now projected into the air:

The D-unk PuT pavern

Traly entered the bar, pulling Norman in close behind. Once the fluorescents had probably lighted the place well, but now only two or three in a far corner were operating.

He pulled Norman around in front of him and seemed eager to announce his discovery of the "talkin' monkey." Then he noticed that the bar was almost empty. No one was sitting at any of the tables, although there were half empty glasses of beer left on a few of them. Four or five men and the barkeeper were engaged in an intense discussion at the far end of the room. "Where is everybody?" Traly was astonished.

The barkeeper looked up. "Jimmy! Right at lunch President Langley came on TV an' said that the government was going to let us buy as many Bender fusion boxes as we want. You could go out an' buy one right now for twenty-five bucks. When everybody heard that, why they just asked themselves what they were doin' sittin' around in a bar when they could have a job an' even be in business for themselves. Not much profit for me this afternoon, but I don't care. I know where I can get some junk copters. Fit 'em out with Bender packs and start a tourist service. You know: See the U.P. with Don Zalevsky." The bartender winked.

Traly's jaw dropped. He forgot Norman. "You really mean that there's no more black market where we can get fusion boxes?"

One of the customers, a short man with a protuberant beak and a bald pate, turned to Traly. "What do you need a black market for when you can go out an' buy a Pack for twenty-five dollars? Well, will you look at that: Traly's disappointed. Now you can do whatcher always bragging about, go out and dig up some fusion boxes and go into business." He turned back to the others.

"And we owe it all to President Langley's fizical and economic policies. Bender's Pack coulda destroyed our nation. Instead we only had a little depression, an' look at us now. Three years after the invention, the economy's on an even keel enough to let us buy as many power packs as we want."

Someone interrupted. "You got rocks in your head, buddy. The government closed down most of the mines so the oil corporations would have a market to make plastics for; we get to produce just enough ore up here so no one starves. Those 'economic measures' have kept us all hungry. If the government had only let us buy as many Packs as we wanted and not interfered with free competition, there wouldna been no depression or nothing."

From the derisive remarks of the other customers, this appeared to be a minority opinion. The Beak slammed his glass of beer down and turned to his opponent. "You know what woulda happened if there wasn't no 'interference'?" He didn't wait for an answer. "Everybody woulda gone out an bought Packs. All the businesses in the U.S. woulda gone bankrupt, 'cause anyone with a Bender and some electric motors would hardly need to buy any regular goods, except food. It wouldn't have been a depression, it woulda been just like a jungle. As it is, we only had a short period of adjustment," he almost seemed to be quoting, "an' now we're back on our feet. We got power to burn; those ore buckets out in the bay can fly through the air and space, and we can take the salt out of the water and—"

"Aw, you're jus' repeating what Langley said in his speech."

"Sure I am, but it's true." Another thought occurred to him. "And *now* we don't even need Public Works Projects."

"Yeah, no more Public Works Projects," Traly put in, disappointed.

"There wouldn't have been no need for PWP if it wasn't for Langley and his loony ideas. My old man said the same thing about Roosevelt." The dissenter was outnumbered but voluble.

Norman had become engrossed in the argument. In fact he was so interested that he had forgotten his danger. Back in the District he had been made to learn some economics as part of his regular course of study—and, of course, he could remember considerably more about the subject. Now he decided to make his contribution. Traly had loosened his grip; the chimpanzee easily broke the hold and jumped to the top of the counter. "This man," he pointed to the Beak, "is right, you know. The Administration's automatic stabilizers and discretionary measures prevented total catastro— "

"What is *this*, Jimmy?" The bartender broke the amazed silence that greeted Norman's sudden action.

"That's what I've been trying to tell you guys. I picked up this monkey back in Ishpeming. He's like a parrot, only better. Jus' listen to him. I figure he could be worth a lot of money."

"Thought you were going into the trucking business, Jimmy."

Traly shrugged. "This could be a lot greener."

"That's no parrot-talk," the Beak opined. "The monkey's *really* talking. He's smart like you and me."

Norman decided that he had to trust someone.

"Yes I am, yes I am! And I need to get into Canada. Otherwise—"

The door to the Drunk Pup Tavern squeaked as a young man in brown working clothes pushed it halfway open. "Hey, Ed, all of you guys. There's a bunch of big Army copters circling the bay, and GI's all over. It doesn't look like any practice maneuver." The man was panting as if he had run several blocks.

"Say, let's see that," moved the Beak. He was informally seconded. Even the bartender seemed ready to leave. Norman started. *They* were still after him, and they were close. He leaped off the counter and ran through the half-open door, right by the knees of the young man who had made the announcement. The man stared at the chimpanzee and made a reflex grab for him. Norman evaded the snatch and scuttled down the street. Behind him, he heard Traly arguing with the man about, "Letting my talking monkey escape."

He had dropped his blanket when he jumped onto the counter. Now the chill drizzle made him regret the loss. Soon he was damp to the skin again, and the water splashed his forearms and legs as he ran through spots where water had collected in the tilted and cracked sections of sidewalk. All the shops and dives along the street were closed and boarded up. Some owners had left in such disgust and discouragement that they had not bothered even to pull in their awnings. He stopped under one such to catch his breath and get out of the rain.

Norman glanced about for some sign of airborne infantrymen, but as far as he could see, the sky was empty of men and aircraft. He examined the awning above him. For several years the once green plastic fabric had been subjected alternately to baking sun and rotting rain. It was cheap plastic and now it hung limp, the gray sky visible through the large holes in the material. Norman looked up, got an idea. He backed away from the awning and then ran toward it. He leaped and caught its rusting metal frame. The shade sagged even more, but held. He eased himself over the frame and rested for an instant on the top; then pulled himself onto the windowsill of a second-story apartment.

Norman looked in, saw nothing but an old bed and a closet with one lonely hangar. He caught the casing above the window and swung up. It was almost like being Tarzan. (Usually, Norman tended to identify himself with Tarzan rather than with the Lord-of-the-Jungle's chimpanzee flunkies.) He caught the casing with his toes, pushed himself upwards until he could grasp the edge of the flat roof. One last heave and he was lying on that tar-and-gravel roofing material. In places where the tar had been worn away, someone had sprayed plastite, but more time had passed and that "miracle construction material" had deteriorated, too.

The roofs provided scant cover from observation. Fifty feet away, Norman saw the spidery black framework of a radio tower mounted on the roof of another building. It was in good repair; probably it was a government navigation beacon. Norman sneezed several times, violently. He crawled warily across the roof toward the tower. The buildings were separated by a two-foot alley which Norman easily swung across.

He arrived at the base of the tower. Its black plastic members gleamed waxily in the dull light. As with many structures built after 1980, Hydrocarbon Products Administration regulations dictated that it be constructed with materials deriving from the crippled petroleum and coal industries, Norman remembered. In any case, the intricate framework provided good camouflage. Norman settled himself among the girders and peered out across Marquette.

*   *   *

There were hundreds of them! In the distance, tiny figures in Allservice green were walking through the streets, inspecting each building. Troop carriers and airtanks hung above them. Other airtanks patrolled some arbitrary perimeter about the city and bay. Norman recognized the setup as one of the standard formations for encirclement and detection of hostile forces. With confident foreknowledge he looked up and examined the sky above him. Every few seconds a buckrogers fell out of the apparently empty grayness. After a free fall of five thousand feet, the airborne infantrymen hit their jets just two or three hundred feet above the city. Already, more than twenty of them were posted over the various intersections.

The chimpanzee squinted, trying to get a clearer view of the nearest buckrogers. Images seen through the air behind and below the soldier seemed to waver. This and a faint screaming sound was the only indication of the superheated air shot from the Bender powered thermal element in the soldier's back pack. The infantryman's shoulders seemed lopsided. On more careful inspection Norman recognized that this was due to a GE fifty-thousand line reconnaissance camera strapped to the soldier's upper arm and shoulder. The camera's eight-inch lens gaped blackly as the soldier turned (rotated?) in the chimp's direction.

Norman froze. He knew that every hyper-resolution picture was being transmitted back to Sawyer AFB where computers and photo-interp teams analyzed them. Under certain conditions just a clear footprint or the beady glint of Norman's eyes within the maze of girders would be enough to bring a most decisive—though somewhat delayed—reaction.

As the buckrogers turned away, Norman sighed with relief. But he knew that he wouldn't remain

safe for long. Sooner or later—most likely sooner—
they would be able to trace him. And then . . . With
horror he remembered once again some of the terrible bits of information that hid in the vast pile he
knew, remembered the punishments for unauthorized knowledge. *He had to escape them!* Norman
considered the means, both fictional and otherwise,
that had been used in the past to elude pursuers. In
the first place, he recognized that some outside help
was needed, or he could never escape from the
country. Erik Satanssen, he remembered, always
played the double agent, gaining advantages from
both sides right up to the denouement. Or take
Slippery Jim DiGriz . . . the point was there are
always some loopholes even in the most mechanized
of traps. What organization would have a secret means
of getting across Lake Superior into Canada? The
Reds, of course!

Norman stopped fiddling with his soaked suspenders, and looked up. That was the pat answer, in some
stories: Pretend to side up with the baddies just long
enough to get out of danger and expose them at the
same time. Turning around, he gazed at the massive
automated pier jutting out into the bay. At its root
were several fourth-class apartments—and in one of
them was the only Soviet agent in the Upper
Peninsula! Norman remembered more about Boris
Kuchenko. What sort of government would employ a
slob like that as a spy? He racked his memory but
could find no other evidence of espionage in the
U.P. area.

Many tiny details seemed to crystallize into an
idea. It was just like in some stories where the hero
appears to pull his hunches out of the thin air. Norman *knew* without any specific reason, that the Sovi-
ets were not as incapacitated as they seemed. Stark,
Borovsky, Ivanov were smart boys, much smarter

than the so-called Bumpkinov incompetents they had
replaced. If Stark had been in power in the first
place, the Soviet Union might have survived Bender's invention without losing more than a few outly-
ing SSR's. As it was the Party bosses controlled only
the area immediately around Moscow and some "hardened" bases in the Urals. Somehow Norman felt
that, if all the mental and physical resources
of the rulers had been used against the counter-
revolutionaries, the Reds' position would have to be
better. Borovsky and Ivanov especially, were noted
for devious, back-door victories. Something smelled
about this spy business.

If Kuchenko was more than he seemed, there
might be a way out even yet. If he could trick the
Reds into thinking he was a stupe or a traitor, they
might take him to some hideout in Canada. He knew
they would be interested in him and his knowledge;
that was his passport and his peril. They must never
know the things *he* knew. And then later, in Canada,
maybe he could expose the Russian spies and gain
forgiveness.

The nearest buckrogers was now facing directly
away from Norman's tower. The chimpanzee moved
away from the tower, hurried to the edge of the roof,
and swung himself over. Now he was out of the line
of sight of the infantryman. He reached the ground
and scampered across the empty street. Soon he was
padding along the base of the huge auto pier. Finally
he reached the point where the street was swallowed
by the enclosed portion of the pier. Norman ran into
the dimness; at least he was out of the rain now.
Along the side of the inner wall was a metal grid
stairway. The chimp clambered up the stairs, found
himself in the narrow corridor serving the cheap
apartments which occupied what otherwise would

have been dead space in the warehouse pier. He paused before turning the doorknob.

". . . Move fast!" The knob was snatched from his fingers, as someone on the other side pulled the door open. Norman all but fell into the room. "What the hell!" The speaker slammed the door shut behind the chimpanzee. Norman glanced about the room, saw Boris Kuchenko frozen in the act of wringing his hands. The other man spun Norman around, and the chimpanzee recognized him as one Ian Sloane, civilian employee No. 36902u at Sawyer AFB; so the hunch had been right! The Reds *were* operating on a larger scale than the government suspected.

Norman assumed his best conspiratorial air. "Good morning, gentlemen . . . or should I say Comrades?"

The older man, Sloane, kept a tight grip on his arm. A look of surprise and triumph and oddly—fear, was on his face. Norman decided to go all the way with the double-agent line. "I'm here to offer my services, uh, Comrades. Perhaps you don't know quite what and who I am . . ." He looked around expectantly for some sign of curiosity. Sloane—that was the only name Norman could remember, but it couldn't be his real one—gazed at him attentively, but kept a tight grip on his arm. Seeing that he was going to get no response, Norman continued less confidently. "I . . . I know who you are. Get me out of the country and you'll never regret it. You must have some way of escaping—at the very least some hiding place." He noticed Boris Kuchenko glance involuntarily at a spot in the ceiling near one of the walls. There was an ill-concealed trap hacked raggedly out of the ceiling. It hardly seemed the work of a master spy.

At last Sloane spoke. "I think we can arrange your escape. And I am sure that we will not regret it."

His tone made Norman realize how naïve his plan

had been. These agents would get the information and secrets from him or they would destroy him, and there was no real possibility that he would have any opportunity to create a third, more acceptable alternative. The fire was much hotter than the frying pan, and fiction was vaporized by reality. He was in trouble.

Pfft.

The tiny sound came simultaneously with a pin-prick in his leg. The curtains drawn before the window jerked slightly. A faint greenish haze seemed to hang in the air for an instant, then disappeared. He scratched his leg with his free hand and dislodged a black pellet. Then he knew that the photo-interpretation group at Sawyer had finally found his trail. They knew exactly where he was, and now they were acting. They had just fired at least two PAX cartridges into the room, one of which had failed to go off. The little black object was a cartridge of that famous nerve gas.

During the Pittsburgh Bread Riots back in '81, screaming mobs, the type that dismember riot police, had been transformed into the most docile groups by a few spoken commands and a couple of grams of PAX diffused over the riot area. The stuff wasn't perfect, of course; in about half a per cent of the population there were undesirable side effects such as pseudo-epilepsy and permanent nerve damage; another half per cent weren't affected by normal dosages at all. But the great majority of people immediately lost all power to resist outside suggestion. He felt Sloane's grip loosening.

Norman pulled away and spoke to both men. "Give me a boost through that trapdoor."

"Yes, sir." The two men agreeably formed a stirrup and raised the chimpanzee toward the ceiling. As they did, Norman suddenly wondered why the gas had not affected him. *Because I'm not all here!*

He answered himself with an almost hysterical chuckle. The gas could only affect the part of him that was physically present. And, though that was a very important part, he still retained some of his own initiative.

As Norman pushed open the trap, there was a splintering crash from the window as a buckrogers in full battle gear came hurtling feet first into the room. With a spastic heave, the chimp drew himself into the darkness above. From below he heard an almost plaintive, "Halt!" then Sloane's formerly menacing voice; "We'll go quietly, Officer."

Norman picked himself up and began running. The way was dimly lit from windows mounted far above. Now that his eyes were adjusted, he could see bulky crates around him and above him. He looked down, and gasped, for he could see crates below him, too. He seemed suspended. Then Norman remembered. In the dim light it wasn't too evident, but the floor and ceiling of this level were composed of heavy wire mesh. From a control board somewhere in the depths of the building, roller segments in the mesh could be turned on, and the bulkiest crates could be shuttled about the auto pier like toys. When in operation the pier could handle one million tons of merchandise a day; receiving products from trucks, storing them for a short time, and then sliding them into the holds of superfreighters. This single pier had been expected to bring the steel industry to Marquette, thus telescoping the mining and manufacturing complexes into one. Perhaps after the Recovery it would fulfill its promise, but at the moment it was dead and dark.

Norman zigzagged around several crates, scampered up an incline. Behind him he could hear the infantrymen, shed of their flying gear, scrambling through the trap door.

They would never believe his honesty now that he had been seen consorting with the communists. Things did indeed look dark—he complimented himself on this pun delivered in the midst of danger—but he still had some slim chance of escaping capture and the terrible punishment that would be sure to follow. He had one undetonated PAX cartridge. Apparently its relatively gentle impact with his flesh had kept it from popping. Perhaps not all the soldiers were wearing the antiPAX nose filters—in which case he might be able to commandeer a helicopter. It was a wild idea, but the time for cautious plans was past.

The pier seemed to extend forever. Norman kept moving. He had to get away; and he was beginning to feel very sick. Maybe it was some effect of the gas. He ran faster, but even so he felt a growing terror. His mind seemed to be dissolving, disintegrating. Could *this* be the effect of PAX? He groped mentally for some explanation, but somehow he was having trouble remembering the most obvious things, while at the same time extraneous memories were swamping him more completely than they had for weeks. He should know what the source of the danger was, but somehow . . . *I'm not all here!* That was the answer! But he couldn't understand what its significance was anymore. He no longer could form rational plans. Only one goal remained—to get away from the things that were stalking him. The dim gray glow far ahead now seemed to offer some kind of safety. If he could only reach it. Intelligence was deserting him, and chaos was creeping in.

Faster!

3,456,628 more shopping days until Christmas . . . Latitude 40.9234°N, Longitude 121.3018°W: Semi-hardened Isis missile warehouse; 102 megatons total . . . Latitude 59.00160°N, Longitude 87.4763°W: Cluster of three Vega class Submarine Launched Ballistic Missiles; 35 megatons total . . . depth 105.4

*fathoms . . . All-serv IFF codes as follows: 1. 398547
. . . 436344 . . . 51 . . .* "Hey, let me out!" *. . .
Master of jungle poised, knife ready as . . the nature
of this rock formation was not realized until the
plutonist theory of Bender's . . . New Zealand Har-
bor Defense of Wellington follows: Three antisubma-
rine detection rings at 10.98 miles from . . . REO
factory depot Boise, Idaho contains 242,925 million-hp
consumer fusion packs; inventory follows.* Cold gray
light shining in the eyes. And I must escape or . . .
"die with a stake driven through his heart," the
professor laughed. STOP or you'll fall; MOVE or
you'll die; escape escape escape seascape orescape
3scape5scape2pecape4ea 1a00p30 689135010112131-
01000101011000010101010000111111010101—

The chimpanzee crouched frozen and glared madly
at the soft gray light coming through the window.

The tiny black face looked up from the starched
white of the pillow and stared dazedly at the ceiling.
Around the bed hung the glittering instruments of
the SOmatic Support unit. Short of brain tissue damage, the SOS could sustain life in the most terribly
mangled bodies. At the moment it was fighting pneu-
monia, TB, and polio in the patient on the bed.

Dunbar sniffed. The medical ward of the Labyrinth used all the latest procedures—gone was the
antiseptic stink of earlier years. The germicidals used
were a very subtle sort—and only a shade different
from antipersonnel gases developed in the '60's and
'70's. William Dunbar turned to Pederson, the only
other human in the room. "According to the doctors,
he'll make it." Dunbar gestured to the unconscious
chimp. "And his reactions to those questions you
asked him under truth drug indicate that no great
damage has been done to his 'amplified personality.' "

"Yeah," Pederson replied, "but we won't know
whether he responded truthfully until I have these

coordinates for his computer checked out." He tapped the sheet of paper on which he had scrawled the numbers Norman had called off. "For all we know, he may be immune to truth drug in the same way he is to PAX."

"No, I think he probably told the truth, General. He is, after all, in a very confused state.

"Now that we know the location of his computer, it should be an easy matter to remove the critical information from it. When we try the invention on a man we can be much more careful with the information initially presented."

Pederson stared at him for a long moment. "I suppose you know that I've always opposed your project."

"Uh, yes," said Dunbar, startled, "though I can't understand why you do."

Pederson continued, apparently without noticing the other's answer, "I've never quite been able to convince my superiors of the dangers inherent in the things you want to do. I think I can convince them now and I intend to do everything in my power to see that your techniques are never tried on a human, or for that matter, on any creature."

Dunbar's jaw dropped. "But why? We *need* this invention! Nowadays there is so much knowledge in so many different areas that it is impossible for a man to become skilled in more than two or three of them. If we don't use this invention, most of that knowledge will sit in electronic warehouses waiting for insights and correlations that will never occur. The human-computer symbiosis can give man the jump on evolution and nature. Man's intellect can be ex—"

Pederson swore. "You and Bender make a pair, Dunbar; both of you see the effects of your inventions with narrow utopian blinders. But yours is by far the more dangerous of the two. Look what this one chimpanzee has done in under six hours—escaped from the most secure post in America, eluded a large armed force, and deduced the existence of an espionage net that we had completely overlooked. Catching him was more an *accident* than anything else. If he had had time to think about it, he probably would have deduced that distance limit and found some way to escape us that really would have worked. And this is what happens with an experimental *animal!* His intelligence has increased steadily as he developed a firmer command of his information banks. We captured him more or less by chance, and unless we act fast while he's drugged, we won't be able to hold him.

"*And you want to try this thing on a man!*

"Tell me, Doctor, who are you going to give godhood to first, hm-m-m? If your choice is wrong, the product will be more satanic than divine. It will be a devil that we can not possibly beat except with the aid of some fortuitous accident, for we can't outthink that which, by definition, is smarter than we. The slightest instability on the part of the person you choose would mean the death or *domestication* of the entire human race."

Pederson relaxed, his voice becoming calmer. "There's an old saw, Doctor, that the only truly dangerous weapon is a man. By that standard, you have made the only advance in weaponry in the last one hundred thousand years!" He smiled tightly. "It may seem strange to you, but I oppose arms races and I intend to see that you don't start one."

William Dunbar stared, pale-faced, entertaining a dream and a nightmare at the same time. Pederson noted the scientist's expression with some satisfaction.

This tableau was interrupted by the buzzing of the comm. Pederson accepted the call. "Yes," he said, recognizing Smith's features on the screen.

"Sir, we just finished with those two fellows we picked up on the auto pier," the aide spoke somewhat nervously. "One is Boris Kuchenko, the yuk we've had spotted all along. The other is Ivan Sliv, who's been working for the last nine months as a code man at Sawyer under the name of Ian Sloane. We didn't suspect him at all before. Anyway, we gave both of them a deep-probe treatment, and then erased their memories of what's happened today, so we could release them and use them as tracers."

"Fine," replied Pederson.

"They've been doing the darndest things, those spies." Smith swallowed. "But that isn't what this call is about."

"Oh?"

"Can I talk? Are you alone?"

"Spit it out, Smith."

"Sir, this Sliv is really a top man. Some of his memories are under blocks that I'm sure the Russkies' never thought we could break. Sir—he knows of a project the Sovs are running in an artificial cave system under the Urals. They've taken a dog and wired it—wired it into a computer. Sliv has heard the dog talk, just like Dunbar's chimp. Apparently this is the big project they're pouring their resources into to the exclusion of all others. In fact, one of Sliv's main duties was to detect and obstruct any similar project here. When all the bugs have been worked out, Stark, or one of the other Red chiefs is going to use it on himself and—"

Pederson turned away from the screen, stopped listening. He half noticed Dunbar's face, even paler than before. He felt the same sinking, empty sensation he had four years before when he had heard of Bender's fusion pack. Always it was the same pattern: The invention, the analysis of the dangers, the attempt at suppression, and then the crushing knowledge that no invention can really be suppressed and that the present case is no exception. Invention came after invention, each with greater changes. Bender's pack would ultimately mean the dissolution of central collections of power, of cities—but Dunbar's invention meant an increased *capability* for invention.

Somewhere under the Urals slept a very smart son of a bitch indeed . . .

And so he must choose between the certain disaster of having a Russian dictator with superhuman intelligence, and the probable disaster involved in beating the enemy to the punch.

He knew what the decision must be; as a practical man he must adapt to changes beyond his control, must plan for the safest possible handling of the unavoidable.

. . . For better or worse, the world would soon be unimaginably different.

Of course, I never wrote the "important" story, the sequel about the first amplified human. Once I tried something similar. John Campbell's letter of rejection began: "Sorry—you can't write this story. Neither can anyone else." The moral: keep your supermen offstage, or deal with them when they are children (Slan). or when they are in disguise (Campbell's own story "The Idealists"). (There is another possibility, one that John never mentioned to me. You can deal with the superman when s/he's senile; this option was used to very amusing effect in one episode of the Quark television series.)

The story and its lesson were important to me. Here I had tried a straightforward extrapolation of technology, and found myself precipitated over an abyss. It's a problem we face every time we consider the creation of intelligences greater than our own. When this happens, human history will have reached a kind of singularity—a place where extrapolation breaks down and new models must be applied—and the world will pass beyond our understanding. In one form or another this Singularity haunts many science-fiction writers: A bright fellow like Mark Twain could predict television, but such extrapolation is forever beyond—say—a dog. The best we writers can do is creep up on the Singularity, and hang ten at its edge.

Fifteen years passed. I went to college, earned some math degrees, but was still very careful not to learn anything about computers. They remained tremendously important in my schemes, but somehow astronomy and math were always the more immediate things. Again I wonder if this ignorance was an advantage, saving me from getting lost in the irrelevancies of the moment. After all, I knew where things were ultimately going!

By 1979, I did know a little about contemporary computing. I had been teaching computer science courses for several years; I did a lot of what is now called "data commuting." One night I was working at home, logged on my school's principal computer (a PDP-11/45 running RSTS . . . wow!). As usual, I sneaked around in anonymous accounts—no need for the whole world to see I was on the machine. Every so often, I'd take a look at the other users, or surface in my official account. Suddenly I was accosted by another user via the TALK program (which for some reason I had left enabled). The TALKer claimed some implausible name, and I responded in kind. We chatted for a bit, each trying to figure out the other's true name. Finally I gave up, and told the other fellow I had to go—that I was actually a personality simulator, and that if I kept talking my artificial nature would become obvious.

Afterwards, I realized that I had just lived a science-fiction story, at least by the standards of my childhood. For several years (ever since reading Ursula K. LeGuin's A Wizard of Earthsea) I'd had the idea that the "true names" of fantasy were like object ID numbers from a big database. Now I saw how easily that could be turned into a story.

Word for word, "True Names" was easier to write than anything I've ever done.

48

TRUE NAMES

In the once-upon-a-time days of the First Age of Magic, the prudent sorcerer regarded his own true name as his most valued possession but also the greatest threat to his continued good health, for—the stories go—once an enemy, even a weak unskilled enemy, learned the sorcerer's true name, then routine and widely known spells could destroy or enslave even the most powerful. As times passed, and we graduated to the Age of Reason and thence to the first and second industrial revolutions, such notions were discredited. Now it seems that the Wheel has turned full circle (even if there never really was a First Age) and we are back to worrying about true names again:

The first hint Mr. Slippery had that his own True Name might be known—and, for that matter, known to the Great Enemy—came with the appearance of two black Lincolns humming up the long dirt driveway that stretched through the dripping pine forest down to Road 29. Roger Pollack was in his garden weeding, had been there nearly the whole morning, enjoying the barely perceptible drizzle and the overcast, and trying to find the initiative to go inside and do work that actually makes money. He looked up the moment the intruders turned, wheels squealing, into his driveway. Thirty seconds passed, the cars came out of the third-generation forest to pull up beside and behind Pollack's Honda. Four heavy-set men and a hard-looking female piled out, started purposefully across his well-tended cabbage patch, crushing tender young plants with a disregard which told Roger that this was no social call.

Pollack looked wildly around, considered making a break for the woods, but the others had spread out and he was grabbed and frog-marched back to his house. (Fortunately the door had been left unlocked. Roger had the feeling that they might have knocked it down rather than ask him for the key.) He was shoved abruptly into a chair. Two of the heaviest and least collegiate-looking of his visitors stood on either side of him. Pollack's protests—now just being voiced—brought no response. The woman and an older man poked around among his sets. "Hey, I remember this, Al: It's the script for *1965*. See?" The woman spoke as she flipped through the holo-scenes that decorated the interior wall.

The older man nodded. "I told you. He's written more popular games than any three men and even more than some agencies. Roger Pollack is something of a genius."

They're novels, damn you, not games! Old irritation flashed unbidden into Roger's mind. Aloud: "Yeah, but most of my fans aren't as persistent as you all."

"Most of your fans don't know that you are a criminal, Mr. Pollack."

"Criminal? I'm no criminal—but I do know my rights. You FBI types must identify yourselves, give me a phone call, and—"

The woman smiled for the first time. It was not a nice smile. She was about thirty-five, hatchet-faced, her hair drawn back in the single braid favored by military types. Even so it could have been a nicer smile. Pollack felt a chill start up his spine. "Perhaps that would be true, if we *were* the FBI or if you were *not* the scum you are. But this is a Welfare Department bust, Pollack, and you are suspected—putting it kindly—of interference with the instrumentalities of National and individual survival."

She sounded like something out of one of those asinine scripts he occasionally had to work on for government contracts. Only now there was nothing to laugh about, and the cold between his shoulder blades spread. Outside the drizzle had become a misty rain sweeping across the Northern California forests. Normally he found that rain a comfort, but now it just added to the gloom. Still, if there was any chance he could wriggle out of this, it would be worth the effort. "Okay, so you have license to hassle innocents, but sooner or later you're going to discover that I *am* innocent and then you'll find out what hostile media coverage can really be like." *And thank God I backed up my files last night. With luck, all they'll find is some out-of-date stock-market schemes.*

"You're no innocent, Pollack. An *honest* citizen is content with an ordinary data set like yours there." She pointed across the living room at the forty-by-fifty-centimeter data set. It was the great-grandchild of the old CRT's. With color and twenty-line-per-millimeter resolution, it was the standard of government offices and the more conservative industries. There was a visible layer of dust on Pollack's model. The femcop moved quickly across the living room and poked into the drawers under the picture window. Her maroon business suit revealed a thin and angular figure. "An *honest* citizen would settle for a standard processor and a few thousand megabytes of

fast storage." With some superior intuition she pulled
open the center drawer—right under the marijuana
plants—to reveal at least five hundred cubic centimeters of optical memory, neatly racked and threaded
through to the next drawer which held correspondingly powerful CPUs. Even so, it was nothing compared to the gear he had buried under the house.

She drifted out into the kitchen and was back in a
moment. The house was a typical airdropped bungalow, small and easy to search. Pollack had spent most
of his money on the land and his . . . hobbies. "And
finally," she said, a note of triumph in her voice, "an
honest citizen does not need one of these!" She had
finally spotted the Other World gate. She waved the
electrodes in Pollack's face.

"Look, in spite of what you may want, all this is
still legal. In fact, that gadget is scarcely more powerful than an ordinary games interface." That should
be a good explanation, considering that he was a
novelist.

The older man spoke almost apologetically, "I'm
afraid Virginia has a tendency to play cat and mouse,
Mr. Pollack. You see, we know that in the Other
World you are Mr. Slippery."

"Oh."

There was a long silence. Even "Virginia" kept her
mouth shut. This had been, of course, Roger Pollack's great fear. They had discovered Mr. Slippery's
True Name and it was Roger Andrew Pollack TIN/
SSAN 0959-34-2861, and no amount of evasion, tricky
programming, or robot sources could ever again protect him from them. "How did you find out?"

A third cop, a technician type, spoke up. "It wasn't
easy. We wanted to get our hands on someone who
was really good, not a trivial vandal—what your Coven would call a lesser warlock." The younger man
seemed to know the jargon, but you could pick that
up just by watching the daily paper. "For the last

three months, DoW has been trying to find the identity of someone of the caliber of yourself or Robin Hood, or Erythrina, or the Slimey Limey. We were having no luck at all until we turned the problem around and began watching artists and novelists. We figured at least a fraction of them must be attracted to vandal activities. And they would have the talent to be good at it. Your participation novels are the best in the world." There was genuine admiration in his voice. *One meets fans in the oddest places.* "So you were one of the first people we looked at. Once we suspected you, it was just a matter of time before we had the evidence."

It was what he had always worried about. A successful warlock cannot afford to be successful in the real world. He had been greedy; he loved both realms too much.

The older cop continued the technician's almost diffident approach. "In any case, Mr. Pollack, I think you realize that if the Federal government wants to concentrate all its resources on the apprehension of a single vandal, we can do it. The vandals' power comes from their numbers rather than their power as individuals."

Pollack repressed a smile. That was a common belief—or faith—within government. He had snooped on enough secret memos to realize that the Feds really believed it, but it was very far from true. He was not nearly as clever as someone like Erythrina. He could only devote fifteen or twenty hours a week to SIG activities. Some of the others must be on welfare, so complete was their presence on the Other Plane. The cops had nailed him simply because he was a relatively easy catch.

"So you have something besides jail planned for me?"

"Mr. Pollack, have you ever heard of the Mailman?"

"You mean on the Other Plane?"

"Certainly. He has had no notoriety in the, uh, real world as yet."

For the moment there was no use lying. They must know that no member of a SIG or coven would ever give his True Name to another member. There was no way he could betray any of the others—*he hoped*.

"Yeah, he's the weirdest of the werebots."

"Werebots?"

"Were-robots, like werewolves—get it? They don't really mesh with coven imagery. They want some new mythos, and this notion that they are humans who can turn into machines seems to suit them. It's too dry for me. This Mailman, for instance, never uses real-time communication. If you want anything from him, you usually have to wait a day or two for each response—just like the old-time hardcopy mail service."

"That's the fellow. How impressed are you by him?"

"Oh, we've been aware of him for a couple years, but he's so slow that for a long time we thought he was some clown on a simple data set. Lately, though, he's pulled some really—" Pollack stopped short, remembering just who he was gossiping with.

"—some really tuppin stunts, eh, Pollack?" The femcop "Virginia" was back in the conversation. She pulled up one of the roller chairs, till her knees were almost touching his, and stabbed a finger at his chest. "You may not know just how tuppin. You vandals have caused Social Security Records enormous problems, and Robin Hood cut IRS revenues by three percent last year. You and your friends are a greater threat than any foreign enemy. Yet you're nothing compared to this Mailman."

Pollack was rocked back. It must be that he had seen only a small fraction of the Mailman's japes. "You're actually scared of him," he said mildly.

Virginia's face began to take on the color of her suit. Before she could reply, the older cop spoke. "Yes, we are scared. We can scarcely cope with the Robin Hoods and the Mr. Slipperys of the world. Fortunately, most vandals are interested in personal gain or in proving their cleverness. They realize that if they cause too much trouble, they could no doubt be identified. I suspect that tens of thousands of cases of Welfare and Tax fraud are undetected, committed by little people with simple equipment who succeed because they don't steal much—perhaps just their own income tax liability—and don't wish the notoriety which you, uh, warlocks go after. If it weren't for their petty individualism, they would be a greater threat than the nuclear terrorists.

"But the Mailman is different; he appears to be ideologically motivated. He is *very* knowledgeable, *very* powerful. Vandalism is not enough for him; he wants control . . ." The Feds had no idea how long it had been going on, at least a year. It never would have been discovered but for a few departments in the Federal Screw Standards Commission which kept their principal copy records on paper. Discrepancies showed up between those records and the decisions rendered in the name of the FSSC. Inquiries were made; computer records were found at variance with the hardcopy. More inquiries. By luck more than anything else, the investigators discovered that decision modules as well as data were different from the hardcopy backups. For thirty years government had depended on automated central planning, shifting more and more from legal descriptions of decision algorithms to program representations that could work directly with data bases to allocate resources, suggest legislation, outline military strategy.

The take-over had been subtle, and its extent was unknown. That was the horror of it. It was not even clear just what groups within the Nation (or without) were benefitting from the changed interpretations of Federal law and resource allocation. Only the decision modules in the older departments could be directly checked, and some thirty percent of them showed tampering. ". . . and that percentage scares us as much as anything, Mr. Pollack. It would take a large team of technicians and lawyers *months* to successfully make just the changes that we have detected."

"What about the military?" Pollack thought of the Finger of God installations and the thousands of missiles pointed at virtually every country on Earth. If Mr. Slippery had ever desired to take over the world, that is what he would have gone for. To hell with pussy-footing around with Social Security checks.

"No. No penetration there. In fact, it was his attempt to infiltrate—" the older cop glanced hesitantly at Virginia, and Pollack realized who was the boss of this operation, "—NSA that revealed the culprit to be the Mailman. Before that it was anonymous, totally without the ego-flaunting we see in big-time vandals. But the military and NSA have their own systems. Impractical though that is, it paid off this time." Pollack nodded. The SIG steered clear of the military, and especially of NSA.

"But if he was about to slide through DoW and Department of Justice defenses so easy, you really don't know how much a matter of luck it was that he didn't also succeed with his first try on NSA. . . . I think I understand now. You need help. You hope to get some member of the Coven to work on this from the inside."

"It's not a *hope*, Pollack," said Virginia. "It's a certainty. Forget about going to jail. Oh, we could put you away forever on the basis of some of Mr. Slippery's pranks. But even if we don't do that, we can take away your license to operate. You know what that means."

It was not a question, but Pollack knew the answer

nevertheless: ninety-eight percent of the jobs in modern society involved some use of a data set. Without a license, he was virtually unemployable—and that left Welfare, the prospect of sitting in some urbapt counting flowers on the wall. Virginia must have seen the defeat in his eyes. "Frankly, I am not as confident as Ray that you are all that sharp. But you are the best we could catch. NSA thinks we have a chance of finding the Mailman's true identity if we can get an agent into your coven. We want you to continue to attend coven meetings, but now your chief goal is not mischief but the gathering of information about the Mailman. You are to recruit any help you can without revealing that you are working for the government—you might even make up the story that you suspect the Mailman of being a government plot. (I'm sure you see he has some of the characteristics of a Federal agent working off a conventional data set.) Above all, you are to remain alert to contact from us, and give us your instant cooperation in anything we require of you. Is all this perfectly clear, Mr. Pollack?"

He found it difficult to meet her gaze. He had never really been exposed to extortion before. There was something . . . dehumanizing about being used so. "Yeah," he finally said.

"Good." She stood up, and so did the others. 'If you behave, this is the last time you'll see us in person."

Pollack stood too. "And afterward, if you're . . . satisfied with my performance?"

Virginia grinned, and he knew he wasn't going to like her answer. "Afterward, we can come back to considering *your* crimes. If you do a good job, I would have no objection to your retaining a standard data set, maybe some of your interactive graphics. But I'll tell you, if it weren't for the Mailman, nabbing Mr. Slippery would make my month. There is no way I'd risk your continuing to abuse the System."

Three minutes later, their sinister black Lincolns were halfway down the drive, disappearing into the pines. Pollack stood in the drizzle watching till long after their sound had faded to nothing. He was barely aware of the cold wet across his shoulders and down his back. He looked up suddenly, feeling the rain in his face, wondering if the Feds were so clever that they had taken the day into account: the military's recon satellites could no doubt monitor their cars, but the civilian satellites the SIG had access to could not penetrate these clouds. Even if some other member of the SIG did know Mr. Slippery's True Name, they would not know that the Feds had paid him a visit.

Pollack looked across the yard at his garden. *What a difference an hour can make.*

By late afternoon, the overcast was gone. Sunlight glinted off millions of waterdrop jewels in the trees. Pollack waited till the sun was behind the tree line, till all that was left of its passage was a gold band across the taller trees to the east of his bungalow. Then he sat down before his equipment and prepared to ascend to the Other Plane. What he was undertaking was trickier than anything he had tried before, and he wanted to take as much time as the Feds would tolerate. A week of thought and research would have suited him more, but Virginia and her pals were clearly too impatient for that.

He powered up his processors, settled back in his favorite chair, and carefully attached the Portal's five sucker electrodes to his scalp. For long minutes nothing happened: a certain amount of self-denial—or at least self-hypnosis—was necessary to make the ascent. Some experts recommended drugs or sensory isolation to heighten the user's sensitivity to the faint, ambiguous signals that could be read from the Portal. Pollack, who was certainly more experienced than any of the pop experts, had found that he could make it simply by staring out into the trees and listening to the wind-surf that swept through their upper branches.

And just as a daydreamer forgets his actual surroundings and sees other realities, so Pollack drifted, detached, his subconscious interpreting the status of the West Coast communication and data services as a vague thicket for his conscious mind to inspect, interrogate for the safest path to an intermediate haven. Like most exurb data-commuters, Pollack rented the standard optical links: Bell, Boeing, Nippon Electric. Those, together with the local West Coast data companies, gave him more than enough paths to proceed with little chance of detection to any accepting processor on Earth. In minutes, he had traced through three changes of carrier and found a place to do his intermediate computing. The comsats rented processor time almost as cheaply as ground stations, and an automatic payment transaction (through several dummy accounts set up over the last several years) gave him sole control of a large data space within milliseconds of his request. The whole process was almost at a subconscious level—the proper functioning of numerous routines he and others had devised over the last four years. Mr. Slippery (the other name was avoided now, even in his thoughts) had achieved the fringes of the Other Plane. He took a quick peek through the eyes of a low-resolution weather satellite, saw the North American continent spread out below, the terminator sweeping through the West, most of the plains clouded over. One never knew when some apparently irrelevant information might help—and though it could all be done automatically through subconscious access, Mr. Slippery had always been a romantic about spaceflight.

He rested for a few moments, checking that his indirect communication links were working and that the encryption routines appeared healthy, untampered with. (Like most folks, honest citizens or warlocks, he had no trust for the government standard encryption routines, but preferred the schemes that had leaked out of academia—over NSA's petulant objections—during the last fifteen years.) Protected now against traceback, Mr. Slippery set out for the Coven itself. He quickly picked up the trail, but this was never an easy trip, for the SIG members had no interest in being bothered by the unskilled.

In particular, the traveler must be able to take advantage of subtle sensory indications, and see in them the environment originally imagined by the SIG. The correct path had the aspect of a narrow row of stones cutting through a gray-greenish swamp. The air was cold but very moist. Weird, towering plants dripped audibly onto the faintly iridescent water and the broad lilies. The subconscious knew what the stones represented, handled the chaining of routines from one information net to another, but it was the conscious mind of the skilled traveler that must make the decisions that could lead to the gates of the Coven, or to the symbolic "death" of a dump back to the real world. The basic game was a distant relative of the ancient Adventure that had been played on computer systems for more than forty years, and a nearer relative of the participation novels that are still widely sold. There were two great differences, though. This game was more serious, and was played at a level of complexity impossible without the use of the EEG input/output that the warlocks and the popular data bases called Portals.

There was much misinformation and misunderstanding about the Portals. Oh, responsible data bases like the *LA Times* and the *CBS News* made it clear that there was nothing supernatural about them or about the Other Plane, that the magical jargon was at best a romantic convenience and at worst obscurantism. But even so, their articles often missed the point and were both too conservative and too extravagant. You might think that to convey the full sense imagery of the swamp, some immense bandwidth would be necessary. In fact, that was not so (and if it were, the Feds would have quickly been able to spot warlock and werebot operations). A typical Portal link was around fifty thousand baud, far narrower than even a flat video channel. Mr. Slippery could feel the damp seeping through his leather boots, could feel the sweat starting on his skin even in the cold air, but this was the response of Mr. Slippery's imagination and subconscious to the cues that were actually being presented through the Portal's electrodes. The interpretation could not be arbitrary or he would be dumped back to reality and would never find the Coven; to the traveler on the Other Plane, the detail was there as long as the cues were there. And there is nothing new about this situation. Even a poor writer—if he has a sympathetic reader and an engaging plot—can evoke complete internal imagery with a few dozen words of description. The difference now is that the imagery has interactive significance, just as sensations in the real world do. Ultimately, the magic jargon was perhaps the closest fit in the vocabulary of millennium Man.

The stones were spaced more widely now, and it took all Mr. Slippery's skill to avoid falling into the noisome waters that surrounded him. Fortunately, after another hundred meters or so, the trail rose out of the water, and he was walking on shallow mud. The trees and brush grew in close around him, and large spider webs glistened across the trail and between some of the trees along the side.

Like a yo-yo from some branch high above him, a red-banded spider the size of a man's fist descended into the space right before the traveler's face. "Beware, beware," the tiny voice issued from dripping mandibles. "Beware, beware," the words were repeated, and the creature swung back and forth, nearer and farther from Mr. Slippery's face. He looked carefully at the spider's banded abdomen. There were many species of deathspider here, and each required a different response if a traveler was to survive. Finally he raised the back of his hand and held it level so that the spider could crawl onto it. The creature raced up the damp fabric of his jacket to the open neck. There it whispered something very quietly.

Mr. Slippery listened, then grabbed the animal before it could repeat the message and threw it to the left, at the same time racing off into the tangle of webs and branches on the other side of the trail. Something heavy and wet slapped into the space where he had been, but he was already gone—racing at top speed up the incline that suddenly appeared before him.

He stopped when he reached the crest of the hill. Beyond it, he could see the solemn, massive fortress that was the Coven's haven. It was not more than five hundred meters away, illuminated as the swamp had been by a vague and indistinct light that came only partly from the sky. The trail leading down to it was much more open than the swamp had been, but the traveler proceeded as slowly as before: the sprites the warlocks set to keep guard here had the nasty—though preprogrammed—habit of changing the rules in deadly ways.

The trail descended, then began a rocky, winding climb toward the stone and iron gates of the castle. The ground was drier here, the vegetation sparse. Leathery snapping of wings sounded above him, but Mr. Slippery knew better than to look up. Thirty meters from the moat, the heat became more than uncomfortable. He could hear the lava popping and hissing, could see occasional dollops of fire splatter up from the liquid to scorch what vegetation still lived. A pair of glowing eyes set in coal-black head rose briefly from the moat. A second later, the rest of the creature came surging into view, cascading sparks and lava down upon the traveler. Mr. Slippery raised his hand just so, and the lethal spray separated over his head to land harmlessly on either side of him. He watched with apparent calm as the creature descended ancient stone steps to confront him.

Alan—that was the elemental's favorite name—peered nearsightedly, his head weaving faintly from side to side as he tried to recognize the traveler. "Ah, I do believe we are honored with the presence of Mr. Slippery, is it not so?" he finally said. He smiled, an open grin revealing the glowing interior of his mouth. His breath did not show flame but did have the penetrating heat of an open kiln. He rubbed his clawed hands against his asbestos T-shirt as though anxious to be proved wrong. Away from his magna moat, the dead black of his flesh lightened, trying to contain his body heat. Now he looked almost reptilian.

"Indeed it is. And come to bring my favorite little gifts." Mr. Slippery threw a leaden slug into the air and watched the elemental grab it with his mouth, his eyes slitted with pleasure—melt-in-your-mouth pleasure. They traded conversation, spells, and counterspells for several minutes. Alan's principal job was to determine that the visitor was a known member of the Coven, and he ordinarily did this with little tests of skill (the magma bath he had tried to give Mr. Slippery) and by asking the visitor questions about previous activities within the castle. Alan was a personality simulator, of course. Mr. Slippery was sure that there had never been a living operator behind that toothless, glowing smile. But he was certainly one of the best, probably the product of many hundreds of blocks of psylisp programming, and certainly superior to the little "companionship" programs you can buy nowadays, which generally become repetitive after a few hours of conversation, which don't grow, and which are unable to counter weird responses. Alan had been with the Coven and the castle since before Mr. Slippery had become a member, and no one would admit to his creation (though Wiley J. was suspected). He hadn't even had a name until this year, when Erythrina had given him that asbestos Alan Turing T-shirt.

Mr. Slippery played the game with good humor, but care. To "die" at the hands of Alan would be a painful experience that would probably wipe a lot of unbacked memory he could ill afford to lose. Such death had claimed many petitioners at this gate, folk who would not soon be seen on this plane again.

Satisfied, Alan waved a clawed fist at the watchers in the tower, and the gate—ceramic bound in wolfram clasps—was rapidly lowered for the visitor. Mr. Slippery walked quickly across, trying to ignore the spitting and bubbling that he heard below him. Alan—now all respectful—waited till he was in the castle courtyard before doing an immense belly-flop back into his magma swimming hole.

Most of the others, with the notable exception of Erythrina, had already arrived. Robin Hood, dressed in green and looking like Errol Flynn, sat across the hall in very close conversation with a remarkably good-looking female (but then they could all be remarkably good-looking here) who seemed unsure whether to project blonde or brunette. By the fireplace, Wiley J. Bastard, the Slimey Limey, and DON. MAC were in animated discussion over a pile of maps. And in the corner, shaded from the fireplace and apparently unused, sat a classic remote printing terminal. Mr. Slippery tried to ignore that teleprinter as he crossed the hall.

"Ah, it's Slip." DON.MAC looked up from the maps and gestured him closer. "Take a look here at what the Limey has been up to."

"Hmm?" Mr. Slippery nodded at the others, then leaned over to study the top map. The margins of the paper were aging vellum, but the "map" itself hung in three dimensions, half sunk into the paper. It was a typical banking defense and cash-flow plot—that is, typical for the SIG. Most banks had no such clever ways of visualizing the automated protection of their assets. (For that matter, Mr. Slippery suspected that most banks still looked wistfully back to the days of credit cards and COBOL.) This was the sort of thing Robin Hood had developed, and it was surprising to see the Limey involved in it. He looked up questioningly. "What's the jape?"

"It's a reg'lar double-slam, Slip. Look at this careful, an' you'll see it's no ord'n'ry protection map. Seems like what you blokes call the Mafia has taken over this banking net in the Maritime states. They must be usin' Portals to do it so slick. Took me a devil of a time to figure out it was them as done it. *Ha ha!* but now that I have . . . look here, you'll see how they've been launderin' funds, embezzlin' from straight accounts.

"They're ever so clever, but not so clever as to know about Slimey." He poked a finger into the map and a trace gleamed red through the maze. "If they're lucky, they'll discover this tap next autumn, when they find themselves maybe three billion dollars short, and not a single sign of where it all disappeared to."

The others nodded. There were many covens and SIGs throughout this plane. Theirs, The Coven, was widely known, had pulled off some of the most publicized pranks of the century. Many of the others were scarcely more than social clubs. But some were old-style criminal organizations which used this plane for their own purely pragmatic and opportunistic reasons. Usually such groups weren't too difficult for the warlocks to victimize, but it was the Slimey Limey who seemed to specialize in doing so.

"But, geez, Slimey, these guys play rough, even rougher than the Great Enemy." That is, the Feds. "If they ever figure out who you really are, you'll die the True Death for sure."

"I may be slimy, but I ain't crazy. There's no way I could absorb three billion dollars—or even three million—without being discovered. But I played it like Robin over there: the money got spread around three million ordinary accounts here and in Europe, one of which just happens to be mine."

Mr. Slippery's ears perked up. "Three million accounts, you say? Each with a sudden little surplus? I'll bet I could come close to finding your True Name from that much, Slimey."

The Limey made a faffling gesture. "It's actually a wee bit more complicated. Face it, chums, none of you has ever come close to sightin' me, an' you know more than any Mafia."

That was true. They all spent a good deal of their time in this plane trying to determine the others' True Names. It was not an empty game, for the knowledge of another's True Name effectively made him your slave—as Mr. Slippery had already discovered in an unpleasantly firsthand way. So the warlocks constantly probed one another, devised immense programs to sieve government-personnel records for the idiosyncracies that they detected in each other. At first glance, the Limey should have been one of the easiest to discover: he had plenty of mannerisms. His Brit accent was dated and broke down every so often into North American. Of all the warlocks, he was the only one neither handsome nor grotesque.

His face was, in fact, so ordinary and real that Mr. Slippery had suspected that it might be his true appearance and had spent several months devising a scheme that searched U.S. and common Europe photo files for just that appearance. It had been for nothing, and they had all eventually reached the conclusion that the Limey must be doubly or triply deceptive.

Wiley J. Bastard grinned, not too impressed. "It's nice enough, and I agree that the risks are probably small, Slimey. But what do you really get? An ego boost and a little money. But we," he gestured inclusively, "are worth more than that. With a little cooperation, we could be the most powerful people in the real world. Right, DON?"

DON.MAC nodded, smirking. His face was really the only part of him that looked human or had much flexibility of expression—and even it was steely gray. The rest of DON's body was modeled after the standard Plessey-Mercedes all-weather robot.

Mr. Slippery recognized the reference. "So you're working with the Mailman now, too, Wiley?" He glanced briefly at the teleprinter.

"Yup."

"And you still won't give us any clue what it's all about?"

Wiley shook his head. "Not unless you're serious about throwing in with us. But you all know this: DON was the first to work with the Mailman, and he's richer than Croesus now."

DON.MAC nodded again, that silly smile still on his face.

"Hmmm." It was easy to get rich. In principle, the Limey could have made three billion dollars off the Mob in his latest caper. The problem was to become that rich and avoid detection and retribution. Even Robin Hood hadn't mastered that trick—but apparently DON and Wiley thought the Mailman had

done that and more. After his chat with Virginia, he
was willing to believe it. Mr. Slippery turned to look
more closely at the teleprinter. It was humming
faintly, and as usual it had a good supply of paper.
The paper was torn neatly off at the top, so that the
only message visible was the Mailman's asterisk
prompt. It was the only way they ever communi-
cated with this most mysterious of their members:
type a message on the device, and in an hour or a
week the machine would rattle and beat, and a response of up to several thousand words would
appear. In the beginning, it had not been very
popular—the idea was cute, but the delays made
conversation just too damn dull. He could remember
seeing meters of Mailman output lying sloppily on
the stone floor, mostly unread. But *now*, every one
of the Mailman's golden words was eagerly sopped
up by his new apprentices, who very carefully removed every piece of output, leaving no clues for the
rest of them to work with.

"Ery!" He looked toward the broad stone stair
that led down from the courtyard. It was Erythrina
the Red Witch. She swept down the stairs, her cos-
tume shimmering, now revealing, now obscuring.
She had a spectacular figure and an excellent sense
of design, but of course that was not what was re-
markable about her. Erythrina was the sort of person
who knew much more than she ever said, even though
she always seemed easy to talk to. Some of her
adventures—though unadvertised—were in a class
with Robin Hood's. Mr. Slippery had known her
well for a year; she was certainly the most interesting
personality on this plane. She made him wish that all
the secrets were unnecessary, that True Names could
be traded as openly as phone numbers. What was
she really?

Erythrina nodded to Robin Hood, then proceeded
down the hall to DON.MAC, who had originally

shouted greetings and now continued, "We've just been trying to convince Slimey and Slip that they are wasting their time on pranks when they could have real power and real wealth."

She glance sharply at Wiley, who seemed strangely irritated that she had been drawn into the conversation. " 'We' meaning you and Wiley and the Mailman?"

Wiley nodded. "I just started working with them last week, Ery," as if to say, *and you can't stop me*.

"You may have something, DON. We all started out as amateurs, doing our best to make the System just a little bit uncomfortable for its bureaucratic masters. But we are experts now. We probably understand the System better than anyone on Earth. That should equate to power." It was the same thing the other two had been saying, but she could make it much more persuasive. Before his encounter with the Feds, he might have bought it (even though he always knew that the day he got serious about Coven activities and went after real gain would also be the day it ceased to be an enjoyable game and became an all-consuming job that would suck time away from the projects that made life entertaining).

Erythrina looked from Mr. Slippery to the Limey and then back. The Limey was an easygoing sort, but just now he was a bit miffed at the way his own pet project had been dismissed. "Not for me, thanky," he said shortly and began to gather up his maps.

She turned her green, faintly oriental eyes upon Mr. Slippery. "How about you, Slip? Have you signed up with the Mailman?"

He hesitated. *Maybe I should*. It seemed clear that the Mailman's confederates were being let in on at least part of his schemes. In a few hours, he might be able to learn enough to get Virginia off his back. And perhaps destroy his friends to boot; it was a hell of a bargain. *God in Heaven, why did they have to get mixed up in this? Don't they realize what the Government will do to them, if they really try to take over, if they ever try to play at being more than vandals?* "Not . . . not yet," he said finally. "I'm awfully tempted, though."

She grinned, regular white teeth flashing against her dark, faintly green face. "I, too. What do you say we talk it over, just the two of us?" She reached out a slim, dark hand to grasp his elbow. "Excuse us, gentlemen; hopefully, when we get back, you'll have a couple of new allies." And Mr. Slippery felt himself gently propelled toward the dark and musty stairs that led to Erythrina's private haunts.

Her torch burned and glowed, but there was no smoke. The flickering yellow lit their path for scant meters ahead. The stairs were steep and gently curving. He had the feeling that they must do a complete circle every few hundred steps: this was an immense spiral cut deep into the heart of the living rock. And it was alive. As the smell of mildew and rot increased, as the dripping from the ceiling grew subtly louder and the puddles in the worn steps deeper, the walls high above their heads took on shapes, and those shapes changed and flowed to follow them. Erythrina protected her part of the castle as thoroughly as the castle itself was guarded against the outside world. Mr. Slippery had no doubt that if she wished, she could trap him permanently here, along with the lizards and the rock sprites. (Of course he could always "escape" simply by falling back into the real world, but until she relented or he saw through her spells, he would not be able to access any other portion of the castle.) Working on some of their projects, he had visited her underground halls, but never anything this deep.

He watched her shapely form preceding him down, down, down. Of all the Coven (with the possible exception of Robin Hood, and of course the Mailman), she was the most powerful. He suspected that she was one of the original founders. If only there were some way of convincing her (without revealing the source of his knowledge) that the Mailman was a threat. If only there was some way of getting her cooperation in nailing down the Mailman's True Name.

Erythrina stopped and he bumped pleasantly into her. Over her shoulder, a high door ended the passage. She moved her hand in a pattern hidden from Mr. Slippery and muttered some unlocking spell. The door split horizontally, its halves pulling apart with oiled and massive precision. Beyond, he had the impression of spots and lines of red breaking a further darkness.

"Mind your step," she said and hopped over a murky puddle that stood before the high sill of the doorway.

As the door slid shut behind them, Erythrina changed the torch to a single searing spot of white light, like some old-time incandescent bulb. The room was bright-lit now. Comfortable black leather chairs sat on black tile. Red engraving, faintly glowing, was worked into the tile and the obsidian of the walls. In contrast to the stairway, the air was fresh and clean—though still.

She waved him to a chair that faced away from the light, then sat on the edge of a broad desk. The point light glinted off her eyes, making them unreadable. Erythrina's face was slim and fine-boned, almost Asian except for the pointed ears. But the skin was dark, and her long hair had the reddish tones unique to some North American blacks. She was barely smiling now, and Mr. Slippery wished again he had some way of getting her help.

"Slip, I'm scared," she said finally, the smile gone.

You're scared! For a moment, he couldn't quite believe his ears. "The Mailman?" he asked, hoping.

She nodded. "This is the first time in my life I've felt outgunned. I need help. Robin Hood may be the most competent, but he's basically a narcissist; I don't think I could interest him in anything beyond his immediate gratifications. That leaves you and the Limey. And I think there's something special about you. We've done a couple things together," she couldn't help herself, and grinned remembering. "They weren't real impressive, but somehow I have a feeling about you: I think you understand what things up here are silly games and what things are really important. If you think something is really important, you can be trusted to stick with it even if the going gets a little . . . bloody."

Coming from someone like Ery, the words had special meaning. It was strange, to feel both flattered and frightened. Mr. Slippery stuttered for a moment, inarticulate. "What about Wiley J? Seems to me you have special . . . influence over him."

"You knew. . . ?"

"Suspected."

"Yes, he's my thrall. Has been for almost six months. Poor Wiley turns out to be a life-insurance salesman from Peoria. Like a lot of warlocks, he's rather a Thurberesque fellow in real life: timid, always dreaming of heroic adventures and grandiose thefts. Only nowadays people like that can realize their dreams. . . . Anyway, he doesn't have the background, or the time, or the skill that I do, and I found his True Name. I enjoy the chase more than the extortion, so I haven't leaned on him too hard; now I wish I had. Since he's taken up with the Mailman, he's been giving me the finger. Somehow Wiley thinks that what they have planned will keep him safe even if I give his True Name to the cops!"

"So the Mailman actually has some scheme for winning political power in the real world?"

She smiled. "That's what Wiley thinks. You see,

poor Wiley doesn't know that there are more uses for
True Names than simple blackmail. I know everything he sends over the data links, everything he has
been told by the Mailman."

"So what are they up to?" It was hard to conceal
his eagerness. *Perhaps this will be enough to satisfy
Virginia and her goons.*

Erythrina seemed frozen for a moment, and he
realized that she too must be using the low-altitude
satellite net for preliminary processing: her task had
just been handed off from one comsat to a nearer
bird. Ordinarily it was easy to disguise the hesita-
tion. She must be truly upset.

And when she finally replied, it wasn't really with
an answer. "You know what convinced Wiley that
the Mailman could deliver on his promises? It was
DON.MAC—and the revolution in Venezuela. Apparently DON and the Mailman had been working
on that for several months before Wiley joined them.
It was to be the Mailman's first demonstration that
controlling data and information services could be
used to take permanent political control of a state.
And Venezuela, they claimed, was perfect: it has
enormous data-processing facilities—all just a bit obsolete, since they were bought when the country was
at the peak of its boom time."

"But that was clearly an internal coup. The present leaders are local—"

"Nevertheless, DON is supposedly down there
now, the real *Jefe*, for the first time in his life able to
live in the physical world the way we do in this
plane. If you have your own country, you are no
longer small fry that must guard his True Name. You
don't have to settle for crumbs."

"You said 'supposedly'."

"Slip, have you noticed anything strange about
DON lately?"

Mr. Slippery thought back. DON.MAC had always

been the most extreme of the werebots—after the Mailman. He was not an especially talented fellow, but he did go to great lengths to sustain the image that he was both machine and human. His persona was always present in this plane, though at least part of the time it was a simulator—like Alan out in the magma moat. The simulation was fairly good, but no one had yet produced a program that could really pass the Turing test: that is, fool a real human for any extended time. Mr. Slippery remembered the silly smile that seemed pasted on DON's face and the faintly repetitive tone of his lobbying for the Mailman. "You think the real person behind DON is gone, that we have a zombie up there?"

"Slip, I think the real DON is *dead*, and I mean the True Death."

"Maybe he just found the real world more delightful than this, now that he owns such a big hunk of it?"

"I don't think he owns anything. It's just barely possible that the Mailman had something to do with that coup; there are a number of coincidences between what they told Wiley beforehand and what actually happened. But I've spent a lot of time floating through the Venezuelan data bases, and I think I'd know if an outsider were on the scene, directing the new order.

"I think the Mailman is taking us on one at a time, starting with the weakest, drawing us in far enough to learn our True Names—and then destroying us. So far he has only done it to one of us. I've been watching DON.MAC both directly and automatically since the coup, and there has never been a real person behind that facade, not once in two thousand hours. Wiley is next. The poor slob hasn't even been told yet what country his kingdom is to be—evidence that the Mailman doesn't really have the power he claims—but even so, he's ready to do practically anything for the Mailman, and against us.

"Slip, we have *got* to identify this *thing*, this Mailman, before he can get us."

She was even more upset than Virginia and the Feds. And she was right. For the first time, he felt more afraid of the Mailman than the government agents. He held up his hands. "I'm convinced. But what should we do? You've got the best angle in Wiley. The Mailman doesn't know you've got a tap through him, does he?"

She shook her head. "Wiley is too chicken to tell him, and doesn't realize that I can do this with his True Name. But I'm already doing everything I can with that. I want to pool information, guesses, with you. Between us maybe we can see something new."

"Well for starters, it's obvious that the Mailman's queer communication style—those long time delays—is a ploy. I know that fellow is listening all the time to what's going on in the Coven meeting hall. And he commands a number of sprites in real time." Mr. Slippery remembered the day the Mailman—or at least his teleprinter—had arrived. The image of an American Van Lines truck had pulled up at the edge of the moat, nearly intimidating Alan. The driver and loader were simulators, though good ones. They had answered all of Alan's questions correctly, then hauled the shipping crate down to the meeting hall. They hadn't left till the warlocks signed for the shipment and promised to "wire a wall outlet" for the device. This enemy definitely knew how to arouse the curiosity of his victims. Whoever controlled that printer seemed perfectly capable of normal behavior. *Perhaps it's someone we already know, like in the mysteries where the murderer masquerades as one of the victims. Robin Hood?*

"I know. In fact, he can do many things faster than I. He must control some powerful processors. But you're partly wrong: the living part of him that's behind it all really does operate with at least a one-hour turnaround time. All the quick stuff is pro-grammed."

Mr. Slippery started to protest, then realized that she could be right. "My God, what could that mean? Why would he deliberately saddle himself with that disadvantage?"

Erythrina smiled with some satisfaction. "I'm con-vinced that if we knew that, we'd have this guy sighted. I agree it's too great a disadvantage to be a simple red herring. I think he must have some time-delay problem to begin with, and—"

"—and he has exaggerated it?" But even if the Mailman were an Australian, the low satellite net made delays so short that he would probably be indistinguishable from a European or a Japanese. There was no place on Earth where . . . *but there are places off Earth!* The mass-transit satellites were in synchronous orbit 120 milliseconds out. There were about two hundred people there. And further out, at L5, there were at least another four hundred. Some were near-permanent residents. A strange idea, but still a possibility.

"*I* don't think he has exaggerated. Slip, I think the Mailman—not his processors and simulators, you understand—is at least a half-hour out from Earth, probably in the asteroid belt."

She smiled suddenly, and Mr. Slippery realized that his jaw must be resting on his chest. Except for the Joint Mars Recon, no human had been anywhere near that far out. *No human.* Mr. Slippery felt his ordinary, everyday world disintegrating into sheer science fiction. This was ridiculous.

"I know you don't believe; it took me a while to. He's not so obvious that he doesn't add in some time delay to disguise the cyclic variation in our relative positions. But it *is* a consistent explanation for the delay. These last few weeks I've been sniffing around the classified reports on our asteroid probes; there are definitely some mysterious things out there."

"Okay. It's consistent. But you're talking about an interstellar *invasion*. Even if NASA had the funding, it would take them decades to put the smallest interstellar probe together—and decades more for the flight. Trying to invade anyone with those logistics would be impossible. And if these aliens have a decent stardrive, why do they bother with deception? They could just move in and brush us aside."

"Ah, that's the point, Slip. The invasion I'm thinking of doesn't need any 'stardrive,' and it works fine against any race at exactly our point of development. Right: most likely interstellar war is a fantastically expensive business, with decade lead times. What better policy for an imperialistic, highly technological race than to lie doggo listening for evidence of younger civilizations? When they detect such, they send only one ship. When it arrives in the victims' solar system, the Computer Age is in full bloom there. We in the Coven know how fragile the present system is; it is only fear of exposure that prevents some warlocks from trying to take over. Just think how appealing our naïveté must be to an older civilization that has thousands of years of experience at managing data systems. Their small crew of agents moves in as close as local military surveillance permits and gradually insinuates itself into the victims' system. They eliminate what sharp individuals they detect in that system—people like us—and then they go after the bureaucracies and the military. In ten or twenty years, another fiefdom is ready for the arrival of the master race."

She lapsed into silence, and for a long moment they stared at each other. It did all hang together with a weird sort of logic. "What can we do, then?"

"That's the question." She shook her head sadly,

came across the room to sit beside him. Now that she had said her piece, the fire had gone out of her. For the first time since he had known her, Erythrina looked depressed. "We could just forsake this plane and stay in the real world. The Mailman might still be able to track us down, but we'd be of no more interest to him than anyone else. If we were lucky, we might have years before he takes over." She straightened. "I'll tell you this: if we want to live as warlocks, we have to stop him soon—within days at most. After he gets Wiley, he may drop the con tactics for something more direct.

"If I'm right about the Mailman, then our best bet would be to discover his communication link. That would be his Achilles' heel; there's no way you can hide in the crowd when you're beaming from that far away. We've got to take some real chances now, do things we'd never risk before. I figure that if we work together, maybe we can lessen the risk that either of us is identified."

He nodded. Ordinarily a prudent warlock used only limited bandwidth and so was confined to a kind of linear, personal perception. If they grabbed a few hundred megahertz of comm space, and a bigger share of rented processors, they could manipulate and search files in a way that would boggle Virginia the femcop. Of course, they would be much more easily identifiable. With two of them, though, they might be able to keep it up safely for a brief time, confusing the government and the Mailman with a multiplicity of clues. "Frankly, I don't buy the alien part. But the rest of what you say makes sense, and that's what counts. Like you say, we're going to have to take some chances."

"Right!" She smiled and reached behind his neck to draw his face to hers. She was a very good kisser. (Not everyone was. It was one thing just to look gorgeous, and another to project and respond to the many sensory cues in something as interactive as kissing.) He was just warming to this exercise of their mutual abilities when she broke off. "And the best time to start is right now. The others think we're sealed away down here. If strange things happen during the next few hours, it's less likely the Mailman will suspect *us*." She reached up to catch the light point in her hand. For an instant, blades of harsh white slipped out from between her fingers; then all was dark. He felt faint air motion as her hands moved through another spell. There were words, distorted and unidentifiable. Then the light was back, but as a torch again, and a door—a second door—had opened in the far wall.

He followed her up the passage that stretched straight and gently rising as far as the torchlight shone. They were walking a path that could not be—or at least that no one in the Coven could have believed. The castle was basically a logical structure "fleshed" out with the sensory cues that allowed warlocks to move about it as one would a physical structure. Its moats and walls were part of that logical structure, and though they had no physical reality outside of the varying potentials in whatever processors were running the program, they were proof against the movement of the equally "unreal" perceptions of the inhabitants of the plane. Erythrina and Mr. Slippery could have escaped the deep room simply by falling back into the real world, but in doing so, they would have left a chain of unclosed processor links. Their departure would have been detected by every Coven member, even by Alan, even by the sprites. An orderly departure scheme, such as represented by this tunnel, could only mean that Erythrina was far too clever to need his help, or that she had been one of the original builders of the castle some four years earlier (lost in the Mists of Time, as the Limey put it).

*   *   *

They were wild dogs now, large enough so as not likely to be bothered, small enough to be mistaken for the amateur users that are seen more and more in the Other Plane as the price of Portals declines and the skill of the public increases. Mr. Slippery followed Erythrina down narrow paths, deeper and deeper into the swamp that represented commercial and government data space. Occasionally he was aware of sprites or simulators watching them with hostile eyes from nests off to the sides of the trail. These were idle creations in many cases—program units designed to infuriate or amuse later visitors to the plane. But many of them guarded information caches, or peepholes into other folks' affairs, or meeting places of other SIGs. The Coven might be the most sophisticated group of users on this plane, but they were far from being alone.

The brush got taller, bending over the trail to drip on their backs. But the water was clear here, spread in quiet ponds on either side of their path. Light came from the water itself, a pearly luminescence that shone upward on the trunks of the waterbound trees and sparkled faintly in the droplets of water in their moss and leaves. That light was the representation of the really huge data bases run by the government and the largest companies. It did not correspond to a specific geographical location, but rather to the main East/West net that stretches through selected installations from Honolulu to Oxford, taking advantage of the time zones to spread the user load.

"Just a little bit farther," Erythrina said over her shoulder, speaking in the beast language (encipherment) that they had chosen with their forms.

Minutes later, they shrank into the brush, out of the way of two armored hackers that proceeded implacably up the trail. The pair drove in single file, the impossibly large eight-cylinder engines on their bikes belching fire and smoke and noise. The one bringing up the rear carried an old-style recoilless rifle decorated with swastikas and chrome. Dim fires glowed through their blackened face plates. The two dogs eyed the bikers timidly, as befitted their present disguise, but Mr. Slippery had the feeling he was looking at a couple of amateurs who were imaging beyond their station in life: the bikes' tires didn't always touch the ground, and the tracks they left didn't quite match the texture of the muck. Anyone could put on a heroic image in this plane, or appear as some dreadful monster. The problem was that there were always skilled users who were willing to cut such pretenders down to size—perhaps even to destroy their access. It befitted the less experienced to appear small and inconspicuous, and to stay out of others' way.

(Mr. Slippery had often speculated just how the simple notion of using high-resolution EEGs as input/output devices had caused the development of the "magical world" representation of data space. The Limey and Erythrina argued that sprites, reincarnation, spells, and castles were the natural tools here, more natural than the atomistic twentieth-century notions of data structures, programs, files, and communications protocols. It was, they argued, just more convenient for the mind to use the global ideas of magic as the tokens to manipulate this new environment. They had a point; in fact, it was likely that the governments of the world hadn't caught up to the skills of the better warlocks simply because they refused to indulge in the foolish imaginings of fantasy. Mr. Slippery looked down at the reflection in the pool beside him and saw the huge canine face and lolling tongue looking up at him; he winked at the image. He knew that despite all his friends' high intellectual arguments, there was another reason for the present state of affairs, a reason that went back to the Moon Lander and Adventure games at the "dawn of time": it was simply a hell of a lot of fun to live in a world as malleable as the human imagination.)

Once the riders were out of sight, Erythrina moved back across the path to the edge of the pond and peered long and hard down between the lilies, into the limpid depths. "Okay, let's do some cross-correlation. You take the JPL data base, and I'll take the Harvard Multispectral Patrol. Start with data coming off space probes out to ten AUs. I have a suspicion the easiest way for the Mailman to disguise his transmissions is to play trojan horse with data from a NASA spacecraft."

Mr. Slippery nodded. One way or another, they should resolve her alien invasion theory first.

"It should take me about half an hour to get in place. After that, we can set up for the correlation. Hmmm . . . if something goes wrong, let's agree to meet at Mass Transmit 3," and she gave a password scheme. Clearly that would be an emergency situation. If they weren't back in the castle within three or four hours, the others would certainly guess the existence of her secret exit.

Erythrina tensed, then dived into the water. There was a small splash, and the lilies bobbed gently in the expanding ring waves. Mr. Slippery looked deep, but as expected, there was no further sign of her. He padded around the side of the pool, trying to identify the special glow of the JPL data base.

There was thrashing near one of the larger lilies, one that he recognized as obscuring the NSA connections with the East/West net. A large bullfrog scrambled out of the water onto the pad and turned to look at him. "Aha! Gotcha, you sonofabitch!"

It was Virginia; the voice was the same, even if the body was different. "*Shhhhhh!*" said Mr. Slippery, and looked wildly about for signs of eavesdroppers. There were none, but that did not mean they were safe. He spread his best privacy spell over her and crawled to the point closest to the lily. They sat glaring at each other like some characters out of La Fontaine: The Tale of the Frog and Dog. How dearly he would love to leap across the water and bite off that fat little head. Unfortunately the victory would be a bit temporary. "How did you find me?" Mr. Slippery growled. If people as inexperienced as the Feds could trace him down in his disguise, he was hardly safe from the Mailman.

"You forget," the frog puffed smugly. "We know your Name. It's simple to monitor your home processor and follow your every move."

Mr. Slippery whined deep in his throat. *In thrall to a frog. Even Wiley has done better than that.* "Okay, so you found me. Now what do you want?"

"To let you know that we want results, and to get a progress report."

He lowered his muzzle till his eyes were even with Virginia's. "Heh heh. I'll give you a progress report, but you're not going to like it." And he proceeded to explain Erythrina's theory that the Mailman was an alien invasion.

"Rubbish," spoke the frog afterward. "Sheer fantasy! You're going to have to do better than that, Pol—er, Mister."

He shuddered. She had almost spoken his Name. Was that a calculated threat or was she simply as stupid as she seemed? Nevertheless, he persisted. "Well then, what about Venezuela?" He related the evidence Ery had that the coup in that country was the Mailman's work.

This time the frog did not reply. Its eyes glazed over with apparent shock, and he realized that Virginia must be consulting people at the other end. Almost fifteen minutes passed. When the frog's eyes cleared, it was much more subdued. "We'll check on that one. What you say is possible. Just barely possible. If true . . . well, if it's true, this is the biggest threat we've had to face this century."

And you see that I am perhaps the only one who can bail you out. Mr. Slippery relaxed slightly. If they only realized it, they were thralled to him as much as the reverse—at least for the moment. Then he remembered Erythrina's plan to grab as much power as they could for a brief time and try to use that advantage to flush the Mailman out. With the Feds on their side, they could do more than Ery had ever imagined. He said as much to Virginia.

The frog croaked, "*You* . . . want . . . *us* . . . to give you carte blanche in the Federal data system? Maybe you'd like to be President and Chair of the JCS, to boot?"

"Hey, that's not what I said. I know it's an extraordinary suggestion, but this is an extraordinary situation. And in any case, you know my Name. There's no way I can get around that."

The frog went glassy-eyed again, but this time for only a couple of minutes. "We'll get back to you on that. We've got a lot of checking to do on the rest of your theories before we commit ourselves to anything. Till further notice, though, you're grounded."

"Wait!" What would Ery do when he didn't show? If he wasn't back in the castle in three or four hours, the others would surely know about the secret exit.

The frog was implacable. "I said, you're grounded, Mister. We want you back in the real world immediately. And you'll stay grounded till you hear from us. Got it?"

The dog slumped. "Yeah."

"Okay." The frog clambered heavily to the edge of the sagging lily and dumped itself ungracefully into the water. After a few seconds, Mr. Slippery followed.

Coming back was much like waking from a deep daydream; only here it was the middle of the night. Roger Pollack stood, stretching, trying to get the kinks out of his muscles. Almost four hours he had been gone, longer than ever before. Normally his concentration began to fail after two or three hours. Since he didn't like the thought of drugging up, this put a definite limit on his endurance in the Other Plane.

Beyond the bungalow's picture window, the pines stood silhouetted against the Milky Way. He cranked open a pane and listened to the night birds trilling in the trees. It was near the end of spring; he liked to imagine he could see dim polar twilight to the north. More likely it was just Crescent City. Pollack leaned close to the window and looked high into the sky, where Mars sat close to Jupiter. It was hard to think of a threat to his own life from as far away as that.

Pollack backed up the spells acquired during this last session, powered down his system, and stumbled off to bed.

The following morning and afternoon seemed the longest of Roger Pollack's life. How would they get in touch with him? Another visit of goons and black Lincolns? What had Erythrina done when he didn't make contact? Was she all right?

And there was just no way of checking. He paced back and forth across his tiny living room, the novel-plots that were his normal work forgotten. *Ah, but there is a way*. He looked at his old data set with dawning recognition. Virginia had said to stay out of the Other Plane. But how could they object to his using a simple data set, no more efficient than millions used by office workers all over the world?

He sat down at the set, scraped the dust from the handpads and screen. He awkwardly entered long-unused call symbols and watched the flow of news across the screen. A few queries and he discovered that no great disasters had occurred overnight, that

the insurgency in Indonesia seemed temporarily
abated. (Wiley J. was not to be king just yet.) There
were no reports of big-time data vandals biting the
dust.

Pollack grunted. He had forgotten how tedious it
was to see the world through a data set, even with
audio entry. In the Other Plane, he could pick up
this sort of information in seconds, as casually as an
ordinary mortal might glance out the window to see
if it is raining. He dumped the last twenty-four hours
of the world bulletin board into his home memory
space and began checking through it. The bulletin
board was ideal for untraceable reception of messages: anyone on Earth could leave a message—
indexed by subject, target audience, and source. If a
user copied the entire board, and *then* searched it,
there was no outside record of exactly what information he was interested in. There were also simple
ways to make nearly untraceable entries on the board.

As usual, there were about a dozen messages for
Mr. Slippery. Most of them were from fans; the
Coven had greater notoriety than any other vandal
SIG. A few were for other Mr. Slipperys. With five
billion people in the world, that wasn't surprising.

And one of the memos was from the Mailman;
that's what it said in the source field. Pollack punched
the message up on the screen. It was in caps, with
no color or sound. Like all messages directly from
the Mailman, it looked as if it came off some incredibly ancient I/O device:

YOU COULD HAVE BEEN RICH. YOU
COULD HAVE RULED. INSTEAD YOU
CONSPIRED AGAINST ME. I KNOW ABOUT
THE SECRET EXIT. I KNOW ABOUT YOUR
DOGGY DEPARTURE. YOU AND THE RED
ONE ARE DEAD NOW. IF YOU EVER SNEAK
BACK ONTO THIS PLANE, IT WILL BE THE

TRUE DEATH—I AM THAT CLOSE TO
KNOWING YOUR NAMES.
*****WATCH FOR ME IN THE NEWS,
    SUCKER*********

Bluff, thought Roger. *He wouldn't be sending out
warnings if he has that kind of power.* Still, there
was a dropping sensation in his stomach. The Mailman shouldn't have known about the dog disguise.
Was he onto Mr. Slippery's connection with the
Feds? If so, he might really be able to find Slippery's
True Name. And what sort of danger was Ery in?
What had she done when he missed the rendezvous
at Mass Transmit 3?

A quick search showed no messages from Erythrina.
Either she was looking for him in the Other Plane,
or she was as thoroughly grounded as he.

He was still stewing on this when the phone rang.
He said, "Accept, no video send." His data set cleared
to an even gray: the caller was not sending video
either.

"You're still there? Good." It was Virginia. Her
voice sounded a bit odd, subdued and tense. Perhaps it was just the effect of the scrambling algorithms. He prayed she would not trust that scrambling.
He had never bothered to make his phone any more
secure than average. (And he had seen the schemes
Wiley J. and Robin Hood had devised to decrypt
thousands of commercial phone messages in real-
time and monitor for key phrases, signaling them
when anything interesting was detected. They couldn't
use the technique very effectively, since it took an
enormous amount of processor space, but the Mailman was probably not so limited.)

Virginia continued, "No names, okay? We checked
out what you told us and . . . it looks like you're
right. We can't be sure about your theory about *his*
origin, but what you said about the international

situation was verified." So the Venezuela coup had been an outside take-over. "Furthermore, we think *he* has infiltrated us much more than we thought. It may be that the evidence we had of unsuccessful meddling was just a red herring." Pollack recognized the fear in her voice now. Apparently the Feds saw that they were up against something catastrophic. They were caught with their countermeasures down, and their only hope lay with unreliables like Pollack.

"Anyway, we're going ahead with what you suggested. We'll provide you two with the resources you requested. We want you in the Other . . . place as soon as possible. We can talk more there."

"I'm on my way. I'll check with my friend and get back to you there." He cut the connection without waiting for a reply. Pollack sat back, trying to savor this triumph and the near-pleading in the cop's voice. Somehow, he couldn't. He knew what a hard case she was; anything that could make her crawl was more hellish than anything he wanted to face.

His first stop was Mass Transmit 3. Physically, MT3 was a two-thousand-tonne satellite in synchronous orbit over the Indian Ocean. The Mass Transmits handled most of the planet's noninteractive communications (and in fact that included a lot of transmission that most people regarded as interactive— such as human/human and the simpler human/computer conversations). Bandwidth and processor space was cheaper on the Mass Transmits because of the 240- to 900-millisecond time delays that were involved.

As such, it was a nice out-of-the-way meeting place, and in the Other Plane it was represented as a five-meter-wide ledge near the top of a mountain that rose from the forests and swamps that stood for the lower satellite layer and the ground-based nets. In the distance were two similar peaks, clear in pale sky.

Mr. Slippery leaned out into the chill breeze that swept the face of the mountain and looked down past the timberline, past the evergreen forests. Through the unnatural mists that blanketed those realms, he thought he could see the Coven's castle.

Perhaps he should go there, or down to the swamps. There was no sign of Erythrina. Only sprites in the forms of bats and tiny griffins were to be seen here. They sailed back and forth over him, sometimes soaring far higher, toward the uttermost peak itself.

Mr. Slippery himself was in an extravagant winged man form, one that subtly projected amateurism, one that he hoped would pass the inspection of the enemy's eyes and ears. He fluttered clumsily across the ledge toward a small cave that provided some shelter from the whistling wind. Fine, wind-dropped snow lay in a small bank before the entrance. The insects he found in the cave were no more than what they seemed—amateur transponders.

He turned and started back toward the drop-off; he was going to have to face this alone. But as he passed the snowbank, the wind swirled it up and tiny crystals stung his face and hands and nose. *Trap!* He jumped backward, his fastest escape spell coming to his lips, at the same time cursing himself for not establishing the spell before. The time delay was just too long; the trap lived here at MT3 and could react faster than he. The little snow-devil dragged the crystals up into a swirling column of singing motes that chimed in near-unison, "W-w-wait-t-t!"

The sound matched deep-set recognition patterns; this was Erythrina's work. Three hundred milliseconds passed, and the wind suddenly picked up the rest of the snow and whirled into a more substantial, taller column. Mr. Slippery realized that the trap had been more of an alarm, set to bring Ery if he should be recognized here. But her arrival was so quick that she must already have been at work somewhere in this plane.

"Where have you been-n-n!" The snow-devil's chime was a combination of rage and concern.

Mr. Slippery threw a second spell over the one he recognized she had cast. There was no help for it: he would have to tell her that the Feds had his Name. And with that news, Virginia's confirmation about Venezuela and the Feds' offer to help.

Erythrina didn't respond immediately—and only part of the delay was light lag. Then the swirling snow flecks that represented her gusted up around him. "So you lose no matter how this comes out, eh? I'm sorry, Slip."

Mr. Slippery's wings drooped. "Yeah. But I'm beginning to believe it will be the True Death for us all if we don't stop the Mailman. He really means to take over . . . everything. Can you imagine what it would be like if all the governments' wee megalomaniacs got replaced by one big one?"

The usual pause. The snow-devil seemed to shudder in on itself. "You're right; we've got to stop him even if it means working for Sammy Sugar and the entire DoW." She chuckled, a near-inaudible chiming. "Even if it means that *they* have to work for *us*." She could laugh; the Feds didn't know her Name. "How did your Federal Friends say we could plug into their system?" Her form was changing again—to a solid, winged form, an albino eagle. The only red she allowed herself was in the eyes, which gleamed with inner light.

"At the Laurel end of the old arpa net. We'll get something near carte blanche on that and on the DoJ domestic intelligence files, but we have to enter through one physical location and with just the password scheme they specify." He and Erythrina would have more power than any vandals in history, but they would be on a short leash, nevertheless.

His wings beat briefly, and he rose into the air. After the usual pause, the eagle followed. They flew almost to the mountain's peak, then began the long, slow glide toward the marshes below, the chill air whistling around them. In principle, they could have made the transfer to the Laurel terminus virtually instantaneously. But it was not mere romanticism that made them move so cautiously—as many a novice had discovered the hard way. What appeared to the conscious mind as a search for air currents and clear lanes through the scattered clouds was a manifestation of the almost-subconscious working of programs that gradually transferred processing from rented space on MT3 to low satellite and ground-based stations. The game was tricky and time-consuming, but it made it virtually impossible for others to trace their origin. The greatest danger of detection would probably occur at Laurel, where they would be forced to access the system through a single input device.

The sky glowed momentarily; seconds passed, and an airborne fist slammed into them from behind. The shock wave sent them tumbling tail over wing toward the forests below. Mr. Slippery straightened his chaotic flailing into a head-first dive. Looking back—which was easy to do in his present attitude—he saw the peak that had been MT3 glowing red, steam rising over descending avalanches of lava. Even at this distance, he could see tiny motes swirling above the inferno. (Attackers looking for the prey that had fled?) Had it come just a few seconds earlier, they would have had most of their processing still locked into MT3 and the disaster—whatever it really was—would have knocked them out of this plane. It wouldn't have been the True Death, but it might well have grounded them for days.

On his right, he glimpsed the white eagle in a controlled dive; they had had just enough communications established off MT3 to survive. As they fell deeper into the humid air of the lowlands, Mr. Slippery dipped into the news channels: word was already coming over the *LA Times* of the fluke accident in which the Hokkaido aerospace launching laser had somehow shone on MT3's optics. The laser had shone for microseconds and at reduced power; the damage had been nothing like a Finger of God, say. No one had been hurt, but wideband communications would be down for some time, and several hundred million dollars of information traffic was stalled. There would be investigations and a lot of very irate customers.

It had been no accident, Mr. Slippery was sure. The Mailman was showing his teeth, revealing infiltration no one had suspected. He must guess what his opponents were up to.

They leveled out a dozen meters above the pine forest that bordered the swamps. The air around them was thick and humid, and the faraway mountains were almost invisible. Clouds had moved in, and a storm was on the way. They were now securely locked into the low-level satellite net, but thousands of new users were clamoring for entry, too. The loss of MT3 would make the Other Plane a turbulent place for several weeks, as heavy users tried to shift their traffic here.

He swooped low over the swamp, searching for the one particular pond with the one particularly large water lily that marked the only entrance Virginia would permit them. There! He banked off to the side, Erythrina following, and looked for signs of the Mailman or his friends in the mucky clearings that surrounded the pond.

But there was little purpose in further caution. Flying about like this, they would be clearly visible to any ambushers waiting by the pond. *Better to move fast now that we're committed.* He signaled the red-eyed eagle, and they dived toward the placid water. That surface marked the symbolic transition to observation mode. No longer was he aware of a winged form or of water coming up and around him. Now he was interacting directly with the I/O protocols of a computing center in the vicinity of Laurel, Maryland. He sensed Ery poking around on her own. This wasn't the arpa entrance. He slipped "sideways" into an old-fashioned government office complex. The "feel" of the 1990-style data sets was unmistakable. He was fleetingly aware of memos written and edited, reports hauled in and out of storage. One of the vandals' favorite sports—and one that even the moderately skilled could indulge in—was to infiltrate one of these office complexes and simulate higher level input to make absurd and impossible demands on the local staff.

This was not the time for such games, and this was still not the entrance. He pulled away from the office complex and searched through some old directories. Arpa went back more than half a century, the first of the serious data nets, now (figuratively) gathering dust. The number was still there, though. He signaled Erythrina, and the two of them presented themselves at the log-in point and provided just the codes that Virginia had given him.

. . . and they were in. They eagerly soaked in the megabytes of password keys and access data that Virginia's people had left there. At the same time, they were aware that this activity was being monitored. The Feds were taking an immense chance leaving this material here, and they were going to do their best to keep a rein on their temporary vandal allies.

In fifteen seconds, they had learned more about the inner workings of the Justice Department and

DoW than the Coven had in fifteen months. Mr. Slippery guessed that Erythrina must be busy plotting what she would do with all that data later on. For him, of course, there was no future in it. They drifted out of the arpa "vault" into the larger data spaces that were the Department of Justice files. He could see that there was nothing hidden from them; random archive retrievals were all being honored and with a speed that would have made deception impossible. They had subpoena power and clearances and more.

"Let's go get 'im, Slip." Erythrina's voice seemed hollow and inhuman in this underimaged realm. (How long would it be before the Feds started to make their data perceivable analogically, as on the Other Plane? It might be a little undignified, but it would revolutionize their operation—which, from the Coven's standpoint, might be quite a bad thing.)

Mr. Slippery "nodded." Now they had more than enough power to undertake the sort of work they had planned. In seconds, they had searched all the locally available files on off-planet transmissions. Then they dove out of the DoJ net, Mr. Slippery to Pasadena and the JPL planetary probe archives, Erythrina to Cambridge and the Harvard Multispectral Patrol.

It should take several hours to survey these records, to determine just what transmissions might be cover for the alien invasion that both the Feds and Erythrina were guessing had begun. But Mr. Slippery had barely started when he noticed that there were dozens of processors within reach that he could just grab with his new Federal powers. He checked carefully to make sure he wasn't upsetting air traffic control or hospital life support, then quietly stole the computing resources of several hundred unknowing users, whose data sets automatically switched to other resources. Now he had more power than he ever would have risked taking in the past. On the other side of the continent, he was aware that Erythrina had done something similar.

In three minutes, they had sifted through five years' transmissions far more thoroughly than they had originally planned.

"No sign of him," he sighed and "looked" at Erythrina. They had found plenty of irregular sources at Harvard, but there was no orbital fit. All transmissions from the NASA probes checked out legitimately.

"Yes." Her face, with its dark skin and slanting eyes, seemed to hover beside him. Apparently with her new power, she could image even here. "But you know, we haven't really done much more than the Feds could—given a couple months of data set work. . . . I know, it's more than we had planned to do. But we've barely used the resources they've opened to us."

It was true. He looked around, feeling suddenly like a small boy let loose in a candy shop: he sensed enormous data bases and the power that would let him use them. Perhaps the cops had not intended them to take advantage of this, but it was obvious that with these powers, they could do a search no enemy could evade. "Okay," he said finally, "let's pig it."

Ery laughed and made a loud snuffling sound. Carefully, quickly, they grabbed noncritical data-processing facilities along all the East/West nets. In seconds, they were the biggest users in North America. The drain would be clear to anyone monitoring the System, though a casual user might notice only increased delays in turnaround. Modern nets are at least as resilient as old-time power nets—but like power nets, they have their elastic limit and their breaking point. So far, at least, he and Erythrina were far short of those.

—but they were experiencing what no human had ever known before, a sensory bandwidth thousands of times normal. For seconds that seemed without end, their minds were filled with a jumble verging on pain, data that was not information and information that was not knowledge. To hear ten million simultaneous phone conversations, to see the continent's entire video output, should have been a white noise. Instead it was a tidal wave of detail rammed through the tiny aperture of their minds. The pain increased, and Mr. Slippery panicked. This could be the True Death, some kind of sensory burnout—

Erythrina's voice was faint against the roar, *"Use everything, not just the inputs!"* And he had just enough sense left to see what she meant. He controlled more than raw data now; if he could master them, the continent's computers could process this avalanche, much the way parts of the human brain preprocess their input. More seconds passed, but now with a sense of time, as he struggled to distribute his very consciousness through the System.

Then it was over, and he had control once more. But things would never be the same: the human that had been Mr. Slippery was an insect wandering in the cathedral his mind had become. There simply was more there than before. No sparrow could fall without his knowledge, via air traffic control; no check could be cashed without his noticing over the bank communication net. More than three hundred million lives swept before what his senses had become.

Around and through him, he felt the other occupant—Erythrina, now equally grown. They looked at each other for an unending fraction of a second, their communication more kinesthetic than verbal. Finally she smiled, the old smile now deep with meanings she could never 'image before. "Pity the poor Mailman now!"

Again they searched, but now it was through all the civil data bases, a search that could only be dreamed of by mortals. The signs were there, a near invisible system of manipulations hidden among more routine crimes and vandalisms. Someone had been at work within the Venezuelan system, at least at the North American end. The trail was tricky to follow—their enemy seemed to have at least some of their own powers—but they saw it lead back into the labyrinths of the Federal bureaucracy: resources diverted, individuals promoted or transferred, not quite according to the automatic regulations that should govern. These were changes so small they were never guessed at by ordinary employees and only just sensed by the cops. But over the months, they added up to an instability that neither of the two searchers could quite understand except to know that it was planned and that it did the status quo no good.

"He's still too sharp for us, Slip. We're all over the civil nets and we haven't seen any living sign of him; yet we know he does heavy processing on Earth or in low orbit."

"So he's either off North America, or else he has penetrated the . . . military."

"I bet it's a little of both. The point is, we're going to have to follow him."

And that meant taking over at least part of the U.S. military system. Even if that was possible, it certainly went far beyond what Virginia and her friends had intended. As far as the cops were concerned, it would mean that the threat against the government was tripled. So far he hadn't detected any objections to their searching, but he was aware of Virginia and her superiors deep in some kind of bunker at Langley, intently watching a whole wall full of monitors, trying to figure out just what he was up to and if it was time to pull the plug on him.

Erythrina was aware of his objections almost as fast as he could bring them to mind. "We don't have any choice, Slip. We have to take control. The Feds aren't the only thing watching us. If we don't get the

Mailman on this try, he is sure as hell going to get us."

That was easy for her to say. None of her enemies yet knew her True Name. Mr. Slippery had somehow to survive *two* enemies. On the other hand, he suspected that the deadlier of those enemies was the Mailman. "Only one way to go and that's up, huh? Okay, I'll play."

They settled into a game that was familiar now, grabbing more and more computing facilities, but now from common Europe and Asia. At the same time, they attacked the harder problem—infiltrating the various North American military nets. Both projects were beyond normal humans or any group of normal humans, but by now their powers were greater than any single civil entity in the world.

The foreign data centers yielded easily, scarcely more than minutes' work. The military was a different story. The Feds had spent many years and hundreds of billions of dollars to make the military command and control system secure. But they had not counted on the attack from all directions that they faced now; in moments more, the two searchers found themselves on the inside of the NSA control system—

—and under attack! Impressions of a dozen sleek, deadly forms converging on them, and sudden loss of control over many of the processors he depended on. He and Erythrina flailed out wildly, clumsy giants hacking at fast-moving hawks. There was imagery here, as detailed as on the Other Plane. They were fighting people with some of the skills the warlocks had developed—and a lot more power. But it was still an uneven contest. He and Erythrina had too much experience and too much sheer processing mass behind them. One by one, the fighters flashed into incandescent destruction.

He realized almost instantly that these were not

the Mailman's tools. They were powerful, but they fought only as moderately skilled warlocks might. In fact, they had encountered the most secret defense the government had for its military command and control. The civilian bureaucracies had stuck with obsolete data sets and old-fashioned dp languages, but the cutting edge of the military is always more willing to experiment. They had developed something like the warlocks' system. Perhaps they didn't use magical jargon to describe their computer/human symbiosis, but the techniques and the attitudes were the same. These swift-moving fighters flew against a background imagery that was like an olive-drab Other Plane.

Compared to his present power, they were nothing. Even as he and Erythrina swept the defenders out of the "sky," he could feel his consciousness expanding further as more and more of the military system was absorbed into their pattern. Every piece of space junk out to one million kilometers floated in crystal detail before his attention; in a fraction of a second he sorted through it all, searching for some evidence of alien intelligence. No sign of the Mailman.

The military and diplomatic communications of the preceding fifty years showed before the light of their minds. At the same time as they surveyed the satellite data, Mr. Slippery and Erythrina swept through these bureaucratic communications, looking carefully but with flickering speed at every requisition for toilet paper, every "declaration" of secret war, every travel voucher, every one of the trillions of pieces of "paper" that made it possible for the machinery of state to creak forward. And here the signs were much clearer: large sections were subtly changed, giving the same feeling the eye's blind spot gives, the feeling that nothing is really obscured but that some things are simply gone. Some of the distortions were immense. Under their microscopic yet global scrutiny, it was obvious that all of Venezuela, large parts of Alaska, and most of the economic base for the low satellite net were all controlled by some single interest that had little connection with the proper owners. Who their enemy was was still a mystery, but his works loomed larger and larger around them.

In a distant corner of what his mind had become, tiny insects buzzed with homicidal fury, tiny insects who knew Mr. Slippery's True Name. They knew what he and Erythrina had done, and right now they were more scared of the two warlocks than they had ever been of the Mailman. As he and Ery continued their search, he listened to the signals coming from the Langley command post, followed the helicopter gunships that were dispatched toward a single rural bungalow in Northern California—and changed their encrypted commands so that the sortie dumped its load of death on an uninhabited stretch of the Pacific.

Still with a tiny fraction of his attention, Mr. Slippery noticed that Virginia—actually her superiors, who had long since taken over the operation—knew of this defense. They were still receiving real-time pictures from military satellites.

He signaled a pause to Erythrina. For a few seconds, she would work alone while he dealt with these persistent antagonists. He felt like a man attacked by several puppies: they were annoying and could cause substantial damage unless he took more trouble than they were worth. They had to be stopped without causing themselves injury.

He should freeze the West Coast military and any launch complexes that could reach his body. Beyond that, it would be a good idea to block recon satellite transmission of the California area. And of course, he'd better deal with the Finger of God installations that were above the California horizon. Already he felt one of those heavy lasers, sweeping along in its ten-thousand-kilometer orbit, go into aiming mode and begin charging. He still had plenty of time—at least two or three seconds—before the weapons laser reached its lowest discharge threshold. Still, this was the most immediate threat. Mr. Slippery sent a tendril of consciousness into the tiny processor aboard the Finger of God satellite—

—and withdrew, bloodied. *Someone was already there*. Not Erythrina and not the little military warlocks. *Someone* too great for even him to overpower.

"*Ery!* I've found him!" It came out a scream. The laser's bore was centered on a spot thousands of kilometers below, a tiny house that in less than a second would become an expanding ball of plasma at the end of a columnar explosion descending through the atmosphere.

Over and over in that last second, Mr. Slippery threw himself against the barrier he felt around the tiny military processor—with no success. He traced its control to the lower satellite net, to bigger processors that were equally shielded. Now he had a feel for the nature of his opponent. It was not the direct imagery he was used to on the Other Plane; this was more like fighting blindfolded. He could sense the other's style. The enemy was not revealing any more of himself than was necessary to keep control of the Finger of God for another few hundred milliseconds.

Mr. Slippery slashed, trying to cut the enemy's communications. But his opponent was strong, much stronger—he now realized—than himself. He was vaguely aware of the other's connections to the computing power in those blind-spot areas he and Erythrina had discovered. But for all that power, he was almost the enemy's equal. There was something missing from the other, some critical element of imagination or originality. If Erythrina would only come, they might be able to stop him. Milliseconds separated him from the True Death. He looked desperately around. *Where is she?*

Military Status announced the discharge of an Orbital Weapons Laser. He cowered even as his quickened perceptions counted the microseconds that remained till his certain destruction, even as he noticed a ball of glowing plasma expanding about what had been a Finger of God—*the Finger that had been aimed at him!*

He could see now what had happened. While he and the other had been fighting, Erythrina had commandeered another of the weapons satellites, one already very near discharge threshold, and destroyed the threat to him.

Even as he realized this, the enemy was on him again, this time attacking conventionally, trying to destroy Mr. Slippery's communications and processing space. But now that enemy had to fight both Erythrina and Mr. Slippery. The other's lack of imagination and creativity was beginning to tell, and even with his greater strength, they could feel him slowly, slowly losing resources to his weaker opponents. There was something familiar about this enemy, something Mr. Slippery was sure he could see, given time.

Abruptly the enemy pulled away. For a long moment, they held each other's sole attention, like cats waiting for the smallest sign of weakness to launch back into combat—only here the new attack could come from any of ten thousand different directions, from any of the communications nodes that formed their bodies and their minds.

From beside him, he felt Erythrina move forward, as though to lock the other in her green-eyed gaze. "You know who we have here, Slip?" He could tell that all her concentration was on this enemy, that she almost vibrated with the effort. "This is our old friend DON.MAC grown up to super size, and doing his best to disguise himself."

The other seemed to tense and move even further in upon himself. But after a moment, he began imaging. There stood DON.MAC, his face and Plessey-Mercedes body the same as ever. DON.MAC, the first of the Mailman's converts, the one Erythrina was sure had been killed and replaced with a simulator. "And all the time he's been the Mailman. The last person we would suspect, the Mailman's first victim."

DON rolled forward half a meter, his motors keening, his hydraulic fists raised. But he did not deny what Mr. Slippery said. After a moment he seemed to relax. "You are very . . . clever. But then, you two have had help; I never thought you and the cops would cooperate. That was the one combination that had any chance against the 'Mailman.' " He smiled, a familiar automatic twitch. "But don't you see? It's a combination with lethal genes. We three have much more in common than you and the government.

"Look around you. If we were warlocks before, we are gods now. Look!" Without letting the center of their attention wander, the two followed his gaze. As before, the myriad aspects of the lives of billions spread out before them. But now, many things were changed. In their struggle, the three had usurped virtually all of the connected processing power of the human race. Video and phone communications were frozen. The public data bases had lasted long enough to notice that something had gone terribly, terribly wrong. Their last headlines, generated a second before the climax of the battle, were huge banners announcing GREATEST DATA OUTAGE OF ALL TIME. Nearly a billion people watched blank data sets, feeling more panicked than any simple power blackout could ever make them. Already the accumulation of lost data and work time would cause a major recession.

"They are lucky the old arms race is over, or else

independent military units would probably have already started a war. Even if we hand back control this instant, it would take them more than a year to get their affairs in order." DON.MAC smirked, the same expression they had seen the day before when he was bragging to the Limey. "There have been few deaths yet. Hospitals and aircraft have some stand-alone capability."

Even so . . . Mr. Slippery could see thousands of aircraft stacked up over major airports from London to Christchurch. Local computing could never coordinate the safe landing of them all before some ran out of fuel.

"*We* caused all that—with just the fallout of our battle," continued DON. "if we chose to do them harm, I have no doubt we could exterminate the human race." He detonated three warheads in their silos in Utah just to emphasize his point. With dozens of video eyes, in orbit and on the ground, Mr. Slippery and Erythrina watched the destruction sweep across the launch sites. "Consider: how are we different from the gods of myth? And like the gods of myth, we can rule and prosper, just so long as we don't fight among ourselves." He looked expectantly from Mr. Slippery to Erythrina. There was a frown on the Red One's dark face; she seemed to be concentrating on their opponent just as fiercely as ever.

DON.MAC turned back to Mr. Slippery. "Slip, you especially should see that we have no choice but to cooperate. *They know your True Name*. Of the three of us, your life is the most fragile, depending on protecting your body from a government that now considers you a traitor. You would have died a dozen times over during the last thousand seconds if you hadn't used your new powers.

"And you can't go back. Even if you play Boy Scout, destroy me, and return all obedient—even then they will kill you. They know how dangerous you are, perhaps even more dangerous than I. They can't afford to let you exist."

And megalomania aside, that made perfect and chilling sense. As they were talking, a fraction of Mr. Slippery's attention was devoted to confusing and obstructing the small infantry group that had been air-dropped into the Arcata region just before the government lost all control. Their superiors had realized how easily he could countermand their orders, and so the troops were instructed to ignore all outside direction until they had destroyed a certain Roger Pollack. Fortunately they were depending on city directories and orbit-fed street maps, and he had been keeping them going in circles for some time now. It was a nuisance, and sooner or later he would have to decide on a more permanent solution.

But what was a simple nuisance in his present state would be near-instant death if he returned to his normal self. He looked at Erythrina. Was there any way around DON's arguments?

Her eyes were almost shut, and the frown had deepened. He sensed that more and more of her resources were involved in some pattern analysis. He wondered if she had even heard what DON.MAC said. But after a moment her eyes came open, and she looked at the two of them. There was triumph in that look. "You know, Slip, I don't think I have ever been fooled by a personality simulator, at least not for more than a few minutes."

Mr. Slippery nodded, puzzled by this sudden change in topic. "Sure. If you talk to a simulator long enough, you eventually begin to notice little inflexibilities. I don't think we'll ever be able to write a program that could pass the Turing test."

"Yes, little inflexibilities, a certain lack of imagination. It always seems to be the tipoff. Of course DON here has always pretended to be a program, so it was hard to tell. But I was sure that for the last few months there has been no living being behind his mask . . .

". . . *and furthermore, I don't think there is anybody there even now.*" Mr. Slippery's attention snapped back to DON.MAC. The other smirked at the accusation. Somehow it was not the right reaction. Mr. Slippery remembered the strange, artificial flavor of DON's combat style. In this short an encounter, there could be no really hard evidence for her theory. She was using her intuition and whatever deep analysis she had been doing these last few seconds.

"But that means we still haven't found the Mailman."

"Right. This is just his best tool. I'll bet the Mailman simply used the pattern he stole from the murdered DON.MAC as the basis for this automatic defense system we've been fighting. The Mailman's time lag is a very real thing, not a red herring at all. Somehow it is the whole secret of who he really is.

"In any case, it makes our present situation a lot easier." She smiled at DON.MAC as though he were a real person. Usually it was easier to behave that way toward simulators; in this case, there was a good deal of triumph in her smile. "You almost won for your master, DON. You almost had us convinced. But now that we know what we are dealing with, it will be easy to—"

Her image flicked out of existence, and Mr. Slippery felt DON grab for the resources Ery controlled. All through near-Earth space, they fought for the weapon systems she had held till an instant before.

And alone, Mr. Slippery could not win. Slowly, slowly, he felt himself bending before the other's force, like some wrestler whose bones were breaking one by one under a murderous opponent. It was all he could do to prevent the DON construct from blasting his home; and to do that, he had to give up progressively more computing power.

Erythrina was gone, gone as though she had never been. Or was she? He gave a sliver of his attention to a search, a sliver that was still many times more powerful than any mere warlock. That tiny piece of consciousness quickly noticed a power failure in southern Rhode Island. Many power failures had developed during the last few minutes, consequent to the data failure. But this one was strange. In addition to power, comm lines were down and even his intervention could not bring them to life. It was about as thoroughly blacked out as a place could be. This could scarcely be an accident.

. . . and there was a voice, barely telephone quality and almost lost in the mass of other data he was processing. *Erythrina!* She had, via some incredibly tortuous detour, retained a communication path to the outside.

His gaze swept the blacked-out Providence suburb. It consisted of new urbapts, perhaps one hundred thousand units in all. Somewhere in there lived the human that was Erythrina. While she had been concentrating on DON.MAC, he must have been working equally hard to find her True Name. Even now, DON did not know precisely who she was, only enough to black out the area she lived in.

It was getting hard to think; DON.MAC was systematically dismantling him. The lethal intent was clear: as soon as Mr. Slippery was sufficiently reduced, the Orbital Lasers would be turned on his body, and then on Erythrina's. And then the Mailman's faithful servant would have a planetary kingdom to turn over to his mysterious master.

He listened to the tiny voice that still leaked out of Providence. It didn't make too much sense. She sounded hysterical, panicked. He was surprised that she could speak at all; she had just suffered—in losing all her computer connections—something roughly analogous to a massive stroke. To her, the world was now seen through a keyhole, incomplete, unknown and dark.

"There is a chance; we still have a chance," the voice went on, hurried and slurred. "An old military communication tower north of here. Damn. I don't know the number or grid, but I can see it from where I'm sitting. With it you could punch through to the roof antenna . . . has plenty of bandwidth, and I've got some battery power here . . . but *hurry*."

She didn't have to tell him that; he was the guy who was being eaten alive. He was almost immobilized now, the other's attack squeezing and stifling where it could not cut and tear. He spasmed against DON's strength and briefly contacted the comm towers north of Providence. Only one of them was in line of sight with the blacked-out area. Its steerable antenna was very, very narrow beam.

"Ery, I'm going to need your house number, maybe even your antenna id."

A second passed, two—a hellish eon for Mr. Slippery. In effect, he had asked her for her True Name—he who was already known to the Feds. Once he returned to the real world, there would be no way he could mask this information from them. He could imagine her thoughts: never again to be free. In her place, he would have paused too, but—

"*Ery!* It's the True Death for both of us if you don't. He's got me!"

This time she barely hesitated. "D-Debby Charteris, 4448 Grosvenor Row. Cut off like this, I don't know the antenna id. Is my name and house enough?"

"Yes. Get ready!"

Even before he spoke, he had already matched the name with an antenna rental and aligned the military antenna on it. Return contact came as he turned his attention back to DON.MAC. With luck, the enemy was not aware of their conversation. Now he must be distracted.

Mr. Slippery surged against the other, breaking communications nodes that served them both. DON shuddered, reorganizing around the resources that were left, then moved in on Mr. Slippery again. Since DON had greater strength to begin with, the maneuver had cost Mr. Slippery proportionately more. The enemy had been momentarily thrown off balance, but now the end would come very quickly.

The spaces around him, once so rich with detail and colors beyond color, were fading now, replaced by the sensations of his true body straining with animal fear in its little house in California. Contact with the greater world was almost gone. He was scarcely aware of it when DON turned the Finger of God back upon him—

Consciousness, the superhuman consciousness of before, returned almost unsensed, unrecognized till awareness brought surprise. Like a strangling victim back from oblivion, Mr. Slippery looked around dazedly, not quite realizing that the struggle continued.

But now the roles were reversed. DON.MAC had been caught by surprise, in the act of finishing off what he thought was his only remaining enemy. Erythrina had used that surprise to good advantage, coming in upon her opponent from a Japanese data center, destroying much of Don's higher reasoning centers before the other was even aware of her. Large, unclaimed processing units lay all about, and as DON and Erythrina continued their struggle, Mr. Slippery quietly absorbed everything in reach.

Even now, DON could have won against either one of them alone, but when Mr. Slippery threw himself back into the battle, they had the advantage. DON.MAC sensed this too, and with a brazenness that was either mindless or genius, returned to his original appeal. "There is still time! The Mailman will still forgive you."

Mr. Slippery and Erythrina ripped at their enemy from both sides, disconnecting vast blocks of communications, processing and data resources. They denied the Mass Transmits to him, and one by one put the low-level satellites out of synch with his data accesses. DON was confined to land lines, tied into a single military net that stretched from Washington to Denver. He was flailing, randomly using whatever instruments of destruction were still available. All across the midsection of the US, silo missiles detonated, ABM lasers swept back and forth across the sky. The world had been stopped short by the beginning of their struggle, but the ending could tear it to pieces.

The damage to Mr. Slippery and Erythrina was slight, the risk that the random strokes would seriously damage them small. They ignored occasional slashing losses and concentrated single-mindedly on dismantling DON.MAC. They discovered the object code for the simulator that was DON, and zeroed it. DON—or his creator—was clever and had planted many copies, and a new one awakened every time they destroyed the running copy. But as the minutes passed, the simulator found itself with less and less to work with. Now it was barely more than it had been back in the Coven.

"*Fools!* The Mailman is your natural ally. The Feds will *kill* you! Don't you underst—"

The voice stopped in midshriek, as Erythrina zeroed the currently running simulator. No other took up the task. There was a silence, an . . . absence . . . throughout. Erythrina glanced at Mr. Slippery, and the two continued their search through the enemy's territory. This data space was big, and there could be many more copies of DON hidden in it. But without the resources they presently held, the simulator could

have no power. It was clear to both of them that no
effective ambush could be hidden in these unmoving
ruins.

And they had complete copies of DON.MAC to
study. It was easy to trace the exact extent of his
infection of the system. The two moved systematically, changing what they found so that it would
behave as its original programmers had intended.
Their work was so thorough that the Feds might
never realize just how extensively the Mailman and
his henchman had infiltrated them, just how close he
had come to total control.

Most of the areas they searched were only slightly
altered and required only small changes. But deep
within the military net, there were hundreds of trillions of bytes of program that seemed to have no
intelligible function yet were clearly connected with
DON's activities. It was apparently object code, but
it was so huge and so ill organized that even they
couldn't decide if it was more than hash now. There
was no possibility that it had any legitimate function;
after a few moments' consideration, they randomized
it.

At last it was over. Mr. Slippery and Erythrina
stood alone. They controlled all connected processing facilities in near-Earth space. There was no place
within that volume that any further enemies could
be lurking. And there was no evidence that there
had ever been interference from beyond.

It was the first time since they had reached this
level that they had been able to survey the world
without fear. (He scarcely noticed the continuing,
pitiful attempts of the American military to kill his
real body.) Mr. Slippery looked around him, using
all his millions of perceptors. The Earth floated serene. Viewed in the visible, it looked like a thousand
pictures he had seen as a human. But in the ultravio-
let, he could follow its hydrogen aura out many

thousands of kilometers. And the high-energy detectors on satellites at all levels perceived the radiation belts in thousands of energy levels, oscillating in the solar wind. Across the oceans of the world, he could feel the warmth of the currents, see just how fast they were moving. And all the while, he monitored the millions of tiny voices that were now coming back to life as he and Erythrina carefully set the human race's communication system back on its feet and gently prodded it into function. Every ship in the seas, every aircraft now making for safe landing, every one of the loans, the payments, the meals of an entire race registered clearly on some part of his consciousness. With perception came power; almost everything he saw, he could alter, destroy, or enhance. By the analogical rules of the covens, there was only one valid word for themselves in their present state: they were gods.

". . . we could rule," Erythrina's voice was hushed, self-frightened. "It might be tricky at first, assuring our bodies protection, but we could rule."

"There's still the Mailman—"

She seemed to wave a hand, dismissingly. "Maybe, maybe not. It's true we still are no closer to knowing who he is, but we do know that we have destroyed all his processing power. We would have plenty of warning if he ever tries to reinsinuate himself into the System." She stared at him intently, and it wasn't until some time later that he recognized the faint clues in her behavior and realized that she was holding something back.

What she said was all so clearly true; for as long as their bodies lived, they could rule. And what DON.MAC had said seemed true: they were the greatest threat the "forces of law and order" had ever faced, and that included the Mailman. How could the Feds afford to let them be free, how could they even afford to let them *live*, if the two of them gave up the power they had now? But—"A lot of people would have to die. if we took over. There are enough independent military entities left on Earth that we'd have to use a good deal of nuclear blackmail, at least at first."

"Yeah," her voice was even smaller than before, and the image of her face was downcast. "During the last few seconds I've done some simulating on that. We'd have to take out four, maybe six, major cities. If there are any command centers hidden from us, it could be a lot worse than that. And we'd have to develop our own human secret-police forces as folks began to operate outside our system. . . . Damn. We'd end up being worse than the human-based government."

She saw the same conclusion in his face and grinned lopsidedly. "You can't do it and neither can I. So the State wins again."

He nodded, "reached" out to touch her briefly. They took one last glorious minute to soak in the higher reality. Then, silently, they parted, each to seek his own way downward.

It was not an instantaneous descent to ordinary humanity. Mr. Slippery was careful to prepare a safe exit. He created a complex set of misdirections for the army unit that was trying to close in on his physical body; it would take them several hours to find him, far longer than necessary for the government to call them off. He set up preliminary negotiations with the Federal programs that had been doing their best to knock him out of power, telling them of his determination to surrender if granted safe passage and safety for his body. In a matter of seconds he would be talking to humans again, perhaps even Virginia, but by then a lot of the basic ground rules would be automatically in operation.

As per their temporary agreements, he closed off first one and then another of the capabilities that he

had so recently acquired. It was like stopping one's
ears, then blinding one's eyes, but somehow much
worse since his very ability to think was being deliberately given up. He was like some lobotomy patient
(victim) who only vaguely realizes now what he has
lost. Behind him the Federal forces were doing their
best to close off the areas he had left, to protect
themselves from any change of heart he might have.

Far away now, he could sense Erythrina going
through a similiar procedure, but more slowly. That
was strange; he couldn't be sure with his present
faculties, but somehow it seemed that she was deliberately lagging behind and doing something more
complicated than was strictly necessary to return
safely to normal humanity. And then he remembered that strange look she had given him while
saying that they had not figured out who the Mailman was.

One could rule as easily as two!

The panic was sudden and overwhelming, all the
more terrible for the feeling of being betrayed by
one so trusted. He struck out against the barriers he
had so recently allowed to close in about him, but it
was too late. He was already weaker than the Feds.
Mr. Slippery looked helplessly back into the gathering dimness, and saw . . .

. . . Ery coming down toward the real world with
him, giving up the advantage she had held all alone.
Whatever problems had slowed her must have had
nothing to do with treachery. And somehow his feeling of relief went beyond the mere fact of death
avoided—Ery was still what he had always thought
her.

He was seeing a lot of Virginia lately, though of
course not socially. Her crew had set up offices in
Arcata, and twice a week she and one of her goons
would come up to the house. No doubt it was one of

the few government operations carried out face-to-face. She or her superiors seemed to realize that anything done over the phone might be subject to trickery. (Which was true, of course. Given several weeks to himself, Pollack could have put together a robot phone connection and—using false ids and priority permits—been on a plane to Djakarta.)

There were a lot of superficial similarities between these meetings and that first encounter the previous spring:

Pollack stepped to the door and watched the black Lincoln pulling up the drive. As always, the vehicle came right into the carport. As always, the driver got out quickly, eyes flickering coldly across Pollack. As always, Virginia moved with military precision (in fact, he had discovered, she had been promoted out of the Army to her present job in DoW intelligence). The two walked purposefully toward the bungalow, ignoring the summer sunlight and the deep wet green of the lawn and pines. He held the door open for them, and they entered with silent arrogance. As always.

He smiled to himself. In one sense nothing had changed. They still had the power of life and death over him. They could still cut him off from everything he loved. But in another sense . . .

"Got an easy one for you today, Pollack," she said as she put her briefcase on the coffee table and enabled its data set. "But I don't think you're going to like it."

"Oh?" He sat down and watched her expectantly.

"The last couple of months, we've had you destroying what remains of the Mailman and getting the National program and data bases back in operation."

Behind everything, there still stood the threat of the Mailman. Ten weeks after the battle—the War, as Virginia called it—the public didn't know any more than that there had been a massive vandalism of the System. Like most major wars, this had left ruination in everyone's camp. The U.S. government and the economy of the entire world had slid far toward chaos in the months after that battle. (In fact, without his work and Erythrina's, he doubted if the U.S. bureaucracies could have survived the Mailman War. He didn't know whether this made them the saviors or the betrayers of America.) But what of the enemy? His power was almost certainly destroyed. In the last three weeks Mr. Slippery had found only one copy of the program kernel that had been DON.MAC, and that had been in nonexecutable form. But the man—or the beings—behind the Mailman was just as anonymous as ever. In that, Virginia, the government, and Pollack were just as ignorant as the general public.

"Now," Virginia continued, "we've got some smaller problems—mopping-up action, you might call it. For nearly two decades, we've had to live with the tuppin vandalism of irresponsible individuals who put their petty self-interest ahead of the public's. Now that we've got you, we intend to put a stop to that:

"We want the True Names of all abusers currently on the System, in particular the members of this so-called coven you used to be a part of."

He had known that the demand would eventually come, but the knowledge made this moment no less unpleasant. "I'm sorry, I can't."

"Can't? Or won't? See here, Pollack, the price of your freedom is that you play things our way. You've broken enough laws to justify putting you away forever. And we both know that you are so dangerous that you *ought* to be put away. There are people who feel even more strongly than that, Pollack, people who are not as soft in the head as I am. They simply want you and your girl friend in Providence safely dead." The speech was delivered with characteristic flat bluntness, but she didn't quite meet his eyes as she spoke. Ever since he had returned from the battle, there had been a faint diffidence behind her bluster.

She covered it well, but it was clear to Pollack that she didn't know if she should fear him or respect him—or both. In any case, she seemed to recognize a basic mystery in him; she had more imagination than he had originally thought. It was a bit amusing, for there was very little special about Roger Pollack, the man. He went from day to day feeling a husk of what he had once been and trying to imagine what he could barely remember.

Roger smiled almost sympathetically. "I can't *and* I won't, Virginia. And I don't think you will harm me for it—Let me finish. The only thing that frightens your bosses more than Erythrina and me is the possibility that there may be other unknown persons—maybe even the Mailman, back from wherever he has disappeared to—who might be equally powerful. She and I are your only real experts on this type of subversion. I bet that even if they could, your people wouldn't train their own clean-cut, braided types as replacements for us. The more paranoid a security organization is, the less likely it is to trust anyone with this sort of power. Mr. Slippery and Erythrina are the known factors, the experts who turned back from the brink. Our restraint was the only thing that stood between the Powers That Be and the Powers That Would Be."

Virginia was speechless for a moment, and Pollack could see that this was the crux of her changed attitude toward him. All her life she had been taught that the individual is corrupted by power: she boggled at the notion that he had been offered mastery of all mankind—and had refused it.

Finally she smiled, a quick smile that was gone

almost before he noticed it. "Okay. I'll pass on what
you say. You may be right. The vandals are a long-
range threat to our basic American freedoms,
but day to day, there are a mere annoyance. My
superiors—the Department of Welfare—are probably willing to fight them as we have in the past.
They'll tolerate your, uh, disobedience *in this single
matter* as long as you and Erythrina loyally protect
us against the superhuman threats."

Pollack felt a great sense of relief. He had been so
afraid DoW would be willing to destroy him for this
refusal. But since the Feds would never be free of
their fear of the Mailman, he and Debby Charteris—
Erythrina—would never be forced to betray their
friends.

"But," continued the cop, "that doesn't mean you
get to ignore the covens. The most likely place for
superhuman threats to resurface is from within them.
The vandals are the people with the most real experience on the System—even the Army is beginning
to see that. And if a superhuman type originates
outside the covens, we figure his ego will still make
him show off to them, just as with the Mailman.

"In addition to your other jobs, we want you to
spend a couple of hours a week with each of the
major covens. You'll be one of the 'boys'—only now
you're under responsible control, watching for any
sign of Mailman-type influence."

"I'll get to see Ery again!"

"No. That rule still stands. And you should be
grateful. I don't think we could tolerate your existence if there weren't two of you. With only one in
the Other Plane at a time, we'll always have a weapon
in reserve. And as long as we can keep you from
meeting there, we can keep you from scheming against
us. This is serious, Roger: if we catch you two or
your surrogates playing around in the Other Plane, it
will be the end."

"Hmm."

She looked hard at him for a moment, then appeared to take that for acquiescence. The next half-hour was devoted to the details of this week's assignments. (It would have been easier to feed him all this when he was in the Other Plane, but Virginia—or at least DoW—seemed wedded to the past.) He was to continue the work on Social Security Records and the surveillance of the South American data nets. There was an enormous amount of work to be done, at least with the limited powers the Feds were willing to give him. It would likely be October before the welfare machinery was working properly again. But that would be in time for the elections.

Then, late in the week, they wanted him to visit the Coven. Roger knew he would count the hours; it had been so long.

Virginia was her usual self, intense and all business, until she and her driver were ready to leave. Standing in the carport, she said almost shyly, "I ran your *Anne Boleyn* last week . . . It's really very good."

"You sound surprised."

"No. I mean yes, maybe I was. Actually I've run it several times, usually with the viewpoint character set to Anne. There seems to be a lot more depth to it than other participation games I've read. I've got the feeling that if I am clever enough, someday I'll stop Henry and keep my head!"

Pollack grinned. He could imagine Virginia, the hard-eyed cop, reading *Anne* to study the psychology of her client-prisoner—then gradually getting caught up in the action of the novel. "It is possible."

In fact, it was possible she might turn into a rather nice human being someday.

But by the time Pollack was starting back up the

walk to his house, Virginia was no longer on his mind. He was going back to the Coven!

A chill mist that was almost rain blew across the hillside and obscured the far distance in shifting patches. But even from here, on the ridge above the swamp, the castle looked different: heavier, stronger, darker.

Mr. Slippery started down the familiar slope. The frog on his shoulder seemed to sense his unease and its clawlets bit tighter into the leather of his jacket. Its beady yellow eyes turned this way and that, recording everything. (Altogether, that frog was much improved—almost out of amateur status nowadays.)

The traps were different. In just the ten weeks since the War, the Coven had changed them more than in the previous two years. Every so often, he shook the gathering droplets of water from his face and peered more closely at a bush or boulder by the side of the path. His advance was slow, circuitous, and interrupted by invocations of voice and hand.

Finally he stood before the towers. A figure of black and glowing red climbed out of the magma moat to meet him. Even Alan had changed: he no longer had his asbestos T-shirt, and there was no humor in his sparring with the visitor. Mr. Slippery had to stare upward to look directly at his massive head. The elemental splashed molten rock down on them, and the frog scampered between his neck and collar, its skin cold and slimy against his own. The passwords were different, the questioning more hostile, but Mr. Slippery was a match for the tests and in a matter of minutes Alan retreated sullenly to his steaming pool, and the drawbridge was lowered for their entrance.

The hall was almost the same as before: perhaps a bit drier, more brightly lit. There were certainly more people. And they were all looking at him as he stood in the entranceway. Mr. Slippery gave his traveling jacket and hat to a liveried servant and started down the steps, trying to recognize the faces, trying to understand the tension and hostility that hung in the air.

"Slimey!" The Limey stepped forward from the crowd, a familiar grin splitting his bearded face.

"Slip! Is that really you?" (Not entirely a rhetorical question, under the circumstances.)

Mr. Slippery nodded, and after a moment, the other did, too. The Limey almost ran across the space that separated them, stuck out his hand, and clapped the other on the shoulder. "Come on, come on! We have rather a lot to talk about!"

As if on cue, the others turned back to their conversations and ignored the two friends as they walked to one of the sitting rooms that opened off the main hall. Mr. Slippery felt like a man returning to his old school ten years after graduation. Almost all the faces were different, and he had the feeling that he could never belong here again. But this was only ten weeks, not ten years.

The Slimey Limey shut the heavy door, and the sounds from the main room were muted. He waved Slip to a chair and made a show of mixing them some drinks.

"They're all simulators, aren't they?" Slip said quietly.

"Uh?" The Limey broke off his stream of chatter and shook his head glumly. "Not all. I've recruited four or five apprentices. They do their best to make the place look thriving and occupied. You may have noticed various improvements in our security."

"It looks stronger, but it's more appearance than fact."

Slimey shrugged. "I really didn't expect it to fool the likes of you."

Mr. Slippery leaned forward. "Who's left from the old group, Slimey?"

"DON's gone. The Mailman is gone. Wiley J. Bastard shows up a couple of times a month, but he's not much fun anymore. I think Erythrina's still on the System, but she hasn't come by. I thought you were gone until today."

"What about Robin Hood?"

"Gone."

That accounted for all the top talents. Virginia the Frog hadn't been giving away all that much when she excused him from betraying the Coven. Slip wondered if there was any hint of smugness in the frog's fixed and lipless smile.

"What happened?"

The other sighed. "There's a depression on down in the real world, in case you hadn't noticed; and it's being blamed on us vandals.

"—I know, that could scarcely explain Robin's disappearance, only the lesser ones. Slip, I think most of our old friends are either dead—Truly Dead—or very frightened that if they come back into this Plane, they will become Truly Dead."

This felt very much like history repeating itself. "How do you mean?"

The Limey leaned forward. "Slip, it's quite obvious the government's feeding us lies about what caused the depression. They say it was a combination of programming errors and the work of 'vandals.' We know that can't be true. No ordinary vandals could cause that sort of damage. Right after the crash, I looked at what was left of the Feds' data bases. Whatever ripped things up was more powerful than any vandal. . . . And I've spoken with—p'raps I should say interrogated—Wiley. I think what we see in the real world and on this plane is in fact the wreckage of a bloody major war."

"Between?"

"Creatures as far above me as I am above a chimp. The names we know them by are the Mailman, Erythrina . . . and just possibly Mr. Slippery."

"Me?" Slip tensed and sent out probes along the communications links which he perceived had created the image before him. Even though on a leash, Mr. Slippery was far more powerful than any normal warlock, and it should have been easy to measure the power of this potential opponent. But the Limey was a diffuse, almost nebulous presence. Slip couldn't tell if he were facing an opponent in the same class as himself; in fact, he had no clear idea of the other's strength, which was even more ominous.

The Limey didn't seem to notice. "That's what I thought. Now I doubt it. I wager you were used—like Wiley and possibly DON—by the other combatants. And I see that now you're in *someone's* thrall." His finger stabbed at the yellow-eyed frog on Mr. Slippery's shoulder, and a sparkle of whiskey flew into the creature's face. Virginia—or whoever was controlling the beast—didn't know what to do, and the frog froze momentarily, then recovered its wits and emitted a pale burst of flame.

The Limey laughed. "But it's no one very competent. The Feds is my guess. What happened? Did they sight your True Name, or did you just sell out?"

"The creature's my familiar, Slimey. We all have our apprentices. If you really believe we're the Feds, why did you let us in?"

The other shrugged. "Because there are enemies and enemies, Slip. Beforetime, we called the government the Great Enemy. Now I'd say they are just one in a pantheon of nasties. Those of us who survived the crash are a lot tougher, a lot less frivolous. We don't think of this as all a wry game anymore. And we're teaching our apprentices a lot more systematically. It's not near so much fun. Now when we talk of traitors in the Coven, we mean real, life-and-death treachery.

"But it's necessary. When it comes to it, if we little people don't protect ourselves, we're going to be eaten up by the government or . . . certain other creatures I fear even more."

The frog shifted restively on Mr. Slippery's shoulder, and he could imagine Virginia getting ready to deliver some speech on the virtue of obeying the laws of society in order to reap its protection. He reached across to pat its cold and pimply back; now was not the time for such debate.

"You had one of the straightest heads around here, Slip. Even if you aren't one of us anymore, I don't reckon you're an absolute enemy. You and your . . . friend may have certain interests in common with us. There are things you should know about—if you don't already. An' p'raps there'll be times you'll help us similarly."

Slip felt the Federal tether loosen. Virginia must have convinced her superiors that there was actually help to be had here. "Okay. You're right. There was a war. The Mailman was the enemy. He lost and now we're trying to put things back together."

"Ah, that's just it, old man. *I don't think the war is over*. True, all that remains of the Mailman's constructs are 'craterfields' spread through the government's program space. But something like him is still very much alive." He saw the disbelief in Mr. Slippery's face. "I know, you an' your friends are more powerful than any of us. But there are many of us—not just in the Coven—and we have learned a lot these past ten weeks. There are signs, so light an' fickle you might call 'em atmosphere, that tell us something like the Mailman is still alive. It doesn't quite have the texture of the Mailman, but it's there."

Mr. Slippery nodded. He didn't need any special explanations of the feeling. *Damn! If I weren't on a leash, I would have seen all this weeks ago, instead of finding it out secondhand.* He thought back to those last minutes of their descent from godhood and felt a chill. He knew what he must ask now, and he had a bad feeling about what the answer might be. Somehow he had to prevent Virginia from hearing that answer. It would be a great risk, but he still had a few tricks he didn't think DoW knew of. He probed back along the links that went to Arcata and D.C., feeling the interconnections and the redundancy checks. If he was lucky, he would not have to alter more than a few hundred bits of the information that would flow down to them in the next few seconds. "So who do you think is behind it?"

"For a while, I thought it might be you. Now I've seen you and, uh, done some tests, I know you're more powerful than in the old days and probably more powerful than I am now, but you're no superman."

"Maybe I'm in disguise."

"Maybe, but I doubt it." The Limey was coming closer to the critical words that must be disguised. Slip began to alter the redundancy bits transmitted through the construct of the frog. He would have to fake the record both before and after those words if the deception was to escape detection completely. "No, there's a certain style to this presence. A style that reminds me of our old friend, REorbyitnh rHionoad." The name he said, and the name Mr. Slippery heard, was "Erythrina." The name blended imperceptibly in its place, the name the frog heard, and reported, was "Robin Hood."

"Hmm, possible. He always seemed to be power hungry." The Limey's eyebrows went up fractionally at the pronoun "he." Besides, Robin had been a fantastically clever vandal, not a power grabber. Slimey's eyes flickered toward the frog, and Mr.

Slippery prayed that he would play along. "Do you really think this is as great a threat as the Mailman?"

"Who knows? The presence isn't as widespread as the Mailman's, and since the crash no more of us have disappeared. Also, I'm not sure that . . . he . . . is the only such creature left. Perhaps the original Mailman is still around."

And you can't decide who it is that I'm really trying to fool, can you?

The discussion continued for another half-hour, a weird three-way fencing match with just two active players. On the one hand, he and the Limey were trying to communicate past the frog, and on the other, the Slimey Limey was trying to decide if perhaps Slip was the real enemy and the frog a potential ally. The hell of it was, Mr. Slippery wasn't sure himself of the answer to that puzzle.

Slimey walked him out to the drawbridge. For a few moments, they stood on the graven ceramic plating and spoke. Below them, Alan paddled back and forth, looking up at them uneasily. The mist was a light rain now, and a constant sizzling came from the molten rock.

Finally Slip said, "You're right in a way, Slimey. I am someone's thrall. But I will look for Robin Hood. If you're right, you've got a couple of new allies. If he's too strong for us, this might be the last you see of me."

The Slimey Limey nodded, and Slip hoped he had gotten the real message: He would take on Ery all by himself.

"Well then, let's hope this ain't good-bye, old man."

Slip walked back down into the valley, aware of the Limey's not unsympathetic gaze on his back.

How to find her, how to speak with her? And survive the experience, that is. Virginia had forbidden him—literally on pain of death—from meeting with Ery on this plane. Even if he could do so, it would be a deadly risk for other reasons. What had Ery been doing in those minutes she dallied, when she had fooled him into descending back to the human plane before her? At the time, he had feared it was a betrayal. Yet he had lived and had forgotten the mystery. Now he wondered again. It was impossible for him to understand the complexity of those minutes. Perhaps she had weakened herself at the beginning to gull him into starting the descent, and perhaps then she hadn't been quite strong enough to take over. Was that possible? And now she was slowly, secretly building back her powers, just as the Mailman had done? He didn't want to believe it, and he knew if Virginia heard his suspicions, the Feds would kill her immediately. There would be no trial, no deep investigation.

Somehow he must get past Virginia and confront Ery—confront her in such a way that he could destroy her if she were a new Mailman. *And there is a way!* He almost laughed: it was absurd and absurdly simply, and it was the only thing that might work. All eyes were on this plane, where magic and power flowed easily to the participants. He would attack from beneath, from the lowly magicless real world!

But there was one final act of magic he must slip past Virginia, something absolutely necessary for a real world confrontation with Erythrina.

He had reached the far ridge and was starting down the hillside that led to the swamps. Even preoccupied, he had given the right signs flawlessly. The guardian sprites were not nearly so vigilant toward contructs moving away from the castle. As the wet brush closed in about them, the familiar red and black spider—or its cousin—swung down from above.

"Beware, beware," came the tiny voice. From the flecks of gold across its abdomen, he knew the right response: left hand up and flick the spider away.

Instead Slip raised his right hand and struck at the creature.

The spider hoisted itself upward, screeching faintly, then dropped toward Slip's neck—to land squarely on the frog. A free-for-all erupted as the two scrambled across the back of his neck, pale flame jousting against venom. Even as he moved to save the frog, Mr. Slippery melted part of his attention into a data line that fed a sporting good store in Montreal. An order was placed and later that day a certain very special package would be in the mail to the Boston International Rail Terminal.

Slip made a great show of dispatching the spider, and as the frog settled back on his shoulder, he saw that he had probably fooled Virginia. That he had expected. Fooling Ery would be much the deadlier, chancier thing.

If this afternoon were typical, then July in Providence must be a close approximation to Hell. Roger Pollack left the tube as it passed the urbapt block and had to walk nearly four hundred meters to get to the tower he sought. His shirt was soaked with sweat from just below the belt line right up to his neck. The contents of the package he had picked up at the airport train station sat heavily in his right coat pocket, tapping against his hip with every step, reminding him that this was high noon in more ways than one.

Pollack quickly crossed the blazing concrete plaza and walked along the edge of the shadow that was all the tower cast in the noonday sun. All around him the locals swarmed, all ages, seemingly unfazed by the still, moist, hot air. Apparently you could get used to practically anything.

Even an urbapt in summer in Providence. Pollack had expected the buildings to be more depressing. Workers who had any resources became data commuters and lived outside the cities. Of course, some of the people here were data-set users too and so could be characterized as data commuters. Many of them worked as far away from home as any exurb dweller. The difference was that they made so little money (when they had a job at all) that they were forced to take advantage of the economies of scale the urbapts provided.

Pollack saw the elevator ahead but had to detour around a number of children playing stickball in the plaza. The elevator was only half-full, so a wave from him was all it took to keep it grounded till he could get aboard.

No one followed him on, and the faces around him were disinterested and entirely ordinary. Pollack was not fooled. He hadn't violated the letter of Virginia's law; he wasn't trying to see Erythrina on the data net. But he was going to see Debby Charteris, which came close to being the same thing. He imagined the Feds debating with themselves, finally deciding it would be safe to let the two godlings get together if it were on this plane where the *State* was still the ultimate, all-knowing god. He and Debby would be observed. Even so, he would somehow discover if she were the threat the Limey saw. If not, the Feds would never know of his suspicions. But if Ery had betrayed them all and meant to set herself up in place of—or in league with—the Mailman, then in the next few minutes one of them would die.

The express slid to a stop with a deceptive gentleness that barely gave a feeling of lightness. Pollack paid and got off.

Floor 25 was mainly shopping mall. He would have to find the stairs to the residential apts between Floors 25 and 35. Pollack drifted through the mall. He was beginning to feel better about the whole thing. *I'm still alive, aren't I?* If Ery had really become what the Limey and Slip feared, then he

probably would have had a little "accident" before
now. All the way across the continent he sat with his
guts frozen, thinking how easy it would be for someone with the Mailman's power to destroy an air
transport, even without resorting to the military's
lasers. A tiny change in navigation or traffic-control
directions, and any number of fatal incidents could
be arranged. But nothing had happened, which meant
that either Ery was innocent or that she hadn't noticed him. (And that second possibility was unlikely
if she were a new Mailman. One impression that
remained stronger than any other from his short time
as godling was the omniscience of it all.)

It turned out the stairs were on the other side of
the mall, marked by a battered sign reminiscent of
old-time highway markers: FOOTS > 26–30. The
place wasn't really too bad, he supposed, eyeing the
stained but durable carpet that covered the stairs.
And the hallways coming off each landing reminded
him of the motels he had known as a child, before
the turn of the century. There was very little trash
visible, the people moving around him weren't poorly
dressed, and there was only the faintest spice of
disinfectant in the air. Apt module 28355, where
Debbie Charteris lived, might be high-class. It
did have an exterior view, he knew that. Maybe
Erythrina—Debbie—*liked* living with all these other
people. Surely, now that the government was so
interested in her, she could move anywhere she
wished.

But when he reached it, he found floor 28 no
different from the others he had seen: carpeted hallway stretching away forever beneath dim lights that
showed identical module doorways dwindling in perspective. What was Debbie/Erythrina like that she
would choose to live here?

"Hold it." Three teenagers stepped from behind
the slant of the stairs. Pollack's hand edged toward

his coat pocket. He had heard of the gangs. These three looked like heavies, but they were well and conservatively dressed, and the small one actually had his hair in a braid. They wanted very much to be thought part of the establishment.

The short one flashed something silver at him. "Building Police." And Pollack remembered the news stories about Federal Urban Support paying youngsters for urbapt security: "A project that saves money and staff, while at the same time giving our urban youth an opportunity for responsible citizenship."

Pollack swallowed. Best to treat them like real cops. He showed them his id. "I'm from out of state. I'm just visiting."

The other two closed in, and the short one laughed. "That's sure. Fact, Mr. Pollack, Sammy's little gadget says you're in violation of Building Ordinance." The one on Pollack's left waved a faintly buzzing cylinder across Pollack's jacket, then pushed a hand into the jacket and withdrew Pollack's pistol, a lightweight ceramic slug-gun perfect for hunting hikes—and which should have been perfect for getting past a building's weapon detectors.

Sammy smiled down at the weapon, and the short one continued, "Thing you didn't know, Mr. Pollack, is Federal law requires a metal tag in the butt of these cram guns. Makes 'em easy to detect." Until the tag was removed. Pollack suspected that somehow this incident might never be reported.

The three stepped back, leaving the way clear for Pollack. "That's all? I can go?"

The young cop grinned. "Sure. You're out-of-towner. How could you know?"

Pollack continued down the hall. The others did not follow. Pollack was fleetingly surprised: maybe the FUS project actually worked. Before the turn of the century, goons like those three would have at least robbed him. Instead they behaved something like real cops.

Or maybe—and he almost stumbled at this new thought—*they all work for Ery now*. That might be the first symptom of conquest: the new god would simply become the government. And he—the last threat to the new order—was being granted one last audience with the victor.

Pollack straightened and walked on more quickly. There was no turning back now, and he was damned if he would show any more fear. Besides, he thought with a sudden surge of relief, it was out of his control now. If Ery was a monster, there was nothing he could do about it; he would not have to try to kill her. If she were not, then his own survival would be proof, and he need think of no complicated tests of her innocence.

He was almost hurrying now. He had always wanted to know what the human being beyond Erythrina was like; sooner or later he would have had to do this anyway. Weeks ago he had looked through all the official directories for the state of Rhode Island, but there wasn't much to find: Linda and Deborah Charteris lived at 28355 Place on 4448 Grosvenor Row. The public directory didn't even show their "interests and occupations."

28313, 315, 317. . . .

His mind had gone in circles, generating all the things Debby Charteris might turn out to be. She would not be the exotic beauty she projected in the Other Plane. That was too much to hope for; but the other possibilities vied in his mind. He had lived with each, trying to believe that he could accept whatever turned out to be the case:

Most likely, she was a perfectly ordinary looking person who lived in an urbapt to save enough money to buy high-quality processing equipment and rent dense comm lines. Maybe she wasn't good-looking, and that was why the directory listing was relatively secretive.

Almost as likely, she was massively handicapped. He had seen that fairly often among the warlocks whose True Names he knew. They had extra medical welfare and used all their free money for equipment that worked around whatever their problem might be—paraplegia, quadriplegia, multiple sense loss. As such, they were perfectly competitive on the job market, yet old prejudices often kept them out of normal society. Many of these types retreated into the Other Plane, where one could completely control one's appearance.

And then, since the beginning of time, there had been the people who simply did not like reality, who wanted another world, and if given half a chance would live there forever. Pollack suspected that some of the best warlocks might be of this type. Such people were content to live in an urbapt, to spend all their money on processing and life-support equipment, to spend days at a time in the Other Plane, never moving, never exercising their real world bodies. They grew more and more adept, more and more knowledgeable—while their bodies slowly wasted. Pollack could imagine such a person becoming an evil thing and taking over the Mailman's role. It would be like a spider sitting in its web, its victims all humanity. He remembered Ery's contemptuous attitude on learning he never used drugs to maintain concentration and so stay longer in the Other Plane. He shuddered.

And there, finally, and yet too soon, the numbers 28355 stood on the wall before him, the faint hall light glistening off their bronze finish. For a long moment, he balanced between the fear and the wish. Finally he reached forward and tapped the door buzzer.

Fifteen seconds passed. There was no one nearby

in the hall. From the corner of his eye, he could see the "cops" lounging by the stairs. About a hundred meters the other way, an argument was going on. The contenders rounded the faraway corner and their voices quieted, leaving him in near silence.

There was a click, and a small section of the door became transparent, a window (more likely a holo) on the interior of the apt. And the person beyond that view would be either Deborah or Linda Charteris.

"Yes?" The voice was faint, cracking with age. Pollack saw a woman barely tall enough to come up to the pickup on the other side. Her hair was white, visibly thin on top, especially from the angle he was viewing.

"I'm . . . I'm looking for Deborah Charteris."

"My granddaughter. She's out shopping. Downstairs in the mall, I think." The head bobbed, a faintly distracted nod.

"Oh. Can you tell me—" *Deborah, Debby*. It suddenly struck him what an old-fashioned name that was, more the name of a grandmother than a granddaughter. He took a quick step to the door and looked down through the pane so that he could see most of the other's body. The woman wore an old-fashioned skirt and blouse combination of some brilliant red material.

Pollack pushed his hand against the immovable plastic of the door. "Ery, please. Let me in."

The pane blanked as he spoke, but after a moment the door slowly opened. "Okay." Her voice was tired, defeated. Not the voice of a god boasting victory.

The interior was decorated cheaply and with what might have been good taste except for the garish excesses of red on red. Pollack remembered reading somewhere that as you age, color sensitivity decreases. This room might seem only mildly bright to the person Erythrina had turned out to be.

The woman walked slowly across the tiny apt and

gestured for him to sit. She was frail, her back curved in a permanent stoop, her every step considered yet tremulous. Under the apt's window, he noticed an elaborate GE processor system. Pollack sat and found himself looking slightly upward into her face.

"Slip—or maybe I should call you Roger here— you always were a bit of a romantic fool." She paused for breath, or perhaps her mind wandered. "I was beginning to think you had more sense than to come out here, that you could leave well enough alone."

"You . . . you mean, you didn't know I was coming?" The knowledge was a great loosening in his chest.

"Not until you were in the building." She turned and sat carefully upon the sofa.

"I had to see who you really are," and that was certainly the truth. "After this spring, there is no one the likes of us in the whole world."

Her face cracked in a little smile. "And now you see how different we are. I had hoped you never would and that someday they would let us back together on the Other Plane. . . . But in the end, it doesn't really matter." She paused, brushed at her temple, and frowned as though forgetting something, or remembering something else.

"I never did look much like the Erythrina you know. I was never tall, of course, and my hair was never red. But I didn't spend my whole life selling life insurance in Peoria, like poor Wiley."

"You . . . you must go all the way back to the beginning of computing."

She smiled again, and nodded just so, a mannerism Pollack had often seen on the Other Plane. "Almost, almost. Out of high school, I was a keypunch operator. You know what a keypunch is?"

He nodded hesitantly, visions of some sort of machine press in his mind.

"It was a dead-end job, and in those days they'd

keep you in it forever if you didn't get out under your own power. I got out of it and into college quick as I could, but at least I can say I was in the business during the stone age. After college, I never looked back; there was always so much happening. In the Nasty Nineties, I was on the design of the ABM and FoG control programs. The whole team, the whole of DoD for that matter, was trying to program the thing with procedural languages; it would take 'em a thousand years and a couple of wars to do it that way, and they were beginning to realize as much. I was responsible for getting them away from CRTs, for getting into really interactive EEG programming—what they call portal programming nowadays. Sometimes . . . sometimes when my ego needs a little help, I like to think that if I had never been born, hundreds of millions more would have died back then, and our cities would be glassy ponds today.

". . . And along the way there was a marriage . . ." her voice trailed off again, and she sat smiling at memories Pollack could not see.

He looked around the apt. Except for the processor and a fairly complete kitchenette, there was no special luxury. What money she had must go into her equipment, and perhaps in getting a room with a real exterior view. Beyond the rising towers of the Grosvenor complex, he could see the nest of comm towers that had been their last-second salvation that spring. When he looked back at her, he saw that she was watching him with an intent and faintly amused expression that was very familiar.

"I'll bet you wonder how anyone so daydreamy could be the Erythrina you knew in the Other Plane."

"Why, no," he lied. "You seem perfectly lucid to me."

"Lucid, yes. I am still that, thank God. But I know—and no one has to tell me—that I can't support a train of thought like I could before. These last two or three years, I've found that my mind can wander, can drop into reminiscence, at the most inconvenient times. I've had one stroke, and about all 'the miracles of modern medicine' can do for me is predict that it will not be the last one.

"But in the Other Plane, I can compensate. It's easy for the EEG to detect failure of attention. I've written a package that keeps a thirty-second backup; when distraction is detected, it forces attention and reloads my short-term memory. Most of the time, this gives me better concentration than I've ever had in my life. And when there is a really serious wandering of attention, the package can interpolate for a number of seconds. You may have noticed that, though perhaps you mistook it for poor communications coordination."

She reached a thin, blue-veined hand toward him. He took it in his own. It felt so light and dry, but it returned his squeeze. "It really is me—Ery—inside, Slip."

He nodded, feeling a lump in his throat.

"When I was a kid, there was this song, something about us all being aging children. And it's so very, very true. Inside I still feel like a youngster. But on this plane, no one else can see . . ."

"But I know, Ery. We knew each other on the Other Plane, and I know what you truly are. Both of us are so much more there than we could ever be here." This was all true: even with the restrictions they put on him now, he had a hard time understanding all he did on the Other Plane. What he had become since the spring was a fuzzy dream to him when he was down in the physical world. Sometimes he felt like a fish trying to imagine what a man in an airplane might be feeling. He never spoke of it like this to Virginia and her friends: they would be sure he had finally gone crazy. It was far beyond what he had known as a warlock. And what they had been

those brief minutes last spring had been equally far
beyond that.

"Yes, I think you do know me, Slip. And we'll be
. . . friends as long as this body lasts. And when I'm
gone—"

"I'll remember; I'll always remember you, Ery."

She smiled and squeezed his hand again. "Thanks.
But that's not what I was getting at. . . ." Her gaze
drifted off again. "I figured out who the Mailman was
and I wanted to tell you."

Pollack could imagine Virginia and the other DoW
eavesdroppers hunkering down to their spy equipment. "I hoped you knew something." He went on
to tell her about the Slimey Limey's detection of
Mailman-like operations still on the System. He spoke
carefully, knowing that he had two audiences.

Ery—even now he couldn't think of her as Debby—
nodded. "I've been watching the Coven. They've
grown, these last months. I think they take themselves more seriously now. In the old days, they
never would have noticed what the Limey warned
you about. But it's not the Mailman he saw, Slip."

"How can you be sure, Ery? We never killed more
than his service programs and his simulators—like
DON.MAC. We never found his True Name. We
don't even know if he's human or some science-
fictional alien."

"You're wrong, Slip. I know what the Limey saw,
and I know who the Mailman is—or was," she spoke
quietly, but with certainty. "It turns out the Mailman
was the greatest cliché of the Computer Age, maybe
of the entire Age of Science."

"Huh?"

"You've seen plenty of personality simulators in
the Other Plane. DON.MAC—at least as he was
rewritten by the Mailman—was good enough to fool
normal warlocks. Even Alan, the Coven's elemental,
shows plenty of human emotion and cunning." Pol-

lack thought of the new Alan, so ferocious and intimidating. The Turing T-shirt was beneath his dignity now. "Even so, Slip, I don't think you've ever believed you could be permanently fooled by a simulation, have you?"

"Wait. Are you trying to tell me that the Mailman was just another simulator? That the time lag was just to obscure the fact that he was a simulator? That's ridiculous. You know his powers were more than human, almost as great as ours became."

"But do you think you could ever be fooled?"

"Frankly, no. If you talk to one of those things long enough, they display a repetitiveness, an inflexibility that's a giveaway. I don't know; maybe someday there'll be programs that can pass the Turing test. But whatever it is that makes a person a person is terribly complicated. Simulation is the wrong way to get at it, because being a person is more than symptoms. A program that was a person would use enormous data bases, and if the processors running it were the sort we have now, you certainly couldn't expect real-time interaction with the outside world." And Pollack suddenly had a glimmer of what she was thinking.

"That's the critical point. Slip: *if you want real-time interaction*. But the Mailman—the sentient, conversational part—never did operate real time. We thought the lag was a communications delay that showed the operator was off-planet, but really he was here all the time. It just took him hours of processing time to sustain seconds of self-awareness."

Pollack opened his mouth, but nothing came out. It went against all his intuition, almost against what religion he had, but it might just barely be possible. The Mailman had controlled immense resources. All his quick time reactions could have been the work of ordinary programs and simulators like DON.MAC. The only evidence they had for his humanity were those teleprinter conversations where his responses were spread over hours.

"Okay, for the sake of argument, let's say it's possible. Someone, somewhere had to write the original Mailman. Who was that?"

"Who would you guess? The government, of course. About ten years ago. It was an NSA team trying to automate system protection. Some brilliant people, but they could never really get it off the ground. They wrote a developmental kernel that by itself was not especially effective or aware. It was designed to live within larger systems and gradually grow in power and awareness, *independent* of what policies or mistakes the operators of the system might make.

"The program managers saw the Frankenstein analogy—or at least they saw a threat to their personal power—and quashed the project. In any case, it was very expensive. The program executed slowly and gobbled incredible data space."

"And you're saying that someone conveniently left a copy running all unknown?"

She seemed to miss the sarcasm. "It's not that unlikely. Research types are fairly careless—outside of their immediate focus. When I was in FoG, we lost thousands of megabytes 'between the cracks' of our data bases. And back then, that was a lot of memory. The development kernel is not very large. My guess is a copy was left in the system. Remember, the kernel was designed to live untended if it ever started executing. Over the years it slowly grew— both because of its natural tendencies and because of the increased power of the nets it lived in."

Pollack sat back on the sofa. Her voice was tiny and frail, so unlike the warm, rich tones he remembered from the Other Plane. But she spoke with the same authority.

Debby's—Erythrina's—pale eyes stared off beyond the walls of the apt, dreaming. "You know, they are right to be afraid," she said finally. "Their world is ending. Even without us, there would still be the Limey, the Coven—and someday most of the human race."

Damn. Pollack was momentarily tongue-tied, trying desperately to think of something to mollify the threat implicit in Ery's words. *Doesn't she understand that DoW would never let us talk unbugged? Doesn't she know how trigger-happy scared the top Feds must be by now?*

But before he could say anything, Ery glanced at him, saw the consternation in his face, and smiled. The tiny hand patted his. "Don't worry, Slip. The Feds are listening, but what they're hearing is tearful chitchat—you overcome to find me what I am, and me trying to console the both of us. They will never know what I really tell you here. They will never know about the gun the local boys took off you."

"What?"

"You see, I lied a little. I know why you really came. I know you thought that *I* might be the new monster. But I don't want to lie to you anymore. You risked your life to find out the truth, when you could have just told the Feds what you guessed." She went on, taking advantage of his stupefied silence. "Did you ever wonder what I did in those last minutes this spring, after we surrendered—when I lagged behind you in the Other Plane?

"It's true, we really did destroy the Mailman; that's what all that unintelligible data space we plowed up was. I'm sure there are copies of the kernel hidden here and there, little cancers in the System, but we can control them one by one as they appear.

"I guessed what had happened when I saw all that space, and I had plenty of time to study what was left, even to trace back to the original research project. Poor little Mailman, like the monsters of fiction—he was only doing what he had been designed to do. He

was taking over the System, protecting it from
everyone—even its owners. I suspect he would have
announced himself in the end and used some sort of
nuclear blackmail to bring the rest of the world into
line. But even though his programs had been running for several years, he had only had fifteen or
twenty hours of human type self-awareness when we
did him in. His personality programs were that slow.
He never attained the level of consciousness you and
I had on the System.

"But he really was self-aware, and that was the
triumph of it all. And in those few minutes, I figured
out how I could adapt the basic kernel to accept any
input personality. . . . That is what I really wanted to
tell you."

"Then what the Limey saw was—"

She nodded. "Me . . ."

She was grinning now, an open though conspiratorial grin that was very familiar. "When Bertrand
Russell was very old, and probably as dotty as I am
now, he talked of spreading his interests and attention out to the greater world and away from his own
body, so that when that body died he would scarcely
notice it, his whole consciousness would be so di-
luted through the outside world.

"For him, it was wishful thinking, of course. But
not for me. My kernel is out here in the System.
Every time I'm there, I transfer a little more of
myself. The kernel is growing into a true Erythrina,
who is also truly me. When this body dies," she
squeezed his hand with hers, "when this body dies, *I*
will still be, and you can still talk to me."

"Like the Mailman?"

"Slow like the Mailman. At least till I design faster
processors. . . .

". . . So in a way, I am everything you and the
Limey were afraid of. *You* could probably still stop
me, Slip." And he sensed that she was awaiting his

judgment, the last judgment any human would ever be allowed to levy upon her.

Slip shook his head and smiled at her, thinking of the slow-moving guardian angel that she would become. *Every race must arrive at this point in its history,* he suddenly realized. A few years or decades in which its future slavery or greatness rests on the goodwill of one or two persons. It could have been the Mailman. Thank God it was Ery instead.

And beyond those years or decades . . . for an instant, Pollack came near to understanding things that had once been obvious. Processors kept getting faster, memories larger. What now took a planet's resources would someday be possessed by everyone. Including himself.

Beyond those years or decades . . . were millennia. And Ery.

—Vernor Vinge
San Diego
June 1979–January 1980

As the years pass, I've been very interested in the reaction of readers to "True Names." I have a knowledgeable friend who first read it in 1980. At that time she liked it but thought the story was a bit "off the wall." She reread it several years later, still liked it, but by then it scarcely seemed radical. In the meantime, the ideas in the story had appeared (independently) all over the place. There are the terrific stories of William Gibson and Bruce Sterling, and lately television shows with many of these ideas. By 1987, the Man on the Street is familiar (in some distorted form) with personality simulators and the Other Plane. It can be a humbling experience to hear accountants argue about megabytes and paging strategies.

One thing to notice about "True Names": it sneaks up on the Singularity from a different direction (a direction made obvious by technological developments of the 70's), but like "Bookworm, Run!" it stops shyly near the edge. We could creep closer, we could talk of normal humans watching events unfold. There are many stories in this vein still to be told, and radically different visions are possible: once begun, the final slip into the Singularity might happen in a matter of hours. Greg Bear's marvelous Blood Music is the first story I know that illustrates this wonderful/terrifying possibility. K. Eric Drexler's The Engines of Creation is a sober, nonfiction description of how a superfast transition could actually happen.

What about futures without a Singularity (or with the Singularity postponed)? Could the trends stop short of true AI/IA? For years, I had been fascinated by Fredric Brown's short story, "Letter to a Phoenix." What if a lone human survived beyond his civilization, and the next, and the next? Brown's protagonist was nearly immortal. A similar effect could be achieved by an ordinary human, using some kind of suspended animation. What motive could such a traveler have—beyond crazed curiosity? Perhaps I could have a merchant who traded down time, like an ancient ship captain. But my merchant could move only in one direction . . . and the problem of estimating "consumer demand" at the next port would be truly enormous.

I worked off and on with the idea in the late 60's; I had part of it written, but the ending was never clear. I put the story aside, and this turned out to be the most clever thing I could have done:

From 1972 to 1979 I was married to Joan D. Vinge. Of course, we talked about our various projects all the time; it was a great pleasure to scheme with such a good writer. Yet for all our plot discussions, only once did we collaborate on a story: I showed Joan my "merchant out of time" fragment, told her my plans for how the story might end. We chatted it up, decided that a story "frame" was needed to hold the loose parts together. (I think this is one of the few times either of us had used that device.) Joan wrote the frame and the latter part of the story, then rewrote my draft. The result appears here. Keep in mind that up to a certain point I was writing (with some latter revision by Joan), and after that it is Joan's writing. Can you spot the break?

THE PEDDLER'S APPRENTICE

Lord Buckry I of Fyffe lounged on his throne, watching his two youngest sons engaged in mock battle in the empty Audience Hall. The daggers were wooden but the rivalry was real, and the smaller boy was at a disadvantage. Lord Buckry tugged on a heavy gold earring; thin, brown-haired Hanaban was his private favorite. The boy took after his father both in appearance and turn of mind.

The lord of the Flatlands was a tall man, his own unkempt brown hair graying now at the temples. The blue eyes in his lean, foxlike face still perceived with disconcerting sharpness, though years of experience kept his own thoughts hidden. More than twenty years had passed since he had won control of his lands; he had not kept his precarious place as lord so long without good reason.

Now his eyes flashed rare approval as Hanaban cried. "Trace, look there!" and, as his brother turned, distracted, whacked him soundly on the chest.

"Gotcha!" Hanaban shrieked delightedly. Trace grimaced with disgust.

Their father chuckled, but his face changed suddenly as the sound of a commotion outside the chamber reached him. The heavy, windowed doors at the far end of the room burst open; the Flatlander courier shook off guards, crossed the high-ceilinged, echoing chamber and flung himself into a bow, his rifle clattering on the floor. "Your lordship!"

Lord Buckry snapped his fingers; his gaping children silently fled the room. "Get up," he said impatiently. "What in tarnation is this?"

"Your lordship." The courier raised a dusty face, wincing mentally at his lord's Highland drawl. "There's word the sea kingdoms have raised another army. They're crossing the coast mountains, and—"

"That ain't possible. We cleaned them out not half a year since."

"They've a lot of folk along the coast, Your Lordship." The horseman stood apologetically. "And Jayley Sharkstooth's made a pact this time with the Southlands."

Lord Buckry stiffened. "They've been at each other's throats long as I can remember." He frowned, pulling at his earring. "Only thing they've got in common is—me. Damn!"

He listened distractedly to the rider's report, then stood abruptly, dismissing the man as an afterthought. As the heavy doors of the hall slid shut he was already striding toward the elevator, past the shaft of the ballistic vehicle exit, unused for more than thirty years. His soft-soled Highlander boots made no sound on the cold polished floor.

From the parapet of his castle he could survey a wide stretch of his domain, the rich, utterly flat farmlands of the hundred-mile-wide valley—the lands the South and West were hungry for. The fields were dark now with turned earth, ready for the spring planting; it·was no time to be calling up an army. He was sure his enemies were aware of that.

The day was exceptionally clear, and at the eastern reaches of his sight he could make out the grayed purple wall of the mountains: the Highlands, that held his birthplace—and something more important to him now.

The dry wind ruffled his hair as he looked back across thirty years; his sunburned hands tightened on the seamless, ancient green-blackness of the parapet. "Damn you, Mr. Jagged," he said to the wind. "Where's your magic when I *need* it?"

The peddler came to Darkwood Corners from the east, on Wim Buckry's seventeenth birthday. It was early summer, and Wim could still see sun flashing on snow up on the pine-wooded hill that towered above the Corners; the snowpack in the higher hills was melting at last, sluicing down gullies that stood dry through most of the year, changing Littlebig Creek into a cold, singing torrent tearing at the earth below the cabins on the north side of the road. Even a week ago the East Pass had lain under more than thirty feet of snow.

Something like silence came over the townspeople as they saw the peddler dragging his cart down the east road toward the Corners. His wagon was nearly ten feet tall and fifteen long, with carved, bright-painted wooden sides that bent sharply out over the wheels to meet a gabled roof. Wim gaped in wonder as he saw those wheels, spindly as willow wood yet over five feet across. Under the cart's weight they sank half a foot and more into the mud of the road, but cut through the mud without resistance, without leaving a rut.

Even so, the peddler was bent nearly double with the effort of pulling his load. The fellow was short and heavy, with skin a good deal darker than Wim had ever seen. His pointed black beard jutted at a

determined angle as he staggered along the rutted
track, up to his ankles in mud. Above his calves the
tooled leather of his leggings gleamed black and clean.
Several scrofulous dogs nosed warily around him as
he plodded down the center of the road; he ignored
them as he ignored the staring townsfolk.

Wim shoved his empty mug back at Ounze Rumpster, sitting nearest the tavern door. "More," he
said. Ounze swore, got up from the steps, and disappeared into the tavern.

Wim's attention never left the peddler for an instant. As the dark man reached the widening in the
road at the center of town, he pulled his wagon into
the muddy morass where the Widow Henley's house
had stood until the Littlebig Creek dragged it to
destruction. The stranger had everyone's attention
now. Even the town's smith had left his fire, and stood
in his doorway gazing down the street at the peddler.

The peddler turned his back on them as he kicked
an arresting gear down from the rear of the painted
wagon and let it settle into the mud. He returned to
the front of the cart and moved a small wheel set in
the wood paneling: a narrow blue pennant sprouted
from the peak of the gable and fluttered briskly; crisp
and metallic, a pinging melody came from the wagon.
That sound emptied the tavern and brought the remainder of the Corners' population onto the street.
Ounze Rumpster nearly fell down the wooden steps in
his haste to see the source of the music; he sat down
heavily, handing the refilled mug to Wim. Wim ignored him.

As the peddler turned back to the crowd the eerie
music stopped, and the creek sounded loud in the
silence. Then the little man's surprising bass voice
rumbled out at them, "Jagit Katchetooriantz is my
name, and fine wrought goods is my trade. Needles,
adze-heads, blades—you need 'em?" He pulled a

latch on the wagon's wall and a panel swung out from its side, revealing rows of shining knifeblades and needles so fine Wim could see only glitter where they caught the sunlight. "Step right on up, folks. Take a look, take a feel. Tell me what they might be worth to you." There was no need to repeat the invitation—in seconds he was surrounded. As the townspeople closed around him, he mounted a small step set in the side of the wagon, so that he could still be seen over the crowd.

Wim's boys were on their feet; but he sat motionless, his sharp face intent. "Set down," he said, just loudly enough. "Your eyes is near busting out of your heads. They'd skin us right fast if we try anything here. There's too many. Set!" He gave the nearest of them, Bathecar Henley, a sideways kick in the shin; they all sat. "Gimme that big ring of yours, Sothead."

Ounze Rumpster's younger brother glared at him, then extended his jeweled fist from a filthy woolen cuff. "How come you're so feisty of a sudden, Wim?" He dropped the ring peevishly into the other's hand. Wim turned away without comment, passing the massive chunk of gold to Bathecar's plump, fair girlfriend.

"All right, Emmy, you just take yourself over to that wagon and see about buying us some knifeblades— not too long, say about so." He stretched his fingers. "And find out how they're fastened on the rack."

"Sure, Wim." She rose from the steps and minced away across the muddy road toward the crowd at the peddler's wagon. Wim grimaced, reflecting that the red knit dress Bathecar had brought her was perhaps too small.

The peddler's spiel continued, all but drowning out the sound of Littlebig Creek: "Just try your blades 'gin mine, friends. Go ahead. Nary a scratch you've made on mine, see? Now how much is it worth, friends? I'll take gold, silver. Or craft items. And I need a horse—lost my own, coming down those blamed trails." He waved toward the East Pass. The townspeople were packed tightly together now as each of them tried for a chance to test the gleaming metal, and to make some bid that would catch the peddler's fancy. Emmy wriggled expertly into the mass; in seconds Wim could see her red dress right at the front of the crowd. She was happily fondling the merchandise, competing with the rest for the stranger's attention.

Hanaban Kroy shifted his bulk on the hard wooden step. "Three gold pigs says that outlander is from down west. He just come in from the east to set us all to talking. Nobody makes knives like them east of the pass."

Wim nodded slightly. "Could be." He watched the peddler and fingered the thick gold earring half-hidden in his shaggy brown hair.

Across the road, the merchant was engaged in a four-way bidding session. Many of the townsfolk wanted to trade furs, or crossbows, but Jagit Katchetooriantz wasn't interested. This narrowed his potential clientele considerably. Even as he argued avidly with those below him, his quick dark eyes flickered up and down the street, took in the gang by the tavern, impaled Wim for a long, cold instant.

The peddler lifted several blades off the rack and handed them down, apparently receiving metal in return. Emmy got at least two. Then he raised his arms for quiet. "Folks, I'm really sorry for dropping in so sudden, when you all wasn't ready for me. Let's us quit now and try again tomorrow, when you can bring what you have to trade. I might even take on some furs. And bring horses, too, if you want to. Seein' as how I'm in need of one, I'll give two, maybe three adze heads for a good horse or mule. All right?"

It wasn't. Several frustrated townsfolk tried to pry merchandise off the rack. Wim noticed that they were unsuccessful. The merchant pulled the lanyard at the front of the cart and the rack turned inward, returning carved wood paneling to the outside. As the crowd thinned, Wim saw Emmy, clutching two knives and piece of print cloth, still talking earnestly to the peddler.

The peddler took a silvery chain from around his waist, passed it through the wheels of his cart and then around a nearby tree. Then he followed Emmy back across the road.

Ounze Rumpster snorted. "That sure is a teensy ketter. Betcha we would bust it right easy."

"Could be . . ." Wim nodded again, not listening. Anger turned his eyes to blue ice as Emmy led the peddler right to the tavern steps.

"Oh, Bathecar, just lookit the fine needles Mr. Ketchatoor sold me."

Sothead struggled to his feet. "You stupid little— little— We told you to buy knives. Knives! And you used my ring to buy needles!" He grabbed the cloth from Emmy's hands and began ripping it up.

"Hey—!" Emmy began to pound him in useless fury, clawing after her prize. "Bathecar, make him stop!" Bathecar and Ounze pulled Sothead down, retrieved needles and cloth. Emmy pouted, "Big lout."

Wim frowned and drank, his attention fixed on the peddlar. The dark man stood looking from one gang member to another, hands loosely at his sides, smiling faintly; the calm black eyes missed nothing. Eyes like that didn't belong in the face of a fat peddler. Wim shifted uncomfortably, gnawed by sudden uncertainty. He shook it off. How many chances did you get up here, to try a contest where the outcome wasn't sure— He stood and thrust out his hand. "Wim Buckry's the name, Mr. Ketchatoor. Sorry about Sothead; he's drunk all the time, 'truth."

The peddler had to reach up slightly to shake his hand. "Folks mostly call me Jagit. Pleased to meet you. Miss Emmy here tells me you and your men sometimes hire out to protect folks such as me."

Behind him, Bathecar Henley was open-mouthed. Emmy simpered; every so often, she proved that she was not as stupid as she looked. Wim nodded judiciously. "We do, and it's surely worth it to have our service. There's a sight of thieves in these hills, but most of them will back down from six good bows." He glanced at Sothead. "Five good bows."

"Well then." The pudgy little man smiled blandly, and for a moment Wim wondered how he could ever have seen anything deadly in that face. "I'd like to give you some of my business."

And so they came down out of the high hills. It was early summer, but in the Highlands more like a boisterous spring: Under the brilliant blue sky, green spread everywhere over the ground, nudging the dingy hummocks of melting snow and outcropping shelves of ancient granite. Full leaping streams sang down the alpine valleys, plunged over falls and rapids that smashed the water to white foam and spread it in glinting veils scarcely an inch deep over bedrock. The ragged peaks skirted with glacier fell further and further behind, yet the day grew no warmer; everywhere the chill water kept the air cool.

The peddler and his six "protectors" followed a winding course through deep soughing pine forest, broken by alpine meadows where bright star-like flowers bloomed and the short hummocky grass made their ankles ache with fatigue. They passed by marshes that even in the coolness swarmed with eager mosquitoes, and Wim's high moccasins squelched on the soft dank earth.

But by late afternoon the party had reached Witch Hollow Trail, and the way grew easier for the horse pulling the merchant's wagon. Somewhere ahead of them Ounze Rumpster kept the point position; off to the side were fat Hanaban, Bathecar, and Shorty, while Sothead Rumpster, now nearly sober, brought up the rear. In the Highlands even the robbers— particularly the robbers—journeyed with caution.

For most of the day Wim traveled silently, listening to the streaming water, the wind, the twittering birds among the pines—listening for sounds of human treachery. But it seemed they were alone. He had seen one farmer about four miles outside of Darkwood Corners and since then, no one.

Yesterday the peddler had questioned him about the area, and how many folk were in the vicinity of the Corners, what they did for a living. He'd seemed disappointed when he'd heard they were mostly poor, scattered farmers and trappers, saying his goods were more the kind to interest rich city folk. Wim had promptly allowed as how he was one of the few Highlanders who had ever been down into the Great Valley, all the way to the grand city of Fyffe; and that they'd be more than glad to guide him down into the Flatlands—for a price. If a little greed would conceal their real intentions, so much the better. And the peddler's partial payment, of strange, jewel-studded silver balls, had only added to the sincerity of their interest in his future plans.

Wim glanced over at the peddler, walking beside him near the dappled cart horse. Up close, the stranger seemed even more peculiar than at a distance. His straight black hair was cut with unbelievable precision at the base of his neck; Wim wondered if he'd set a bowl on his head and cut around it. And he smelled odd; not unpleasant, but more like old pine-needles than man. The silver thread stitched into the peddler's soft leather shirt was finer than Wim had ever seen. That would be a nice shirt to have— Wim tugged absently at the loops of bead and polished metal hanging against his own worn linen shirt.

Though short and heavy, the stranger walked briskly and didn't seem to tire; in fact, became friendlier and more talkative as the afternoon passed. But when they reached Witch Hollow he fell silent again, looking first at the unusual smoothness of the path, then up at the naked bedrock wall that jutted up at the side of the narrow trail.

They had walked for about half a mile when Wim volunteered, "This here's called Witch Hollow. There's a story, how once folk had magic to fly through the air in strange contraptions. One of them lost his magic hereabouts—up till twenty years ago, there was still a place you could see the bones, and pieces of steel, they say, all rusted up. Some say this trail through the holler ain't natural, either."

Jagit made no reply, but walked with his head down, his pointy black beard tucked into his chest. For the first time since they had begun the journey he seemed to lose interest in the scenery. At last he said, "How long you figure it's been since this flying contraption crashed here?"

Wim shrugged. "My granther heard the story from his own granther."

"Hmm. And that's all the . . . magic you've heard tell of?"

Wim decided not to tell the peddler what he knew about Fyffe. That might scare the little man into turning back, and force a premature confrontation. "Well, we have witches in these hills, like Widow

Henley's cousin, but they're most of them fakes—
least the ones I seen. Outside of them and the bad
luck that folks claim follows sin"—a grin twitched his
mouth—"well, I don't know of no magic. What was
you expecting?"

Jagit shook his head. "Something more than a
piddling failed witch, that's sure. The more I see of
this country, the more I know it ain't the place I
started out for."

They walked the next mile in silence. The trail
pierced a granite ridge; Wim glimpsed Hanaban
high up on their left, paralleling the wagon. Red-
faced with exertion, he waved briefly down at them,
indicating no problems. Wim returned the signal,
and returned to his thoughts about the peculiar little
man who walked at his side. Somehow he kept remembering yesterday, Hanaban whining, "Wim, that
there little man smells rotten to me. I say we should
drop him," and the unease that had crept back into
his own mind. Angry at himself as much as anything,
he'd snapped, "You going yellow, Han? Just because
a feller's strange don't mean he's got an evil eye."
And known it hadn't convinced either of them . . .

Perhaps sensing the drift of his silence, or perhaps
for some other reason, the peddler began to talk
again. This time it was not of where he was going,
however, but rather about himself, and where he
had come from—a place called Sharn, a land of such
incredible wonders that if Wim had heard the tale
from someone else he would have laughed.

For Sharn was a land where true magicians ruled,
where a flying contraption of steel would be remark-
able only for its commonness. Sharn was an immense
land—but a city also, a city without streets, a single
gleaming sentient crystal that challenged the sky with
spears of light. And the people of Sharn by their
magic had become like gods; they wore clothing like

gossamer, threw themselves across the sky in lightning while thunder followed, spoke to one another over miles. They settled beneath the warm seas of their borders, the weather obeyed them, and they remained young as long as they lived. And their magic made them dreadful warriors and mighty conquerors, for they could kill with scarcely more than a thought and a nod. If a mountain offended them they could destroy it in an instant. Wim thought of his Highlands, and shuddered, touching the bone hilt of the knife strapped to his leg.

Jagit had come to Sharn from a land still further east, and much more primitive. He had stayed and learned what he could of Sharn's magic. The goods he brought to Sharn were popular and had brought high prices; during the time he had spent in the enchanted land he had acquired a small collection of the weaker Sharnish spells. Then he left, to seek a market for these acquisitions—some land where magic was known, but not so deeply as in Sharn.

As the peddler finished his tale, Wim saw that the sun had nearly reached the ridge of the hills to the west before them. He walked on for several minutes, squinting into the sunset for traces of lost Sharn.

The trail curved through ninety degrees, headed down across a small valley. Half hidden in the deepening shadow that now spread over the land, a precarious wooden bridge crossed a stream. Beyond the bridge the pines climbed the darkened hillside into sudden sunlight. Along the far ridgeline, not more than a mile away, ten or twelve immense, solitary trees caught the light, towering over the forest.

"Mr. Jagged, you're the best liar I ever met." Stubbornly Wim swallowed his awe, felt the peddler's unnerving eyes on his face as he pointed across the valley. "Just beyond that ridgeline's where we figure on putting up tonight. A place called Grandfa-

ther Grove. Could be you never seen trees that big
even in Sharn!"

The peddler peered into the leveling sunlight.
"Could be," he said. "I'd surely like to see such
trees, anyhow."

They descended from the sunlight into rising darkness. Wim glimpsed Ounze's high felt hat as he
walked out of the shadow on the other side of the
valley, but none of the other gang members were
visible. Wim and the peddler were forced to leave
Witch Hollow Trail, and the going became more
difficult for horse and wagon; but they reached the
edge of the Grandfather Grove in less than half an
hour, passing one of the soaring trees, and then two,
and three. The dwarfed, spindly pines thinned and
finally were gone. Ahead of them were only the
grandfather trees, their shaggy striated trunks russet
and gold in the dying light. The breeze that had
crossed the valley with them, the roaring of the
stream behind them, all sounds faded into cathedral
silence, leaving only the cool, still air and the golden
trees. Wim stopped and bent his head back to catch
even a glimpse of the lowest branches, needled with
pungent golden-green. This was their land, and he
knew more than one tale that told of how the trees
guarded it, kept pestiferous creatures away, kept
the air cool and the soil fragrant and faintly moist
throughout the summer.

"Over here." Hanaban's voice came muted from
their left. They rounded the twenty-foot base of a
tree, and found Hanaban and Bathecar, setting a
small fire with kindling they had carried into the
grove—Wim knew the bark of the grandfather trees
was almost unburnable. The struggling blaze illuminated an immense pit of darkness behind them: the
gutted trunk of an ancient grandfather tree, that
formed a living cave-shelter for the night's camp.

By the time they had eaten and rotated lookouts, the sun had set. Wim smothered the fire, and the only light was from the sickle moon following the sun down into the west.

The peddler made no move to bed down, Wim noticed with growing irritation. He sat with legs crossed under him in the shadow of his wagon; motionless and wearing a dark coat against the chill, he was all but invisible, but Wim thought the little man was looking up into the sky. His silence stretched on, until Wim thought he would have to pretend to sleep himself before the peddler would. Finally Jagit stood and walked to the rear of his wagon. He opened a tiny hatch and removed two objects.

"What's them?" Wim asked, both curious and suspicious.

"Just a bit of harmless magic." He set one of the contraptions down on the ground, what seemed to be a long rod with a grip at one end. Wim came up to him, as he put the second object against his eye. The second contraption looked much more complex. It glinted, almost sparkled in the dim moonlight, and Wim thought he saw mirrors and strange rulings on its side. A tiny bubble floated along the side in the tube. The peddler stared through the gadget at the scattering of pale stars visible between the trees. At last he set the device back inside the wagon, and picked up the rod. Wim watched him cautiously as the other walked toward the cave tree; the rod looked too much like a weapon.

Jagit fiddled at the grip of the rod, and an eerie whine spread through the grove. The screaming faded into silence again, but Wim was sure that now the front of the rod was spinning. Jagit set it against the moon-silvered bark of the cave tree, and the tip of the rod began to bore effortlessly into the massive trunk.

Wim's voice quavered faintly. "That . . . that there some of your Sharnish magic, Mr. Jagged?"

The peddler chuckled softly, finishing his experiment. "It ain't hardly that. A Sharnish enchantment is a lot craftier, a lot simpler *looking*. This here's just a simple spell for reading the Signs."

"Um." Wim wavered almost visibly, his curiosity doing battle with his fear. There was a deep, precise hole in the cave tree. *Just because a fellow's strange, Han, don't mean he's got an evil eye* . . . instinctively Wim's fingers crossed. Because it looked like the peddler might not be the world's biggest liar; and that meant— "Maybe I better check how the boys is settled."

When the peddler didn't answer, Wim turned and walked briskly away. At least he hoped that was how it looked; he felt like running. He passed Ounze, half-hidden behind a gigantic stump; Wim said nothing, but motioned for him to continue his surveillance of the peddler and his wagon. The rest stood waiting at a medium-sized grandfather tree nearly a hundred yards from the cave tree, the spot they had agreed on last night in Darkwood Corners. Wim moved silently across the springy ground, rounding the ruins of what must once have been one of the largest trees in the grove: a four-hundred-foot giant that disease and the years had brought crashing down. The great disc of its shattered root system rose more than thirty feet into the air, dwarfing him as he dropped down heavily beside Hanaban.

Bathecar Henley whispered. "Ounze and Sothead I left out as guards."

Wim nodded. "It don't hardly matter. We're not going to touch that peddler."

"What!" Bathecar's exclamation was loud with surprise. He lowered his voice only slightly as he continued. "One man? You're ascared of one man?"

Wim motioned threateningly for silence. "You heard me. Hanaban here was right—that Jagged is just too damn dangerous. He's a warlock, he's got an evil eye. And he's got some kind of knife back there that can cut clean through a grandfather tree! And the way he talks, that's just the least . . ."

The others' muttered curses cut him off. Only Hanaban Kroy kept silent.

"You're crazy, Wim," the hulking shadow of Shorty said. "We've walked fifteen miles today. And you're telling us it was for nothing! It'd be easier to farm for a living."

"We'll still get something, but it looks like we'll have to go honest for a while. I figure on guiding him down, say to where the leaf forests start, and then asking pretty please for half of what he promised us back at the Corners."

"I sure as hell ain't going to follow nobody that far down toward the Valley." Bathecar frowned.

"Well, then, you can just turn around and head back. I'm running this here gang, Bathecar, don't you forget it. We already got something out of this deal, them silver balls he give us as first payment—"

Something went *hisss* and then *thuk:* Hanaban sprawled forward, collapsed on the moonlit ground beyond the tree's shadow. A crossbow bolt protruded from his throat.

As Wim and Bathecar scrabbled for the cover of the rotting root system, Shorty rose and snarled, "That damn peddler!" It cost him his life; three arrows smashed into him where he stood, and he collapsed across Hanaban.

Wim heard their attackers closing in on them, noisily confident. From what he could see, he realized they were all armed with crossbows; his boys didn't stand a chance against odds like that. He burrowed his way deeper into the clawing roots, felt a string of beads snap and shower over his hand. Behind him Bathecar unslung his own crossbow and cocked it.

Wim looked over his shoulder, and then, for the length of a heartbeat, he saw the silvery white of the moon-painted landscape blaze with harshly shadowed blue brilliance. He shook his head, dazzled and wondering; until amazement was driven from his mind by sudden screams. He began to curse and pray at the same time.

But then their assailants had reached the fallen tree. Wim heard them thrusting into the roots, shrank back further out of reach of their knives. Another scream echoed close and a voice remarked, "Hey, Rufe, I got the bastard as shot Rocker last fall."

A different voice answered, "That makes five then. Everybody excepting the peddler and Wim Buckry."

Wim held his breath, sweating. He recognized the second voice—Axl Bork, the oldest of the Bork brothers. For the last two years Wim's gang had cut into the Bork clan's habitual thievery, and up until tonight his quick-wittedness had kept them safe from the Bork's revenge. But tonight—how had he gone so wrong tonight? Damn that peddler!

He heard hands thrusting again among the roots, closer now. Then abruptly fingers caught in his hair. He pulled away, but another pair of hands joined the first, catching him by the hair and then the collar of his leather jerkin. He was hauled roughly from the tangle of roots and thrown down. He scrambled to his feet, was kicked in the stomach before he could run off. He fell gasping back onto the ground, felt his knife jerked from the sheath; three shadowy figures loomed over him. The nearest placed a heavy foot on his middle and said, "Well, Wim Buckry. You just lie still, boy. It's been a good night, even if we don't catch that peddler. You just got a little crazy with greed, boy. My cousins done killed every last one of your gang." Their laughter raked him. "Fifteen minutes and we done what we couldn't do the last two years.

"Lew, you take Wim here over to that cave tree. Once we find that peddler we're going to have us a little fun with the both of them."

Wim was pulled to his feet and then kicked, sprawling over the bodies of Hanaban and Shorty. He struggled to his feet and ran, only to be tripped and booted by another Bork. By the time he reached the cave tree his right arm hung useless at his side, and one eye was blind with warm sticky blood.

The Borks had tried to rekindle the campfire. Three of them stood around him in the wavering light; he listened to the rest searching among the trees. He wondered dismally why they couldn't find one wagon on open ground, when they'd found every one of his boys.

One of the younger cousins—scarcely more than fifteen—amused himself half-heartedly by thrusting glowing twigs at Wim's face. Wim slapped at him, missed, and at last one of the other Borks knocked the burning wood from the boy's hand; Wim remembered that Axl Bork claimed first rights against anyone who ran afoul of the gang. He squirmed back away from the fire and propped himself against the dry resilient trunk of the cave tree, stunned with pain and despair. Through one eye he could see the other Borks returning empty-handed from their search. He counted six Borks altogether, but by the feeble flame-cast light he couldn't make out their features. The only one he could have recognized for sure was Axl Bork, and his runty silhouette was missing. Two of the clansmen moved past him into the blackness of the cave tree's heart, he heard them get down on their hands and knees to crawl around the bend at the end of the passage. The peddler could have hidden back there, but his wagon would have filled the cave's entrance. Wim wondered again why the Borks couldn't find that wagon; and wished again that he'd never seen it at all.

The two men emerged from the tree just as Axl limped into the shrinking circle of firelight. The stubby bandit was at least forty years old, but through those forty years he had lost his share of fights, and walked slightly bent-over; Wim knew that his drooping hat covered a hairless skull marred with scars and even one dent. The eldest Bork cut close by the fire, heedlessly sending dust and unburnable bark into the guttering flames. "Awright, where in the mother-devil blazes you toad-gets been keeping your eyes? You was standing ever' whichway from this tree, you skewered every one of that damn Buckry gang excepting Wim here. Why ain't you found that peddler?"

"He's gone, Ax', gone." The boy who had been playing with Wim seemed to think that was a revelation. But Axl was not impressed, his backhand sent the boy up against the side of the tree.

One of the other silhouetted figures spoke hesitantly. "Don't go misbelieving me when I tell you this, Axl . . . but I was looking straight at this here cave tree when you went after them others. I could see that peddler clear as I see you now, standing right beside his wagon and his horse. Then all of a sudden there was this blue flash—I tell you. Ax', it was *bright*—and for a minute I couldn't see nothing, and then when I could again, why there wasn't hide nor hair of that outlander."

"Hmm." The elder Bork took this story without apparent anger. He scratched under his left armpit and began to shuffle around the dying fire toward where Wim lay. "Gone, eh? Just like that. He sounds like a right good prize . . ." He reached suddenly and caught Wim by the collar, dragged him toward the fire. Stopping just inside the ring of light, he pulled Wim up close to his face. The wide, sagging brim of his hat threw his face into a hollow blackness that was somehow more terrible than any reality.

Seeing Wim's expression, he laughed raspingly, and did not turn his face toward the fire. "It's been a long time, Wim, that I been wanting to learn you a lesson. But now I can mix business and pleasure. We're just gonna burn you an inch at a time until you tell us where your friend lit out to."

Wim barely stifled the whimper he felt growing in his throat; Axl Bork began to force his good hand inch by inch into the fire. All he wanted to do was to scream the truth, to tell them the peddler had never made him party to his magic. But he knew the truth would no more be accepted than his cries for mercy; the only way out was to lie—to lie better than he ever had before. The tales the peddler had told him during the day rose from his mind to shape his words, "Just go ahead. Axl Get your fun. I know I'm good as dead. But so's all of you—" The grip stayed firm on his shoulders and neck, but the knotted hand stopped forcing him toward the fire. He felt his own hand scorching in the super-heated air above the embers. Desperately he forced the pain into the same place with his fear and ignored it. "Why d'you think me and my boys didn't lay a hand on that peddler all day long? Just so's we could get ambushed by you?" His laughter was slightly hysterical. "The truth is we was scared clean out of our wits! That foreigner's a warlock, he's too dangerous to go after. He can reach straight into your head, cloud your mind, make you see what just plain isn't. He can kill you, just by looking at you kinda mean-like. Why"—and true inspiration struck him—"why, he could even have killed one of your perty cousins, and be standing here right now pretending to be a Bork, and you'd never know it till he struck *you* dead . . ."

Axl swore and ground Wim's hand into the embers. Even expecting it, Wim couldn't help himself; his scream was loud and shrill. After an instant as long as forever Axl pulled his hand from the heat. The motion stirred the embers, sending a final spurt of evil reddish flame up from the coals before the fire guttered out, leaving only dim ruby points to compete with the moonlight. For a long moment no one spoke; Wim bit his tongue to keep from moaning. The only sounds were a faint rustling breeze, hundreds of feet up among the leafy crowns of the grandfather trees—and the snort of a horse somewhere close by.

"Hey, we ain't got no horses," someone said uneasily.

Seven human figures stood in the immense spreading shadow of the cave tree, lined in faint silver by the setting moon. The Borks stood very still, watching one another—and then Wim realized what they must just have noticed themselves: there should have been eight Bork kinsmen. Somehow the peddler had eliminated one of the Borks during the attack, so silently, so quickly, that his loss had gone unnoticed. Wim shuddered, suddenly remembering a flare of unreal blue-white light, and the claims he had just made for the peddler. If one Bork could be killed so easily, why not two? In which case—

"He's here, pretending to be one of you!" Wim cried, his voice cracking.

And he could almost feel their terror echoing back and forth, from one to another, growing—until one of the shortest of the silhouettes broke and ran out into the moonlight. He got only about twenty feet, before he was brought down by a crossbow quarrel in the back. Even as the fugitive crumpled onto the soft, silver dirt a second crossbow thunked and another of the brothers fell dead across Wim's feet.

"That was Clyne, you . . . warlock!" More bows lowered around the circle.

"Hold on now!" shouted Axl. There were five Borks left standing; two bodies sprawled unmoving on the ground. "The peddler got us in his spell. We got to keep our sense and figure out which of us he's pretendin' to be."

"But Ax', he ain't just in disguise, we woulda seen which one he is . . . he—he can trick us into believing he's anybody!"

Trapped beneath the corpse, all Wim could see were five shadows against the night. Their faces were hidden from the light, and bulky clothing disguised any differences. He bit his lips against the least sound of pain; now was no time to remind the remaining Borks of Wim Buckry— But the agony of his hand pulsed up his arm until he felt a terrible dizziness wrench the blurring world away and his head drooped . . .

He opened his eyes again and saw that only three men stood now in the glade. Two more had died; the newest corpse still twitched on the ground.

Axl's voice was shrill with rage. "You . . . monster! You done tricked all of us into killing each other!"

"No, Ax', I had to shoot him. It was the peddler, I swear. Turn him over. Look! He shot Jan after you told us to hold off—"

"Warlock!" a third voice cried. "All of them dead—!" Two crossbows came down and fired simultaneously. Two men fell.

Axl stood silent and alone among the dead for a long moment. The moon had set at last, and the starlight was rare and faint through the shifting branches of the grandfather tree far overhead. Wim lay still as death, aware of the smell of blood and sweat and burned flesh. And the sound of footsteps, approaching. Sick with fear he looked up at the dark stubby form of Axl Bork.

"Still here? Good." A black-booted foot rolled the dead body from his legs. "Well, boy, you better leave me look at that hand." The voice belonged to Jagit Katchetooriantz.

"Uh." Wim began to tremble. "Uh. Mr. Jagged . . . is that . . . you?"

A light appeared in the hand of the peddler who had come from Sharn.

Wim fainted.

Early morning filled the Grandfather Grove with dusty shafts of light. Wim Buckry sat propped against the cave tree's entrance, sipping awkwardly at a cup of something hot and bitter held in a bandaged hand. His other hand was tucked through his belt, to protect a sprained right shoulder. Silently he watched the peddler grooming the dappled cart horse; glanced for the tenth time around the sunlit grove, where no sign of the last night's events marred the quiet tranquility of the day. Like a bad dream the memory of his terror seemed unreal to him now, and he wondered if that was more witchery, like the drink that had eased the pains of his body. He looked down, where dried blood stained his pants. *I'll take care of the remains*, the peddler had said. It was real, all right—all of the Borks. And all of his boys. He thought wistfully for a moment of the jewelry that had gone into the ground with them; shied away from a deeper sense of loss beneath it.

The peddler returned to the campfire, kicked dirt over the blaze. He had had no trouble in getting a fire to burn. Wim drew his feet up; the dark eyes looked questioningly at his sullen face.

"Mr. Jagged"—there was no trace of mockery in that title now—"just what do you want from me?"

Jagit dusted off his leather shirt. "Well, Wim—I was thinking if you was up to it, maybe you'd want to go on with our agreement."

Wim raised his bandaged hand. "Wouldn't be much pertection, one cripple."

"But I don't know the way down through that there Valley, which you do."

Wim laughed incredulously. "I reckon you could fly over the moon on a broomstick and you wouldn't need no map. And you sure as hell don't need pertecting! Why'd you ever take us on, Mr. Jagged?" Grief sobered him suddenly, and realization— "You knew all along, didn't you? What we were fixing to do. You took us along so's you could watch us, and maybe scare us off. Well, you needn't be watching me no more. I—we already changed our minds, even before what happened with them Borks. We was fixing to take you on down like we said, all honest."

"I know that." The peddler nodded. "You ever hear an old saying, Wim: 'Two heads are better than one'? You can't never tell; you might just come in handy."

Wim shrugged ruefully, and wondered where the peddler ever heard that "old saying." "Well . . . ain't heard no better offers this morning."

They left the grandfather trees and continued the descent toward the Great Valley. Throughout the early morning the pine woods continued to surround them, but as the morning wore on Wim noticed that the evergreens had given way to oak and sycamore, as the air lost its chill and much of its moistness. By late in the day he could catch glimpses between the trees of the green and amber vastness that was the valley floor, and pointed it out to the peddler. Jagit nodded, seeming pleased, and returned to the aimless humming that Wim suspected covered diabolical thoughts. He glanced again at the round, stubby merchant, the last man in the world a body'd suspect of magical powers. Which was perhaps what made them so convincing . . . "Mr. Jagged? How'd you do it? Hex them Borks, I mean."

Jagit smiled and shook his head. "A good magician never tells how. What, maybe, but never how. You have to watch, and figure how for yourself. That's how you get to *be* a good magician."

Wim sighed, shifted his hand under his belt. "Reckon I don't want to know, then."

The peddler chuckled. "Fair enough."

Surreptitiously, Wim watched his every move for the rest of the day.

After the evening meal the peddler again spent time at his wagon in the dark. Wim, sprawled exhausted by the campfire, saw the gleam of a warlock's wand but this time made no move to investigate, only crossing his fingers as a precautionary gesture. Inactivity had left him with too much else to consider. He stared fixedly into the flames, his hand smarting.

"Reckon we should be down to the valley floor in about an hour's travel, tomorrow. Then you say we head northwest, till we come to Fyffe?"

Wim started at the sound of the peddler's voice. "Oh . . . yeah, I reckon. Cut north and any road'll get you there; they all go to Fyffe."

" 'All roads lead to Fyffe'?" The peddler laughed unexpectedly, squatted by the fire.

Wim wondered what was funny. "Anybody can tell you the way from here, Mr. Jagged. I think come morning I'll be heading back; I . . . we never figured to come this far. Us hill folk don't much like going down into the Flatlands."

"Hm. I'm sorry to hear that, Wim." Jagit pushed another branch into the fire. "But somehow I'd figured it you'd really been to Fyffe?"

"Well, yeah. I was . . . almost." He looked up, surprised. "Three, four years ago, when I was hardly more'n a young'un, with my pa and some other men. See, my granther was the smith at Darkwood Corners, and he got hold of a gun—" And he found himself telling a peddler-man things everyone knew, and things he'd never told to anyone: How his grandfather had discovered gunpowder, how the Highlanders had plotted to overthrow the lords at Fyffe and take the rich valley farmlands for themselves. And how horsemen had come out from the city to meet them, with guns and magic, how the amber fields were torn and reddened and his pa had died when his homemade gun blew up in his face. How a bloody, tight-lipped boy returning alone to Darkwood Corners had filled its citizens with the fear of the Lord, and of the lords of Fyffe . . . He sat twisting painfully at a golden earring. "And—I heard tell as how they got dark magics down there that we never even saw, so's to keep all the Flatlanders under a spell . . . Maybe you oughta think again 'bout going down there too, Mr. Jagged."

"I thank you for the warning, Wim." Jagit nodded. "But I'll tell you—I'm a merchant by trade, and by inclination. If I can't sell my wares, I got no point in being, and I can't sell my wares in these hills."

"You ain't afraid they'll try to stop you?"

He smiled. "Well, now, I didn't say that. Their magic ain't up to Sharn, I'm pretty sure. But it is an unknown . . . Who knows—they may turn out to be my best customers; lords are like to be free with their money." He looked at Wim with something like respect, "But like I say, two heads are better than one. I'm right sorry you won't be along. Mayhap in the morning we can settle accounts—"

In the morning the peddler hitched up his wagon and started down toward the Great Valley. And not really undertanding why, Wim Buckry went with him.

Early in the day they left the welcome shelter of the last oak forest, started across the open rolling hills of ripening wild grasses, until they struck a rutted track heading north. Wim stripped off his jerkin and loosened his shirt, his pale Highland skin turning red under the climbing sun of the Valley. The dark-skinned peddler in his leather shirt smiled at him, and Wim figured, annoyed, that he must enjoy the heat. By noon they reached the endless green corduroy fringe of the cultivated Flatlands, and with a jolt they found themselves on paved road. Jagit knelt and prodded the resilient surface before they continued on their way. Wim vaguely remembered the soft pavement, a bizarre luxury to Highland feet, stretching all the way to Fyffe; this time he noticed that in places the pavement was eaten away by time, and neatly patched with smooth-cut stone.

The peddler spoke little to him, only humming, apparently intent on searching out signs of Flatlander magic. *A good magician watches* . . . Wim forced himself to study the half-remembered landscape. The ripening fields and pasturelands blanketed the Valley to the limit of his sight, like an immense, living crazy-quilt in greens and gold, spread over the rich dark earth. In the distance he could see pale mist hovering over the fields, wondered if it was a trick of witchery or only the heat of the day. And he saw the Flatlanders at work in the fields by the road, well-fed and roughly dressed; tanned, placid faces that regarded their passage with the resigned disinterest that he would have expected of a plowmule. Wim frowned.

"A rather curious lack of curiosity, I'd say, wouldn't you?" The peddler glanced at him. "They're going to make bad customers."

"Look at 'em!" Wim burst out angrily. "How could they do all of this? They ain't no better farmers 'n Highlanders; in the hills you work your hands to the bone to farm, and you get nothing, stones— And look at them, they're fat. How, Mr. Jagged?"

"How do *you* think they do it, Wim?"

"I—" He stopped. *Good magicians figure it out* . . . "Well—they got better land."

"True."

"And . . . there's magic."

"Is there now?"

"You saw it—them smooth-bedded streams, this here road; it ain't natural. But . . . they all look as how they're bewitched, themselves, just like I heard. Mayhap it's only the lords of Fyffe as have all the magic—it's them we got to watch for?" He crossed his fingers.

"Maybe so. It looks like they may be the only customers I'll have, too, if this doesn't change." The peddler's face was devoid of expression. "Quit crossing your fingers, Wim; the only thing that'll ever save you from is the respect of educated men."

Wim uncrossed his fingers. He walked on for several minutes before he realized the peddler spoke like a Flatlander now, as perfectly as he'd spoken the Highland talk before.

Late in the afternoon they came to a well, at one of the farm villages that centered like a hub in a great wheel of fields. The peddler dipped a cup into the dripping container, and then Wim took a gulp straight from the bucket. A taste of bitter metal filled his mouth, and he spat in dismay, looking back at the merchant. Jagit was passing his hand over—no, dropping something *into* the cup—and as Wim watched the water began to foam, and suddenly turned bright red. The peddler's black brows rose with interest, and he poured the water slowly out onto the ground. Wim blanched and wiped his mouth hard on his sleeve. "It *tastes* like poison!"

Jagit shook his head. "That's not poison you taste; I'd say farming's just polluted the water table some. But it is drugged." He watched the villagers standing with desultory murmurs around his wagon.

"Sheep," Wim's face twisted with disgust.

The peddler shrugged. "But all of them healthy, wealthy, and wise . . . well, healthy and wise, anyway . . . healthy—?" He moved away to offer his wares. There were few takers. As Wim returned to the wagon, taking a drink of stale mountain water from the barrel on the back, he heard the little man muttering again, like an incantation, "Fyffe . . . Fyffe . . . Dyston-Fyffe, they call it here . . . *District Town Five?* . . . Couldn't be." He frowned, oblivious. "But then again, why couldn't it—?"

For the rest of that day the peddler kept his thoughts to himself, looking strangely grim, only pronouncing an occasional curse in some incomprehensible language. And that night, as they camped, as Wim's weary mind unwillingly relived the loss of the only friends he had, he wondered if the dark silent stranger across the fire shared his loneliness; a peddler was always a stranger, even if he was a magician. "Mr. Jagged, you ever feel like going home?"

"Home?" Jagit glanced up. "Sometimes. Tonight, maybe. But I've come so far, I guess that would be impossible. When I got back, it'd all be gone." Suddenly through the flames his face looked very old. "What made it home was gone before I left . . . But maybe I'll find it again, somewhere else, as I go."

"Yeah . . ." Wim nodded, understanding both more and less than he realized. He curled down into his blanket, oddly comforted, and went soundly to sleep.

*   *   *

Minor wonders continued to assail him on their journey, and also the question, "Why?"; until gradually Jagit's prodding transformed his superstitious awe into a cocky curiosity that sometimes made the peddler frown, though he made no comment.

Until the third morning, when Wim finally declared, "Everything's a trick, if'n you can see behind it, just like with them witches in the hills. Everything's got a—reason. I think there ain't no such thing as magic!"

Jagit fixed him with a long mild look, and the specter of the night in the Grandfather Grove seemed to flicker in the dark eyes. "You think not, eh?"

Wim looked down nervously.

"There's magic, all right, Wim; all around you here. Only now you're seeing it with a magician's eyes: Because there's a reason behind everything that happens; you may not know what it is, but it's there. And knowing that doesn't make the thing less magic, or strange, or terrible—it just makes it easier to deal with. That's something to keep in mind, wherever you are . . . Also keep in mind that a *little* knowledge is a dangerous thing."

Wim nodded, chastened, felt his ears grow red as the peddler muttered, "So's a little ignorance . . ."

The afternoon of the third day showed them Fyffe, still a vague blot wavering against the horizon. Wim looked back over endless green toward the mountains, but they were hidden from him now by the yellow Flatland haze. Peering ahead again toward the city, he was aware that the fear that had come with him into the Great Valley had grown less instead of greater as they followed the familiar-strange road to Fyffe. The dappled cart horse snorted loudly in the hot, dusty silence, and he realized it was the peddler with his wagon full of magics that gave him his newfound courage.

He smiled, flexing his burned hand. Jagit had never made any apology for what he'd done, but Wim was not such a hypocrite that he really expected one, under the circumstances. And the peddler had treated his wounds with potions, so that bruises began to fade and skin to heal almost while he watched. It was almost—

Wim's thoughts were interrupted as he stumbled on a rough patch in the road. The city, much closer now, lay stolidly among the fields in the lengthening shadows of the hot afternoon. He wondered in which field his father—abruptly turned his thoughts ahead again, noticing that the city was without walls or other visible signs of defense. *Why?* Mayhap because they had nothing to fear— He felt his body tighten with old terrors. But Jagit's former grim mood had seemingly dropped away as his goal drew near, as though he had reached some resolution. If the peddler was confident, then Wim would be, too. He looked on the city with magician's eyes; and it struck him that a more outlandish challenge had most likely never visited the lords of Fyffe.

They entered Fyffe, and though the peddler seemed almost disappointed, Wim tried to conceal his gaping with little success. The heavy stone and timber buildings crowded the cobble-patched street, rising up two and three stories to cut off his view of the fields. The street's edge was lined with shop fronts; windows of bullseyed glass and peeling painted signs advertised their trade. The levels above the shops, he supposed, were where the people lived. The weathered stone of the curbs had been worn to hollows from the tread of countless feet, and the idea of so many people—5,000, the peddler had guessed—in so little area made him shudder.

They made their way past dully-dressed, well-fed townsfolk and farmers finishing the day's commerce in the cooling afternoon. Wim caught snatches of sometimes heated bargaining, but he noticed that the town showed little more interest in the bizarre spectacle of himself and the peddler than had the folk they dealt with on their journey. Children at least ought to follow the bright wagon—he was vaguely disturbed to realize he'd scarcely seen any, here or anywhere, and those he saw were kept close by parents. It seemed the peddler's business would be no better here than in the hills after all. *Like hogs in a pen . . .* He glanced down the street, back over his shoulder. "Where's all the hogs?"

"What?" The peddler looked at him.

"It's clean. All them folk living here and there ain't any garbage. How can that be, less'n they keep hogs to eat it? But I don't see any hogs. Nor—hardly any young'uns."

"Hmm." The peddler shrugged, smiling. "Good questions. Maybe we should ask the lords of Fyffe."

Wim shook his head. Yet he had to admit that the city so far, for all its strangeness, had shown him no signs of any magic more powerful or grim than that he'd seen in the fields. Perhaps the lords of Fyffe weren't so fearsome as the tales claimed; their warriors weren't bewitched, but only better armed.

The street curved sharply, and ahead the clustered buildings gave way on an open square, filled with the covered stalls of a public marketplace. And beyond it—Wim stopped, staring. Beyond it, he knew, stood the dwelling of the lords of Fyffe. Twice as massive as any building he had seen, its pilastered green-black walls reflected the square like a dark, malevolent mirror. The building had the solidity of a thing that had grown from the earth, a permanence that made the town itself seem ephemeral. Now, he knew, he looked on the house for magic that might match the peddler and Sharn.

Beside him, Jagit's smile was genuine and unreadable. "Pardon me, ma'm," the peddler stopped a passing woman and child, "but we're strangers. What's that building there called?"

"Why, that's Government House." The woman looked only mildly surprised. Wim admired her stocking-covered ankles.

"I see. And what do they do there?"

She pulled her little girl absently back from the wagon. "That's where the governors are. Folks go there with petitions and such. They—they govern, I suppose. Lissy, keep away from that dusty beast."

"Thank you, ma'm. And could I show you—"

"Not today. Come on, child, we'll be late."

The peddler bowed in congenial exasperation as she moved on. Wim sighed, and he shook his head. "Hardly a market for Sharnish wonders here, either, I begin to think. I may have outfoxed myself for once. Looks like my only choice is to pay a call on your lords of Fyffe over there; I might still have a thing or two to interest them." His eyes narrowed in appraisal as he looked across the square.

At a grunt of disapproval from Wim, Jagit glanced back, gestured at the lengthening shadows. "Too late to start selling now, anyway. What do you say we just take a look—" Suddenly he fell silent.

Wim turned. A group of half a dozen dour-faced men were approaching them; the leader bore a crest on his stiff brimmed hat that Wim remembered. They were unslinging guns from their shoulders. Wim's question choked off as they quietly circled the wagon, cut him off from the peddler. The militia-man addressed Jagit, faintly disdainful. "The Governors—"

Wim seized the barrel of the nearest rifle, slinging its owner into the man standing next to him. He wrenched the gun free and brought it down on the head of a third gaping guard.

"Wim!" He froze at the sound of the peddler's voice, turned back. "Drop the gun." The peddler stood unresisting beside his wagon. And the three remaining guns were pointing at Wim Buckry. Face filled with angry betrayal, he threw down the rifle.

"Tie the hillbilly up . . . The Governors require a few words with you two, peddler, as I was saying. You'll come with us." The militia leader stood back, unperturbed, as his townsman guards got to their feet.

Wim winced as his hands were bound roughly before him, but there was no vindictiveness on the guard's bruised face. Pushed forward to walk with the peddler, he muttered bitterly, "Whyn't you use your magic!"

Jagit shook his head. "Would've been bad for business. After all, the lords of Fyffe have come to *me*."

Wim crossed his fingers, deliberately, as they climbed the green-black steps of Government House.

The hours stretched interminably in the windowless, featureless room where they were left to wait, and Wim soon tired of staring at the evenness of the walls and the smokeless lamps. The peddler sat fiddling with small items left in his pockets; but Wim had begun to doze in spite of himself by the time guards returned at last, to take them to their long-delayed audience with the lords of Fyffe.

The guards left them to the lone man who rose, smiling, from behind a tawny expanse of desk as they entered the green-walled room. "Well, at last!" He was in his late fifties and plainly dressed like the townsmen, about Wim's height but heavier, with graying hair. Wim saw that the smiling face held none of the dullness of their captors' faces. "I'm Charl Aydricks, representative of the World Government. My apologies for keeping you waiting, but I was—out of town. We've been following your progress with some interest."

Wim wondered what in tarnation this poor-man governor took himself for, claiming the Flatlands was the whole world. He glanced past Aydricks into the unimpressive, lamp-lit room. On the governor's desk he noticed the only sign of a lord's riches he'd yet seen—a curious ball of inlaid metals, mostly blue but blotched with brown and green, fixed on a golden stand. He wondered with more interest where the other lords of Fyffe might be; Aydricks was alone, without even guards . . . Wim suddenly remembered that whatever this man wasn't, he was a magician, no less than the peddler.

Jagit made a polite bow. "Jagit Katchetooriantz, at your service. Merchant by trade, and flattered by the interest. This is my apprentice—"

"—Wim Buckry." The governor's appraising glance moved unexpectedly to Wim. "Yes, we remember you, Wim. I must say I'm surprised to see you here again. But pleased—we've been wanting to get ahold of you." A look of too much interest crossed Aydricks' face.

Wim eyed the closed door with longing.

"Please be seated." The governor returned to his desk. "We rarely get such . . . intriguing visitors—"

Jagit took a seat calmly, and Wim dropped into the second chair, knees suddenly weak. As he settled into the softness he felt a sourceless pressure bearing down on him, lunged upward like a frightened colt only to be forced back into the seat. Panting, he felt the pressure ease as he collapsed in defeat.

Jagit looked at him with sympathy before glancing back at the governor; Wim saw the peddler's fingers twitch impotently on the chair-arm. "Surely you don't consider us a threat?" His voice was faintly mocking.

The governor's congeniality stopped short of his eyes. "We know about the forces you were using in the Grandfather Grove."

"Do you now! That's what I'd hoped." Jagit met the gaze and held it. "Then I'm obviously in the presence of some technological sophistication, at last. I have some items of trade that might interest you . . ."

"You may be sure they'll receive our attention. But let's just be honest with each other, shall we? You're no more a peddler than I am; not with what we've seen you do. And if you'd really come from the east—from anywhere—I'd know about it; our communications network is excellent. You simply appeared from nowhere, in the Highlands Preserve. And it really was nowhere on this earth, wasn't it?"

Jagit said nothing, looking expectant. Wim stared fixedly at the textured green of the wall, trying to forget that he was witness to a debate of warlocks.

Aydricks stirred impatiently. "From nowhere on this earth. Our moon colony is long gone; that means no planet in this system. Which leaves the Lost Colonies—you've come from one of the empire's colony worlds, from another star system, Jagit; and if you expected that to surprise us after all this time, you're mistaken."

Jagit attempted a shrug. "No—I didn't expect that, frankly. But I didn't expect any of the rest of this, either; things haven't turned out as I'd planned at all . . ."

Wim listened in spite of himself, in silent wonder. Were there worlds beyond his own, that were no more than sparks in the black vastness of earth's night? Was that where Sharn was, then, with its wonders; beyond the sky, where folks said was heaven—?

". . . Obviously," the governor was saying, "you're a precedent-shattering threat to the World Government. Because this is a *world* government, and it has maintained peace and stability over millennia. Our space defense system sees to it that—outsiders don't upset that peace. At least it always has until now; you're the first person to penetrate our system, and we don't even know how you did it. That's what we want to know—*must* know, Jagit, not who you represent, or where, or even why, so much as *how*. We can't allow anything to disrupt our stability." Aydricks leaned forward across his desk; his hand tightened protectively over the stand of the strange metal globe. His affability had disappeared entirely, and Wim felt his own hopes sink, realizing the governor somehow knew the peddler's every secret. Jagit wasn't infallible, and this time he had let himself be trapped.

But Jagit seemed undismayed. "If you value your stability that much, then I'd say it's time somebody did disturb it."

"That's to be expected." Aydricks sat back, his expression relaxing into contempt. "But you won't be the one. We've had ten thousand years to perfect our system, and in that time no one else has succeeded in upsetting it. We've put an end at last to all the millennia of destructive waste on this world . . ."

Ten thousand years—? As Aydricks spoke, Wim groped to understand a second truth that tore at the very roots of his comprehension:

For the history of mankind stretched back wonder on wonder for unimaginable thousands of years, through tremendous cycles filled with lesser cycles. Civilization reached highs where every dream was made a reality and humanity sent offshoots to the stars, only to fall back, through its own folly, into abysses of loss when men forgot their humanity and reality became a nightmare. Then slowly the cycle would change again, and in time mankind would reach new heights, that paradoxically it could never maintain. Always men seemed unable in the midst of their creation to resist the urge to destroy, and always they found the means to destroy utterly.

Until the end of the last great cyclical empire, when a group among the ruling class saw that a new decline was imminent, and acted to prevent it. They had forced the world into a new order, one of patternless stability at a low level, and had stopped it there. ". . . And because of us that state, free from strife and suffering, has continued for ten thousand years, unchanged. Literally unchanged. I am one of the original founders of the World Government."

Wim looked unbelievingly into the smiling, unremarkable face; found the eyes of a fanatic and incredible age.

"You're well preserved," Jagit said.

The governor burst into honest laughter. "This isn't my original body. By using our computer network we're able to transfer our memories intact into the body of an 'heir': someone from the general population, young and full of potential. As long as the individual's personality is compatible, it's absorbed into the greater whole, and he becomes a revitalizing part of us. That's why I've been keeping track of Wim, here; he has traits that should make him an excellent governor." The too-interested smile showed on the governor's face again.

Wim's bound hands tightened into fists—the invisible pressure forced him back down into the seat, his face stricken.

Aydricks watched him, amused. "Technological initiative and personal aggressiveness are key factors that lead to an unstable society. Since, to keep stability, we have to suppress those factors in the population, we keep control groups free from interference— like the hill folk, the Highlanders—to give us a dependable source of the personality types we need ourselves.

"But the system as a whole really is very well designed. Our computer network provides us with our continuity, with the technology, communications, and—sources of power we need to maintain stability. We in turn ensure the computer's continuity, since we preserve the knowledge to keep it functioning. There's no reason why the system can't go on forever."

Wim looked toward the peddler for some sign of reassurance; but found a grimness that made him look away again as Jagit said, "And you think that's a feat I should appreciate: that you've manipulated the fate of every being on this planet for ten thousand years, to your own ends, and that you plan to go on doing it indefinitely?"

"But it's for their own good, can't you see that? We ask nothing from this, no profit for ourselves, no reward other than knowing that humanity will never be able to throw itself into barbarism again, that the cycle of destructive waste, of rise and fall, has finally been stopped on earth. The people are secure, their world is stable, they know it will be safe for future generations. Could your own world claim as much? Think of the years that must have passed on your journey here—would you even have a civilization to return to by now?"

Wim saw Jagit forcibly relax; the peddler's smile reappeared, full of irony. "But the fact remains that a cycle of rise and fall is the natural order of things— life and death, if you want to call it that. It gives humanity a chance to reach new heights, and gives an old order a clean death. Stasis is a coma—no lows, but no highs either, no *choice*. Somehow I think that Sharn would have preferred a clean death to this—"

"Sharn? What do you know about the old empire?" The governor leaned forward, complaisance lost.

"Sharn—?" Wim's bewilderment was lost on the air.

"They knew everything about Sharn, where I come from. The crystal city with rot at its heart, the Games of Three. They were even seeing the trends that would lead to this, though they had no idea it would prove so eminently successful."

"Well, this gets more and more interesting." The governor's voice hardened. "Considering that there should be no way someone from outside could have known of the last years of the empire. But I suspect we'll only continue to raise more questions this way. I think it's time we got some answers."

Wim slumped in his seat, visions of torture leaping into his mind. But the governor only left his desk, passing Wim with a glance that suggested hunger, and placed a shining band of filigreed metal on Jagit's head.

"You may be surprised at what you get." Jagit's expression remained calm, but Wim thought strain tightened his voice.

The governor returned to his chair. "Oh, I don't think so. I've just linked you into our computer net—"

Abruptly Jagit went rigid with surprise, settled back into a half-smile; but not before Aydricks had seen the change. "Once it gets into your mind you'll have considerable difficulty concealing anything at all. It's quick and always effective; though unfortunately I can't guarantee that it won't drive you crazy."

The peddler's smile faded. "How civilized," he said quietly. He met Wim's questioning eyes. "Well, Wim, you remember what I showed you. And crossing your fingers didn't help, did it?"

Wim shook his head. "Whatever you say, Mr. Jagged . . ." He suspected he'd never have an opportunity to remember anything.

Suddenly the peddler gasped, and his eyes closed, his body went limp in the seat. "Mr. Jagged—?" But there was no response. Alone, Wim wondered numbly what sort of terrible enchantment the metal crown held, and whether it would hurt when the computer—whatever that was—swallowed his own soul.

"Are you monitoring? All districts? Direct hookup, yes." The governor seemed to be speaking to his desk. He hesitated as though listening, then stared into space.

Wim sagged fatalistically against his chair, past horror now, ignoring—and ignored by—the two entranced men. Silence stretched in the green room. Then the light in the room flickered and dimmed momentarily. Wim's eyes widened as he felt the unseen pressure that held him down weaken slightly, then return with the lighting. The governor frowned at nothing, still staring into space. Wim began ineffectually to twist at his bound hands. However the magic worked in this room, it had just stopped working; if it stopped again he'd be ready . . . He glanced at Jagit. Was there a smile—?"

"District Eighteen here. Aydricks, what is this?"

Wim shuddered. The live disembodied head of a red-haired youth had just appeared in a patch of sudden brightness by the wall. The governor turned blinking toward the ghost.

"Our reception's getting garbled. This data can't be right, it says he's . . ." The ghostly face wavered and the voice was drowned in a sound like water rushing. ". . . it, what's wrong with the transmission? Is he linked up directly? We aren't getting anything now—"

Two more faces—one old, with skin even darker than the peddler's, and one a middle-aged woman—appeared in the wall, protesting. And Wim realized then that he saw the other lords of Fyffe—and truly of the world—here and yet not here, transported by their magic from the far ends of the earth. The red-haired ghost peered at Wim, who shrank away from the angry, young-old eyes, then looked past to Jagit. The frown grew fixed and then puzzled, was transformed into incredulity. "No, that's impossible!"

"What is it?" Aydricks looked harrassed.

"I know that man."

The black-haired woman turned as though she could see him. "What do you mean you—"

"I know that man too!" Another dark face appeared. "From Sharn, from the empire. But . . . after ten thousand years, how can he be the *same* . . . Aydricks! Remember the Primitive Arts man, he was famous, he spent . . ." the voice blurred, " . . . got to get him out of the comm system! He knows the comm-sat codes, he can—" The ghostly face dematerialized entirely.

Aydricks looked wildly at the unmoving peddler, back at the remaining governors.

Wim saw more faces appear, and another face flicker out; *the same man* . . .

"Stop him, Aydricks!" The woman's voice rose. "He'll ruin us. He's altering the comm codes, killing the tie-up!"

"I can't cut him off!"

"He's into my link now, I'm losing con—" The red-haired ghost disappeared.

"Stop him, Aydricks, or we'll burn out Fyffe!"

"Jagged! Look out!" Wim struggled against his invisible bonds as he saw the governor reach with grim resolution for the colored metal globe on his desk. He knew Aydricks meant to bash in the peddler's skull, and the helpless body in the chair couldn't stop him. "Mr. Jagged, wake up!" Desperately Wim stuck out his feet as Aydricks passed; the governor stumbled. Another face disappeared from the wall, and the lights went out. Wim slid from the chair, free and groping awkwardly for a knife he no longer had. Under the faltering gaze of the ghosts in the wall, Aydricks fumbled toward Jagit.

Wim grabbed at Aydricks' feet just as the light returned, catching an ankle. The governor turned back, cursing, to kick at him, but Wim was already up, leaping away from a blow with the heavy statue.

"Aydricks, stop the peddler!"

Full of sudden fury, Wim gasped, "Damn you, you won't stop it this time!" As the governor turned away Wim flung himself against the other's back, staggering him, and hooked his bound hands over Aydricks' head. Aydricks fought to pull him loose, dropping the globe as he threw himself backward to slam his attacker against the desk. Wim groaned as his backbone grated against the desk edge, and lost his balance. He brought his knee up as he fell; there was a sharp *crack* as the governor landed beside him, and lay still. Wim got to his knees; the ancient eyes stabbed him with accusation and fear, "No. Oh, *no.*" The eyes glazed.

A week after his seventeenth birthday, Wim Buckry had killed a ten-thousand-year-old man. And, unknowingly, helped to destroy an empire. The room was quiet; the last of the governors had faded from the wall. Wim got slowly to his feet, his mouth pulled back in a grin of revulsion. All the magic in the world hadn't done this warlock any good. He moved to where Jagit still sat entranced, lifted his hands to pull the metal crown off and break the spell. And hesitated, suddenly unsure of himself. Would breaking the spell wake the peddler, or kill him? They had to get out out of here; but Jagit was somehow fighting the bewitchment, that much he understood, and if he stopped him now—His hands dropped, he stood irresolutely, waiting. And waiting.

His hands reached again for the metal band, twitching with indecision; jerked back as Jagit suddenly smiled at him. The dark eyes opened and the peddler sat forward, taking the metal band gently from his own head with a sigh. "I'm glad you waited. You'll probably never know how glad." Wim's grin became real, and relieved.

Jagit got unsteadily to his feet, glanced at Aydricks' body and shook his head; his face was haggard. "Said you might be a help, didn't I?" Wim stood phlegmatically while the peddler who was as old as Sharn itself unfastened the cords on his raw wrists. "I'd say our business is finished. You ready to get out of here? We don't have much time."

Wim started for the door in response, opened it, and came face to face with the unsummoned guard standing in the hall. His fist connected with the gaping jaw; the guard's knees buckled and he dropped to the floor, unconscious. Wim picked up the guard's rifle as Jagit appeared beside him, motioning him down the dim hallway.

"Where is everybody?"

"Let's hope they're home in bed; it's four-thirty in the morning. There shouldn't be any alarms."

Wim laughed giddily. "This's a sight easier than getting away from the Borks!"

"We're not away yet; we may be too late already. Those faces on the wall were trying to drop a—piece of sun on Fyffe. I think I stopped them, but I don't know for sure. If it wasn't a total success, I don't want to find out the hard way." He led Wim back down the wide stairway, into the empty hall where petitioners had gathered during the day. Wim started across the echoing floor but Jagit called him back, peering at something on the wall; they went down another flight into a well of darkness, guided by the peddler's magic light. At the foot of the stairs the way was blocked by a door, solidly shut. Jagit looked chagrined, then suddenly the beam of his light shone blue; he flashed it against a metal plate set in the door. The door slid back and he went through it.

Wim followed him, into a cramped, softly glowing cubicle nearly filled by three heavily padded seats around a peculiar table. Wim noticed they seemed to be bolted to the floor, and suddenly felt claustrophobic.

"Get into a seat, Wim. Thank God I was right about this tower being a ballistic exit. Strap in, because we're about to use it." He began to push lighted buttons on the table before him.

Wim fumbled with the restraining straps, afraid to wonder what the peddler thought they were doing, as a heavy inner door shut the room off from the outside. Why weren't they out of the building, running? How could this— Something pressed him down into the seat cushions like a gentle, insistent hand. His first thought was of another trap; but as the pressure continued, he realized this was something new. And then, glancing up past Jagit's intent face, he saw that instead of blank walls, they were now surrounded by the starry sky of night. He leaned forward—and below his feet was the town of Fyffe, shrinking away with every heartbeat, disappearing into the greater darkness. He saw what the eagle saw . . . he was flying. He sat back again, feeling for the reassuring hardness of the invisible floor, only to discover suddenly that his feet no longer touched it. There was no pressure bearing him down now, there was nothing at all. His body drifted against the restraining straps, lighter than a bird. A small sound of incredulous wonder escaped him as he stared out at the unexpected stars.

And saw a brightness begin to grow at the opaque line of the horizon, spreading and creeping upward second by second, blotting out the stars with the fragile hues of dawn. The sun's flaming face thrust itself up past the edge of the world, making him squint, rising with arcane speed and uncanny brilliance into a sky that remained stubbornly black with night. At last the whole sphere of the sun was revealed, and continued to climb in the midnight sky while now Wim could see a thin streak of sky-blue stretched along the horizon, left behind with the citron glow of dawn still lighting its center. Above the line in darkness the sun wore the pointed crown of a star that dimmed all others, and below it he could see the world at the horizon's edge moving into day. And the horizon did not lie absolutely flat, but was bowing gently downward now at the sides . . . Below his feet was still the utter darkness that had swallowed Fyffe. He sighed.

"Quite a view." Jagit sat back from the glowing table, drifting slightly above his seat, a tired smile on his face.

"You see it too?" Wim said hoarsely.

The peddler nodded. "I felt the same way, the first time. I guess everyone always has. Every time civilization has gained space flight, it's been rewarded again by that sight."

Wim said nothing, unable to find the words. His view of the bowed horizon had changed subtly, and now as he watched there came a further change—the sun began, slowly but perceptibly, to move backward down its track, sinking once more toward the point of dawn that had given it birth. Or, he suddenly saw, it was they who were slipping, back down from the heights of glory into his world's darkness once more. Wim waited while the sun sank from the black and alien sky, setting where it had risen, its afterglow reabsorbed into night as the edge of the world blocked his vision again. He dropped to the seat of his chair, as though the world had reclaimed him, and the stars reappeared. A heavy lurch, like a blow, shook the cubicle, and then all motion stopped.

He sat still, not understanding, as the door slid back in darkness and a breath of cold, sharp air filled the tiny room. Beyond the doorway was darkness again, but he knew it was not the night of a building hallway.

Jagit fumbled wearily with the restraining straps on his seat. "Home the same day . . ."

Wim didn't wait, but driven by instinct freed himself and went to the doorway. And jerked to a stop as he discovered they were no longer at ground level. His feet found the ladder, and as he stepped down from its bottom rung he heard and felt the gritty shifting of gravel. The only other sounds were the sigh of the icy wind, and water lapping. As his eyes adjusted they told him what his other senses already knew—that he was home. Not Darkwood Corners, but somewhere in his own cruelly beautiful Highlands. Fanged shadow peaks rose up on either hand, blotting out the stars, but more stars shone in the smooth waters of the lake; they shivered slightly, as he shivered in the cold breeze, clammy with sweat under his thin shirt. He stood on the rubble of a mountain pass somewhere above the treeline, and in the east the gash between the peaks showed pinkish-gray with returning day.

Behind him he heard Jagit, and turned to see the peddler climbing slowly down the few steps to the ground. From outside, the magician's chamber was the shape of a truncated rifle bullet. Jagit carried the guard's stolen rifle, leaning on it now like a walking stick. "Well, my navigation hasn't failed me yet." He rubbed his eyes, stretched.

Wim recalled making a certain comment about flying over the moon on a broomstick, too long ago, and looked again at the dawn, this time progressing formally and peacefully up a lightening sky. "We flew here. Didn't we, Mr. Jagged?" His teeth chattered. "Like a bird. Only . . . we f-flew right off the world." He stopped, awed by his own revelation. For a moment a lifetime of superstitious dread cried that he had no right to know of the things he had seen, or to believe— The words burst out in a defiant rush. "That's it. Right off the world. And . . . and it's all true: I heard how the world's round like a stone. It must be true, how there's other worlds, that's what you said back there, with people just like here; I seen it, the sun's like all them other stars, only it's bigger . . ." He frowned. "It's—closer? I—"

Jagit was grinning, his teeth showed white in his beard. "Magician, first-class."

Wim looked back up into the sky. "If that don't beat all—" he said softly. Then, struck by more practical matters, he said. "What about them ghosts? Are they going to come after us?"

Jagit shook his head. "No. I think I laid those ghosts to rest pretty permanently. I changed the code words in their communications system. A good part of it is totally unusable now. Their computer net is broken up, and their space defense system must be out for good, because they didn't destroy Fyffe. I'd say the World Government is finished; they don't know it yet, and they may not go for a few hundred years, but they'll go in the end. Their grand 'stability' machine has a monkey wrench in its works at last . . . They won't be around to use their magic in these parts any more, I expect."

Wim considered, and then looked hopeful. "You going to take over back there, Mr. Jagged? Use your magic on them Flatlanders? We could—"

But the peddler shook his head. "No, I'm afraid that just doesn't interest me, Wim. All I really wanted was to break the hold those other magician sorts had on this world; and I've done that already."

"Then . . . you mean you really did all that, you risked our necks, for nothing? Like you said, because it just wasn't right, for them to use their magic on folks who couldn't stop them? You did it for us—and you didn't want *any*thing? You must be crazy."

Jagit laughed. "Well, I wouldn't say that. I told you before: All I want is to be able to see new sights, and sell my wares. And the World Government was bad for my business."

Wim met the peddler's gaze, glanced away undecided. "Where you going to go now?" He half expected the answer to be, Back beyond the sky.

"Back to bed." Jagit left the ballistic vehicle, and began to climb the rubbly slope up from the lake; he gestured for Wim to follow.

Wim followed, breathing hard in the thin air, until they reached a large fall of boulders before a sheer granite wall. Only when he was directly before it did he realize they had come on the entrance to a cave hidden by the rocks. He noticed that the opening was oddly symmetrical; and there seemed to be a rainbow shimmering across the darkness like mist. He stared at it uncomprehendingly, rubbing his chilled hands.

"This is where I came from, Wim. Not from the East, as you figured, or from space as the governor thought." The peddler nodded toward the dark entrance. "You see, the World Government had me entirely misplaced—they assumed I could only have come from somewhere outside their control. But actually I've been here on earth all the time; this cave has been my home for fifty-seven thousand years. There's a kind of magic in there that puts me into an 'enchanted' sleep for five or ten thousand years at a time here. And meanwhile the world changes. When it's changed enough, I wake up again and go out to see it. That's what I was doing in Sharn, ten thousand years ago: I brought art works from an earlier, primitive era; they were popular, and I got to be something of a celebrity. That way I got access to my new items of trade—my Sharnish magics—to take somewhere else, when things changed again.

"That was the problem with the World Government—they interrupted the natural cycles of history that I depend on, and it threw me out of synch. They'd made stability such a science they might have kept things static for fifty or a hundred thousand years. Ten or fifteen thousand, and I could have come back here and outwaited them, but fifty thousand was just too long. I had to get things moving again, or I'd have been out of business."

Wim's imagination faltered at the prospect of the centuries that separated him from the peddler, that separated the peddler from everything that had ever been a part of the man, or ever could be. What kind of belief did it take, what sort of a man, to face that alone? And what losses or rewards to drive him to it? There must be something, that made it all worthwhile—

"There have been more things *done*, Wim, than the descendants of Sharn have *dreamed*. I am surprised at each new peak I attend . . . I'll be leaving you now. You were a better guide than I expected; I thank you for it. I'd say Darkwood Corners is two or three days journey northwest from here."

Wim hesitated, half afraid, half longing. "Let me go with you—?"

Jagit shook his head. "There's only room for one, from here on. But you've seen a few more wonders than most people already; and I think you've learned a few things, too. There are going to be a lot of opportunities for putting it all to use right here, I'd say. You helped change your world, Wim—what are you going to do for an encore?"

Wim stood silent with indecision; Jagit lifted the rifle, tossed it to him.

Wim caught the gun, and a slow smile, filled with possibilities, grew on his face.

"Good-bye, Wim."

"Good-bye, Mr. Jagged." Wim watched the peddler move away toward his cave.

As he reached the entrance, Jagit hesitated, looking back. "And Wim—there are more wonders in this cave than you've ever dreamed of. I haven't been around this long because I'm an easy mark. Don't be tempted to grave-rob." He was outlined momentarily by rainbow as he passed into the darkness.

Wim lingered at the entrance, until at last the cold forced him to move and he picked his way back down the sterile gray detritus of the slope. He stopped again by the mirror lake, peering back past the magician's bullet-shaped vehicle at the cliff face. The rising sun washed it in golden light, but now somehow he really wasn't even sure where the cave had been.

He sighed, slinging his rifle over his shoulder, and began the long walk home.

Lord Buckry sighed as memories receded, and with them the gnawing desire to seek out the peddler's cave again; the desire that had been with him for thirty years. There lay the solutions to every problem he had ever faced, but he had never tested Jagged's warning. It wasn't simply the risk, though the risk was both deadly and sufficient—it was the knowledge that however much he gained in this life, it was ephemeral, less than nothing, held up to a man whose life spanned half that of humanity itself. Within the peddler's cave lay the impossible, and that was why he would never try to take it for his own.

Instead he had turned to the possible and made it fact, depending on himself, and on the strangely clear view of things the peddler had left him. He had solved every problem alone, because he had had to, and now he would just have to solve this one alone too.

He stared down with sudden possessive pride over the townfolk in the square, his city of Fyffe now ringed by a sturdy wall . . . So the West and the South were together, for one reason, and one alone. It balanced the scales precariously against plenty of old hatreds, and if something were to tip them back again— A few rumors, well-placed, and they'd be at each other's throats. Perhaps he wouldn't even need to raise an army. They'd solve that problem for him. And afterward—

Lord Buckry began to smile. He'd always had a hankering to visit the sea.

I think most readers expect that authors have solutions to mysteries posed in their stories, and think it cheating if they discover the author is just as mystified as anyone. Well, I confess, I don't know Jagit's real motives, and I suspect he's not telling the whole truth at the end of the story. I can imagine the character, what he said and did, but as far as motive. . . . Jagit's explanation for overthrowing the World Government is certainly reasonable: that government was destroying whatever reason Jagit had for traveling down time. Maybe he was just a merchant with a desire to see new things, but I think he had an additional agenda: Perhaps he wondered why the Singularity never occurred, and was searching for a civilization that would finally break free from the wheel of fate. Perhaps all the previous civilizations had ended in Singularities, leaving Jagit to make sure that it could happen again. Rereading the story, I feel very much like Wim at the end, awed . . . and a little afraid to learn the truth.

Did you guess where I stopped writing and Joan began? The last thing I did was the rescue from Axl Bork's gang. I wrote my part of the story over a summer, one page per day (for me, a strange way to write—but fun). Beyond the rescue scene I had only general ideas, and things stagnated; finishing the story was a fortunate and interesting collaboration.

There are other, less subtle ways to stop our fall into the Singularity. World war could bring progress to a stop, for a decade or forever. Lots of writers have earned their fortunes "in the aftermath" when high tech and medievalism can be jumbled in many *different proportions (though not as many as some believe).*

I think there is a lot of misunderstanding about the long-range effects of a general war. The war and the years immediately after would be as terrible as advertised. But the race would probably survive, as would technology. Such a war would be a great detour into darkness, but as the years passed and the survivors grew old, and their children's children became adults . . . the bad times would be remembered as a distant misfortune. There could be happiness, and bright times for those descendents; the war would be the end of our world, but not of theirs. And I don't buy the arguments that technology couldn't restart because we 20th-century folks had consumed all the easily accessible resources. With the exception of petroleum, post-debacle civilizations might well find Earth's resources more accessible than before. (Non-poisoned urban ruins make great open pit mines.)

Besides low population density, postwar civilization would likely have high levels of education, and a clear vision of the past. Depending on the depth of the catastrophe, it might be a while before progress neared the edge of the Singularity. This is the sort of background I have in the next story: I suppose that luck finally runs out for us 20th-century types, that we have a general war and worse times than I can describe (or want to imagine). Yet at the far end of it all there is opportunity for happiness and progress. I especially wanted to investigate two questions in this story: What sort of government might exist in such an era? How would the new civilization deal with nuclear weapons, and the possibility that everything gained could be lost again? The story's title reveals my answer to the first question. My answer to the second is equally radical.

THE UNGOVERNED

Al's Protection Racket operated out of Manhattan, Kansas. Despite the name, it was a small, insurance-oriented police service with about 20,000 customers, all within 100 kilometers of the main ship. But apparently "Al" was some kind of humorist: His ads had a gangster motif with his cops dressed like 20th century hoodlums. Wil Brierson guessed that it was all part of the nostalgia thing. Even the Michigan State Police—Wil's outfit—capitalized on the public's feeling of trust for old names, old traditions.

Even so, there's something more dignified about a company with a name like "Michigan State Police," thought Brierson as he brought his flier down on the pad next to Al's HQ. He stepped out of the cockpit into an eerie morning silence: It was close to sunrise, yet the sky remained dark, the air humid. Thunderheads marched around half the horizon. A constant flicker of lightning chased back and forth within those clouds, yet there was not the faintest sound of thunder. He had seen a tornado killer on his way in, a lone eagle in the far sky. The weather was almost as ominous as the plea East Lansing HQ had received from Al's just four hours earlier.

A spindly figure came bouncing out of the shadows. "Am I glad to see you! The name's Alvin Swensen. I'm the proprietor." He shook Wil's hand enthusiastically. "I was afraid you might wait till the front passed through." Swensen was dressed in baggy pants and a padded jacket that would have made Frank Nitti proud. The local police chief urged the other officer up the steps. No one else was outside; the place seemed just as deserted as one might expect a rural police station to be early on a weekday morning. Where was the emergency?

Inside, a clerk (cop?) dressed very much like Al sat before a comm console. Swensen grinned at the other. "It's the MSP, all right. They're really coming, Jim. They're really coming! Just come down the hall, Lieutenant. I got my office back there. We should clear out real soon, but for the moment, I think it's safe."

Wil nodded, more puzzled than informed. At the far end of the hall, light spilled from a half-open door. The frosted glass surface was stenciled with the words "Big Al." A faint smell of mildew hung over the aging carpet and the wood floor beneath settled perceptibly under Wil's 90 kilo tread. Brierson almost smiled: maybe Al wasn't so crazy. The gangster motif excused absolutely slovenly maintenance. Few customers would trust a normal police organization that kept its buildings like this.

Big Al urged Brierson into the light and waved him to an overstuffed chair. Though tall and angular, Swensen looked more like a school teacher than a cop—or a gangster. His reddish-blond hair stood out raggedly from his head, as though he had been pulling at it, or had just been wakened. From the man's fidgety pacing about the room, Wil guessed the first possibility more likely. Swensen seemed about at the end of his rope, and Wil's arrival was some kind of reprieve. He glanced at Wil's name plate and his grin spread even further. "W. W. Brierson. I've heard of you. I knew the Michigan State Police wouldn't let me down; they've sent their best."

Wil smiled in return, hoping his embarrassment didn't show. Part of his present fame was a company hype that he had come to loathe. "Thank you, uh, Big Al. We feel a special obligation to small police companies that serve no-right-to-bear-arms customers. But you're going to have to tell me more. Why so secretive?"

Al waved his hands. "I'm afraid of blabbermouths. I couldn't take a chance on the enemy learning I was bringing you into it until you were on the scene and in action."

Strange that he says "enemy," and not "crooks" or "bastards" or "hustlers." "But even a large gang might be scared off knowing—"

"Look, I'm not talking about some punk gang. I'm talking about the Republic of New Mexico. Invading us." He dropped into his chair and continued more calmly. It was almost as if passing the information on had taken the burden off him. "You're shocked?"

Brierson nodded dumbly.

"Me, too. Or I would have been up till a month ago. The Republic has always had plenty of internal troubles. And even though they claim all lands south of the Arkansas River, they have no settlements within hundreds of kilometers of here. Even now I think this is a bit of adventurism that can be squelched by an application of point force." He glanced at his watch. "Look, no matter how important speed is, we've got to do some coordinating. How many attack patrols are coming in after you?"

He saw the look on Brierson's face. "What? Only

one? Damn. Well, I suppose it's my fault, being secret like, but—"

Wil cleared his throat. "Big Al, there's only me. I'm the only agent MSP sent."

The other's face seemed to collapse, the relief changing to despair, then to a weak rage. "G-God d-damn you to hell, Brierson. I may lose everything I've built here, and the people who trusted me may lose everything they own. But I swear I'm going to sue your Michigan State Police into oblivion. Fifteen years I've paid you guys premiums and never a claim. And now when I need max firepower, they send me one asshole with a 10-millimeter popgun."

Brierson stood, his nearly two-meter bulk towering over the other. He reached out a bearlike hand to Al's shoulder. The gesture was a strange cross between reassurance and intimidation. Wil's voice was soft but steady. "The Michigan State Police hasn't let you down, Mr. Swensen. You paid for protection against wholesale violence—and we intend to provide that protection. MSP has *never* defaulted on a contract." His grip on Alvin Swensen's shoulder tightened with these last words. The two eyed each other for a moment. Then Big Al nodded weakly, and the other sat down.

"You're right. I'm sorry. I'm paying for the results, not the methods. But I know what we're up against, and I'm damned scared."

"And that's one reason why I'm here, Al: to find out exactly what we're up against before we jump in with our guns blazing and our pants down. What are you expecting?"

Al leaned back in the softly creaking chair. He looked out through the window into the dark silence of the morning, and for a moment seemed to relax. However improbably, someone else was going to take on his problems. "They started about three years ago. It seemed innocent enough, and it was certainly legal." Through the Republic of New Mexico claimed the lands from the Colorado on the west to the Mississippi on the east, and north to the Arkansas, in fact, most of their settlements were along the Gulf Coast and Rio Grande. For most of a century, Oklahoma and northern Texas had been uninhabited. The "border" along the Arkansas River had been of no real cpncern to the Republic, which had plenty of problems with its Water Wars on the Colorado, and of even less concern to the farmers at the southern edge of the ungoverned lands. During the last 10 years, immigration from the Republic toward the more prosperous north had been steadily increasing. Few of the southerners stayed in the Manhattan area: most jobs were farther north. But during these last three years, wealthy New Mexicans had moved into the area, men willing to pay almost any price for farmland.

"It's clear now that these people were stooges for the Republic government. They paid more money than they could reasonably recoup from farming, and the purchases started right after the election of their latest president. You know—Hastings Whatever-his-name-is. Anyway, it made a pleasant boom time for a lot of us. If some wealthy New Mexicans wanted isolated estates in the ungoverned lands, that was certainly their business. All the wealth in New Mexico couldn't buy one tenth of Kansas, anyway." At first, the settlers had been model neighbors. They even signed up with Al's Protection Racket and Midwest Jurisprudence. But as the months passed, it became obvious that they were neither farmers nor leisured rich. As near as the locals could figure out, they were some kind of labor contractors. An unending stream of trucks brought raggedly dressed men and women from the cities of the south: Galveston, Corpus Christi, even from the capital, Albuquerque. These folk were housed in barracks the owners had built on the farms. Anyone could see, looking in from above, that the newcomers spent long hours working in the fields.

Those farms produced on a scale that surprised the locals, and though it was still not clear that it was a profitable operation, there was a ripple of interest in the Grange journals; might manual labor hold an economic edge over the automatic equipment rentals? Soon the workers were hiring out to local farmers. "Those people work harder than any reasonable person, and they work dirt cheap. Every night, their contract bosses would truck 'em back to the barracks, so our farmers had scarcely more overhead than they would with automatics. Overall, the NMs underbid the equipment rental people by five percent or so."

Wil began to see where all this was leading. Someone in the Republic seemed to understand Midwest Jurisprudence. "Hmm, you know, Al, if I were one of those laborers, I wouldn't hang around in farm country. There are labor services up north that can get an apprentice butler more money than some rookie cops make. Rich people will always want servants, and nowadays the pay is tremendous."

Big Al nodded. "We've got rich folks, too. When they saw what these newcomers would work for, they started drooling. And that's when things began to get sticky." At first, the NM laborers could scarcely understand what they were being offered. They insisted that they were required to work when and where they were told. A few, a very few at first, took the job offers. "They were really scared, those first ones. Over and over, they wanted assurances that they would be allowed to return to their families at the end of the work day. They seemed to think the deal was some kidnap plot rather than an offer of employment. Then it was like an explosion: they couldn't wait to drop the farm jobs. They wanted to bring their families with them."

"And that's when your new neighbors closed up the camps?"

"You got it, pal. They won't let the families out. And we know they are confiscating the money the workers bring in."

"Did they claim their people were on long-term contracts?"

"Hell, no. It may be legal under Justice, Inc., but indentured servitude isn't under Midwest—and that's who they signed with. I see now that even that was deliberate.

"It finally hit the fan yesterday. The Red Cross flew a guy out from Topeka with a writ from a Midwest judge: He was to enter each of the settlements and explain to those poor folks how they stood with the law. I went along with a couple of my boys. They refused to let us in and punched out the Red Cross fellow when he got insistent. Their chief thug—fellow named Strong—gave me a signed policy cancellation, and told me that from now on they would handle all their own police and justice needs. We were then escorted off the property—at gunpoint."

"So they've gone armadillo. That's no problem. But the workers are still presumptively customers of yours?"

"Not just presumptively. Before this blew up, a lot of them had signed individual contracts with me and Midwest. The whole thing is a setup, but I'm *stuck*."

Wil nodded. "Right. Your only choice was to call in someone with firepower, namely my company."

Big Al leaned forward, his indignation retreating before fear. "Of course. But there's more, Lieutenant. Those workers—those slaves—were part of the trap that was set for us. But most of them are brave, honest people. They know what's happening, and they aren't any happier about it than I am. Last night, after we got our butts kicked, three of them escaped. They walked fifteen kilometers into Manhattan to see me, to beg me *not* to intervene. To beg me not to honor the contract.

"And they told me why: For a hundred kilometer stretch of their truck ride up here, they weren't allowed to see the country they were going through. But they heard plenty. And one of them managed to work a peephole in the side of the truck. He saw armored vehicles and attack aircraft under heavy camouflage just south of the Arkansas. The damn New Mexicans have taken part of their Texas garrison force and holed it up less than ten minutes flying time from Manhattan. And they're ready to move."

It was possible. The Water Wars with Aztlán had been winding down these last few years. The New Mexicans should have equipment reserves, even counting what they needed to keep the Gulf Coast cities in line. Wil got up and walked to the window. Dawn was lighting the sky above the far cloud banks. There was green in the rolling land that stretched away from the police post. Suddenly he felt very exposed here: Death could come out of that sky with precious little warning. W. W. Brierson was no student of history, but he was an old-time movie freak, and he had seen plenty of war stories. Assuming the aggressor had to satisfy some kind of public or world opinion, there had to be a provocation, an excuse for the massive violence that would masquerade as self-defense. The New Mexicans had cleverly created a situation in which Wil Brierson—or someone like him—would be contractually obligated to use force against their settlements.

"So. If we hold off on enforcement, how long do

you think the invasion would be postponed?" It hurt to suggest bending a contract like that, but there was precedent: In hostage cases, you often used time as a weapon.

"It wouldn't slow 'em up a second. One way or another they're moving on us. I figure if we don't do anything, they'll use my 'raid' yesterday as their excuse. The only thing I can see is for MSP to put everything it can spare on the line when those bastards come across. That sort of massive resistance might be enough to scare 'em back."

Brierson turned from the window to look at Big Al. He understood now the shaking fear in the other. It had taken guts for the other to wait here through the night. But now it was W. W. Brierson's baby. "Okay, Big Al. With your permission, I'll take charge."

"You got it, Lieutenant!" Al was out of his chair, a smile splitting his face.

Wil was already starting for the door. "The first thing to do is get away from this particular ground zero. How many in the building?"

"Just two besides me."

"Round 'em up and bring them to the front room. If you have any firearms, bring them, too."

Wil was pulling his comm equipment out of the gunship when the other three came out the front door of Al's HQ and started toward him. He waved them back. "If they play as rough as you think, they'll grab for air superiority first thing. What kind of ground vehicles do you have?"

"Couple of cars. A dozen motorbikes. Jim, open up the garage." The zoot-suited trooper hustled off. Will looked with some curiosity at the person remaining with Al. This individual couldn't be more than 14 years old. She (?) was weighted down with five boxes, some with makeshift carrying straps, others even less portable. Most looked like communications gear. The kid was grinning from ear to ear. Al said, "Kiki van Steen, Lieutenant. She's a war-game fanatic—for once, it may be worth something."

"Hi, Kiki."

"Pleased to meetcha, Lieutenant." She half-lifted one of the suitcase-size boxes, as though to wave. Even with all the gear, she seemed to vibrate with excitement.

"We have to decide where to go, and how to get there. The bikes might be best, Al. They're small enough to—"

"Nah." It was Kiki. "Really, Lieutenant, they're almost as easy to spot as a farm wagon. And we don't have to go far. I checked a couple minutes ago, and no enemy aircraft are up. We've got at least five minutes."

He glanced at Al, who nodded. "Okay, the car it is."

The girl's grin widened and she waddled off at high speed toward the garage. "She's really a good kid, Lieutenant. Divorced though. She spends most of what I pay her on that war-game equipment. Six months ago she started talking about strange things down south. When no one would listen, she shut up. Thank God she's here now. All night she's been watching the south. We'll know the second they jump off."

"You have some hidey-hole already set, Al?"

"Yeah. The farms southwest of here are riddled with tunnels and caves. The old Fort Riley complex. Friend of mine owns a lot of it. I sent most of my men out there last night. It's not much, but at least they won't be picking us up for free."

Around them insects were beginning to chitter, and in the trees west of the HQ there was a dove. Sunlight lined the cloud tops. The air was still cool, humid. And the darkness at the horizon remained. Twister weather. *Now who will benefit from that?*

The relative silence was broken by the sharp coughing of a piston engine. Seconds later, an incredible antique nosed out of the gargage onto the driveway. Wil saw the long black lines of a pre-1950 Lincoln. Brierson and Big Al dumped their guns and comm gear into the back seat and piled in.

This nostalgia thing can be carried too far, Wil thought. A restored Lincoln would cost as much as all the rest of Al's operation. The vehicle pulled smoothly out onto the ag road that paralleled the HQ property, and Wil realized he was in an inexpensive reproduction. He should have known Big Al would keep costs down.

Behind him the police station dwindled, was soon lost in the rolling Kansas landscape. "Kiki. Can you get a line-of-sight on the station's mast?"

The girl nodded. "Okay. I want a link to East Lansing that looks like it's coming from your station-house."

"Sure." She phased an antenna ball on the mast, then gave Wil her command mike. In seconds he had spoken the destination codes and was talking first to the duty desk in East Lansing—and then to Colonel Potts and several of the directors.

When he had finished, Big Al looked at him in awe. "One hundred assault aircraft! Four thousand troopers! My God. I had no idea you could call in that sort of force."

Brierson didn't answer immediately. He pushed the mike into Kiki's hands and said, "Get on the loudmouth channels, Kiki. Start screaming bloody murder to all North America." Finally he looked back at Al, embarrassed. "We don't, Al. MSP has maybe thirty assault aircraft, twenty of them helicopters. Most of the fixed-wing jobs are in the Yukon.

We could put guns on our search and rescue ships—we do have hundreds of those—but it will take weeks."

Al paled, but the anger he had shown earlier was gone. "So it was a bluff?"

Wil nodded. "But we'll get everything MSP has, as fast as they can bring it in. If the New Mexican investment isn't too big, this may be enough to scare 'em back." Big Al seemed to shrink in on himself. He gazed listlessly over Jim's shoulder at the road ahead. In the front seat, Kiki was shrilly proclaiming the details of the enemy's movements, the imminence of their attack. She was transmitting call letters and insignia that could leave no doubt that her broadcast came from a legitimate police service.

The wind whipped through the open windows, brought the lush smells of dew and things dark green. In the distance gleamed the silver dome of a farm's fresh produce bobble. They passed a tiny Methodist church, sparkling white amidst flowers and lawn. In back, someone was working in the pastor's garden.

The road was just good enough to support the big tires of farm vehicles. Jim couldn't do much over 50 kph. Every so often, a wagon or tractor would pass them going the other way—going off to work in the fields. The drivers waved cheerfully at the Lincoln. It was a typical farm country morning in the ungoverned lands. How soon it would change. The news networks should have picked up on Kiki by now. They would have their own investigative people on the scene in hours with live holo coverage of whatever the enemy chose to do. Their programming, some if it directed into the Republic, might be enough to turn the enemy's public opinion against its government. *Wishful thinking*.

More likely the air above them would soon be filled with screaming metal—the end of a generation of peace.

Big Al gave a short laugh. When Wil looked at him questioningly, the small-town cop shrugged. "I was just thinking. This whole police business is something like a lending bank. Instead of gold, MSP backs its promises with force. This invasion is like a run on your 'bank of violence.' You got enough backing to handle normal demands, but when it all comes due at once . . ."

. . . *you wind up dead or enslaved*. Wil's mind shied away from the analogy. "Maybe so, but like a lot of banks, we have agreements with others. I'll bet Portland Security and the Mormons will loan us some aircraft. In any case, the Republic can never hold this land. You run a no-right-to-bear-arms service; but a lot of people around here are armed to the teeth."

"Sure. My biggest competitor is Justice, Inc. They encourage their customers to invest in handguns and heavy home security. Sure. The Republic will get their asses kicked eventually. But we'll be dead and bankrupt by then—and so will a few thousand other innocents."

Al's driver glanced back at them. "Hey, Lieutenant, why doesn't MSP pay one of the big power companies to retaliate—bobble places way inside the Republic?"

Wil shook his head. "The New Mexico government is sure to have all its important sites protected by Wáchendon suppressors."

Suddenly Kiki broke off her broadcast monologue and let out a whoop. "Bandits! Bandits!" She handed a display flat over the seat to Al. The format was familiar, but the bouncing, jostling ride made it hard to read. The picture was based on a sidelooking radar view from orbit, with a lot of data added. Green denoted vegetation and pastel overlays showed cloud cover. It was a jumble till he noticed that Manhattan and the Kansas River were labeled. Kiki zoomed up the magnification. Three red dots were visibly accelerating from a growing pockwork of red dots to the south. The three brightened, still accelerating. "They just broke cloud cover," she explained. Beside each of the dots a moving legend gave what must be altitude and speed.

"Is this going out over your loudmouth channel?"

She grinned happily. "Sure is! But not for long." She reached back to point at the display. "We got about two minutes before Al's stationhouse goes boom. I don't want to risk a direct satellite link from the car, and anything else would be even more dangerous."

Point certain, thought Wil.

"Geez, this is incredible, just incredible. For two years the Warmongers—that's my club, you know—been watching the Water Wars. We got software, hardware, cryptics—everything to follow what's going on. We could predict, and bet other clubs, but we could never actually participate. And now we have a real *war*, right *here!*" She lapsed into awed silence, and Wil wondered fleetingly if she might be psychopathic, and not merely young and naive.

"Do you have outside cameras at the police station?" He was asking Kiki as much as Al. "We should broadcast the actual attack."

The girl nodded. "I grabbed two channels. I got the camera on the comm mast pointing southwest. We'll have public opinion completely nailed on this."

"Let's see it."

She made a moue. "Okay. Not much content to it, though." she flopped back onto the front seat. Over her shoulder, Wil could see she had an out-sized display flat on her lap. It was another composite picture, but this one was overlaid with cryptic legends. They looked vaguely familiar. Then he recognized them from the movies: They were the old, old shorthand for describing military units and capabilities. The Warmongers Club must have software for translating multispec satellite observations into such displays. Hell, they might even be able to listen in on military communications. And what the girl had said about public opinion—the club seemed to play war in a very universal way. They *were* crazy, but they might also be damned useful.

Kiki mumbled something into her command mike, and the flat Al was holding split down the middle: On the left they could follow the enemy's approach with the map; on the right they saw blue sky and farmland and the parking lot by the stationhouse. Wil saw his gunship gleaming in the morning sunlight, just a few meters below the camera's viewpoint.

"Fifteen seconds. They might be visible if you look south."

The car swerved toward the shoulder as Jim pointed out the window. "I see 'em!"

Then Wil did, too. A triple of black insects, silent because of distance and speed. They drifted westward, disappeared behind trees. But to the camera on the comm mast, they did not drift: They seemed to hang in the sky above the parking lot, death seen straight on. Smoke puffed from just beneath them and things small and black detached from the bodies of the attack craft, which now pulled up. The planes were so close that Wil could see shape to them, could see sun glint from canopies. Then the bombs hit.

Strangely, the camera scarcely jolted, but started slowly to pan downward. Fire and debris roiled up around the viewpoint. A rotor section from his flier flashed past, and then the display went gray. He realized that the panning had not been deliberate: The high comm mast had been severed and was toppling.

Seconds passed and sharp thunder swept over the car, followed by the fast-dying scream of the bombers climbing back into the sky.

"So much for the loudmouth channels," said Kiki. "I'm for keeping quiet till we get underground."

Jim was driving faster now. He hadn't seen the display, but the sounds of the explosions were enough to make all but the least imaginative run like hell. The road had been bumpy, but now seemed like washboard. Wil gripped the seat ahead of him. If the enemy connected them with the broadcasts . . .

"How far, Al?"

"Nearest entrance is about four kilometers as the crow flies, but we gotta go all around the Schwartz farm to get to it." He waved at the high, barbed-wire fence along the right side of the road. Corn fields stretched away north of it. In the distance, Wil saw something—a harvester?—amidst the green. "It'll take us fifteen minutes—"

"Ten!" claimed Jim emphatically, and the ride became still wilder.

"—to make it around the farm."

They crested a low hill. Not more than 300 meters distant, Wil could see a side road going directly north. "But we could take that."

"Not a chance. That's on Schwartz land." Big Al glanced at the state trooper. "And I ain't just being law-abiding, Lieutenant. We'd be as good as dead to do that. Jake Schwartz went armadillo about three years ago. See that hulk out there in the field?" He tried to point, but his arm waved wildly.

"The harvester?"

"That's no harvester. It's armor. Robot, I think. If you look careful you may see the gun tracking us." Wil looked again. What he had thought was a chaff exhaust now looked more like a high-velocity catapult.

Their car zipped past the T-intersection with the Schwartz road; Wil had a glimpse of a gate and keep-out signs surmounted by what looked like human skulls. The farm west of the side road seemed undeveloped. A copse at the top of a near hill might have hid farm buildings.

"The expense. Even if it's mostly bluff—"

"It's no bluff. Poor Jake. He always was self-righteous and a bit of a bully. His police contract was with Justice, Inc., and he claimed even they were too bleedin' heart for him. Then one night his kid— who's even stupider than Jake—got pig drunk and killed another idiot. Unfortunately for Jake's boy, the victim was one of my customers. There are no amelioration clauses in the Midwest/Justice, Inc. agreements. Reparations aside, the kid will be locked up for a long time. Jake swore he'd never contract his rights to a court again. He has a rich farm, and since then he's spent every gAu from it on more guns, more traps, more detectors. I hate to think how they live in there. There are rumors he's brought in deathdust from the Hanford ruins, just in case anybody succeeds in getting past everything else."

Oh boy. Even the armadillos up north rarely went that far.

The last few minutes Kiki had ignored them, all her attention on the strategy flat on her lap. She wore a tiny headset and was mumbling constantly into her command mike. Suddenly she spoke up. "Oops. We're not going to make it, Big Al." She began folding the displays, stuffing them back into her equipment boxes. "I monitored. They just told their chopper crews to pick us up. They got us spotted easy. Two, three minutes is all we have."

Jim slowed, shouted over his shoulder. "How about if I drop you and keep going? I might be kilometers gone before they stop me." Brierson had never noticed any lack of guts among the unarmed police services.

"Good idea! Bye!" Kiki flung open her door and rolled off into the deep and apparently soft vegetation that edged the road.

"Kiki!" screamed Big Al, turning to look back down the road. They had a brief glimpse of comm and processor boxes bouncing wildly through the brush. Then Kiki's blond form appeared for an instant as she dragged the equipment deeper into the green.

From the trees behind them they could hear the *thup thupthup* of rotors. Two minutes had been an overstatement. Wil leaned forward. "No, Jim. Drive like hell. And remember: There were only three of us."

The other nodded. The car squealed out toward the center of the road, and accelerated up past 80. The roar and thump of their progress momentarily drowned out the sound of pursuit. Thirty seconds passed, and three helicopters appeared over the tree line behind them. *Do we get what they gave the stationhouse?* An instant later white flashed from their belly guns. The road ahead erupted in a geyser of dirt and rock. Jim stepped on the brakes and the car swerved to a halt, dipping and bobbing among the craters left by the shells. The car's engine died and the thumping of rotors was a loud, almost physical pressure around them. The largest craft settled to earth amidst its own dust devil. The other two circled, their autocannons locked on Big Al's Lincoln.

The passenger hatch on the grounded chopper slid back and two men in body armor hopped out. One waved his submachine gun at them, motioning them out of the car. Brierson and the others were hustled across the road, while the second soldier went to pick up the equipment they had in the car. Wil looked back at the scene, feeling the dust in his mouth and on his sweating face—the ashes of humiliation.

His pistol was pulled from its holster. "All aboard, gentlemen." The words were spoken with a clipped, Down West accent.

Wil was turning when it happened. A flash of fire and a muffled thud came from one of the hovering choppers. Its tail rotor disappeared in a shower of debris. The craft spun uncontrollably on its main rotor and fell onto the roadway behind them. Pale flame spread along fuel lines, sputtering in small explosions. Wil could see injured crew trying to crawl out.

"I said *get aboard*." The gunman had stepped back from them, his attention and the muzzle of his gun still on his captives. Wil guessed the man was a veteran of the Water Wars—that institutionalized gangsterism that New Mexico and Aztlán called "warfare between nations." Once given a mission, he would not be distracted by incidental catastrophes.

The three "prisoners of war" stumbled into the relative darkness of the helicopter's interior. Wil saw the soldier—still standing outside—look back toward the wreck, and speak emphatically into his helmet mike. Then he hopped on and pulled the hatch to. The helicopter slid into the air, hanging close to the ground as it gradually picked up speed. They were moving westward from the wreck, and there was no way they could look back through the tiny windows.

An accident? Who could have been equipped to shoot down an armored warcraft in the middle of Kansas fields? Then Wil remembered: Just before it lost its tail, the chopper had drifted north of the roadway, past the high fence that marked Armadillo Schwartz's land. He looked at Big Al, who nodded slightly. Brierson sat back in the canvas webbing and suppressed a smile. It was a small thing on the scale of the invasion, but he thanked God for armadillos. Now it was up to organizations like the Michigan State Police to convince the enemy that this was just the beginning, that every kilometer into the ungoverned lands would cost them similarly.

* * *

One hundred and eighty kilometers in six hours. Republican casualties: one motorcycle/truck collision, and one helicopter crash—that probably a mechanical failure. Edward Strong, Special Advisor to the President, felt a satisfied smile come to his lips every time he glanced at the situation board. He had seen more casualties on a Freedom Day parade through downtown Albuquerque. His own analysis for the President—as well as the larger, less imaginative analysis from JCS—had predicted that extending the Republic through Kansas to the Mississippi would be almost trivial. Nevertheless, after having fought meter by bloody meter with the fanatics of Aztlán, it was a strange feeling to be advancing hundreds of kilometers each day.

Strong paced down the narrow aisle of the Command and Control van, past the analysts and clerks. He stood for a moment by the rear door, feeling the air-conditioning billow chill around his head. Camouflage netting had been laid over the van, but he could see through it without difficulty: Green leaves played tag with shadows across pale yellow limestone. They were parked in a wooded creek bed on the land Intelligence had bought several years earlier. Somewhere to the north were the barracks that now confined the people Intelligence had imported, allegedly to work the farms. Those laborers had provided whatever legal justification was needed for this move into the ungoverned lands. Strong wondered if any of them realized their role—and realized that in a few months they would be free of poverty, realized that they would own farms in a land that could be made infinitely more hospitable than the deserts of the Southwest.

Sixteen kilometers to the northeast lay Manhattan. It was a minor goal, but the Republic's forces were cautious. It would be an important—though small—test of their analysis. There were Tinkers in that town and in the countryside beyond. The precision electronics and related weapons that came out of the Tinkers' shops were worthy of respect and caution. Privately, Strong considered them to be the only real threat to the success of the invasion he had proposed to the President three years earlier. (Three years of planning, of cajoling resources from other departments, of trying to inject imagination into minds that had been closed for decades. By far, the easiest part had been the operations here in Kansas.)

The results of the move on Manhattan would be relayed from here to General Crick at the head of the armor driving east along Old70. Later in the afternoon, Crick's tank carriers should reach the outskirts of Topeka. The Old U.S. highway provided a mode of armored operations previously unknown to warfare. If the investiture of Manhattan went as planned, then Crick might have Topeka by nightfall and be moving the remainder of his forces on to the Mississippi.

Strong looked down the van at the time posted on the situation board. The President would be calling in 20 minutes to witness the move against Manhattan. Till then, a lull gapped in Strong's schedule. Perhaps there was time for one last bit of caution. He turned to the bird colonel who was his military liaison. "Bill, those three locals you picked up—you know, the protection racket people—I'd like to talk to them before the Chief calls in."

"Here?"

"If possible."

"Okay." There was faint disapproval in the officer's voice. Strong imagined that Bill Alvarez couldn't quite see bringing enemy agents into the C&C van. But what the hell, they were clean—and there was no way that they could report what they saw here. Besides, he had to stay in the van in case the Old Man showed up early.

Minutes later, the three shuffled into the conference area at the front of the van. Restraints glinted at their hands and ankles. They stood in momentary blindness in the darkness of the van, and Strong had a chance to look them over; three rather ordinary human beings, dressed in relatively extraordinary ways. The big black wore a recognizable uniform, complete with badges, sidearm holster, and what appeared to be riding boots. He looked the model fascist. Strong recognized the Michigan State "Police" insignia on his sleeve. MSP was one of the most powerful gangster combines in the ungoverned lands. Intelligence reported they had some modern weapons—enough to keep their "clients" in line, anyway.

"Sit down, gentlemen." Amidst a clanking of shackles, the three sat, sullen. Behind them an armed guard remained standing. Strong glanced at the intelligence summary he had punched up. "Mr., uh, Lieutenant Brierson, you may be interested to know that the troops and aircraft you asked your bosses for this morning have not materialized. Our intelligence people have not changed their estimate that you were making a rather weak bluff."

The northerner just shrugged, but the blond fellow in the outrageously striped shirt—Alvin Swensen, the report named him—leaned forward and almost hissed. "Maybe, maybe not, Asshole! But it doesn't matter. You're going to kill a lot of people, but in the end you'll be dragging your bloody tail back south."

Figuratively speaking, Strong's ears perked up. "How is that, Mr. Swensen?"

"Read your history. You're stealing from a free people now—not a bunch of Aztlán serfs. Every single farm, every single family is against you, and these are educated people, many with weapons. It may take a while. It may destroy a lot of things we value. But every day you stay here, you'll bleed. And when you've bled enough to see this; then you'll go home."

Strong glanced at the casualty report on the situation board, and felt laughter stealing up. "You poor fool. What free people? We get your video, your propaganda, but what does it amount to? There hasn't been a government in this part of the continent for more than eighty years. You petty gangsters have the guns and have divided up the territory. Most of you don't even allow your 'clients' firearms. I'll wager that the majority of your victims will welcome a government where there is a franchise to be exercised, where ballots, and not MSP bullets, decide issues.

"No, Mr. Swensen, the little people in the ungoverned lands have no stake in your *status quo*. And as for the armed groups fighting some kind of guerrilla war against us— Well, you've had it easier than you know for a long time. You haven't lived in a land as poor as old New Mexico. Since the Bobble War, we've had to fight for every liter of water, against an enemy far more determined and bloodthirsty than you may imagine. We have prevailed, we have revived and maintained democratic government, and we have remained free men."

"*Sure*. Free like the poor slobs you got locked up over there." Swensen waved in the direction of the workers' barracks.

Strong leaned across the narrow conference table to pin Swensen with his glare. "Mister, I grew up as one of 'those slobs.' In New Mexico, even people that poor have a chance to get something better. This land you claim is practically empty—you don't know how to farm it, you don't have a government to manage large dam and irrigation projects, you don't

even know how to use government agriculture policy
to encourage its proper use by individuals.

"Sure, those workers couldn't be told why they
were brought here. But when this is over, they will
be heroes, with homesteads they had never imagined being able to own."

Swensen rocked back before the attack, but was
plainly unconvinced. *Which makes sense*, thought
Strong. *How can a wolf imagine anyone sincerely
wishing good for sheep?*

An alert light glowed on Strong's display and one
of the clerks announced, "Presidential transmission
under way, Mr. Strong." He swore behind his teeth.
The Old Man was early. He'd hoped to get some
information out of these three, not just argue politics.

A glowing haze appeared at the head of the
conference table and quickly solidified into the image of the fourth President of the Republic. Hastings
Martinez was good-looking with bio-age around 50
years—old enough to inspire respect, young enough
to appear decisive. In Strong's opinion, he was not
the best president the Republic had seen, but he had
the advisor's respect and loyalty nevertheless. There
was something in the very responsibility of the office
of the Presidency that made its holder larger than
life.

"Mr. President," Strong said respectfully.

"Ed," Martinez's image nodded. The projection
was nearly as substantial as the forms of those truly
present; Strong didn't know whether this was because of the relative darkness within the van, or
because Martinez was transmitting via fiber from his
estate in Alva, just 300 kilometers away.

Strong waved at the prisoners. "Three locals, sir. I
was hoping to—"

Martinez leaned forward. "Why, I think I've seen
you before." He spoke to the MSP officer. "The ads

Michigan State Police uses; our intelligence people have shown me some. You protect MSP's client mobs from outside gangs."

Brierson nodded, smiled wryly. Strong recognized him now and kicked himself for not noticing earlier. If those ads were correct, then Brierson was one of the top men in the MSP.

"They make you out to be some sort of superman. Do you honestly think your people can stop a modern, disciplined army?"

"Sooner or later, Mr. Martinez. Sooner or later."

The President smiled, but Strong wasn't sure whether he was piqued or truly amused. "Our armor is approaching Manhattan on schedule, sir. As you know, we regard this action as something of a bench mark. Manhattan is almost as big as Topeka, and has a substantial cottage electronics industry. It's about the closest thing to a city you'll find in the ungoverned lands." Strong motioned for the guard to remove the three prisoners, but the President held up his hand.

"Let 'em stay, Ed. The MSP man should see this firsthand. These people may be lawless, but I can't believe they are crazy. The sooner they realize that we have overwhelming force—and that we use it fairly—the sooner they'll accept the situation."

"Yes, sir." Strong signaled his analysts, and displays came to life on the situation board. Simultaneously, the conference table was overhung with a holographic relief map of central Kansas. The northerners looked at the map and Strong almost smiled. They obviously had no idea of the size of the New Mexican operation. For months the Republic had been building reserves along the Arkansas. It couldn't be entirely disguised; these three had known something about the forces. But until the whole military machine was in motion, its true size had escaped them. Strong was honest with himself. It was not New Mexican cleverness that had outwitted northern electronics. The plan could never have worked without advanced countermeasures equipment—some of it bought from the northerners themselves.

Computer-selected radio traffic became a background noise. He had rehearsed all this with the technicians earlier; there was not a single aspect of the operation that the President would miss. He pointed at the map. "Colonel Alvarez has one armored force coming north from Old70. It should enter Manhattan from the east. The other force left here a few minutes ago, and is approaching town along this secondary road." Tiny silver lights crept along the map where he pointed. A few centimeters above the display, other lights represented helicopter and fixed-wing cover. These coasted gracefully back and forth, occasionally swooping close to the surface.

A voice spoke against a background of turbine noise, to announce no resistance along the eastern salient. "Haven't really seen anyone. People are staying indoors, or else bobbled up before we came in range. We're avoiding houses and farm buildings, sticking to open fields and roads."

Strong expanded one of the views from the western salient. The situation board showed a picture taken from the air: A dozen tanks moved along a dirt road, trails of dust rising behind them. The camera chopper must have been carrying a mike, for the rumbling and clanking of treads replaced the radio traffic for a moment. Those tanks were the pride of New Mexico. Unlike the aircraft, their hulls and engines were 100 percent Product of the Republic. New Mexico was poor in most resources, but like Japan in the 20th century, and Great Britain before that, she was great in people and ingenuity. Someday soon, she would be great in electronics. For now, though, all the best reconnaissance and communication gear came from Tinkers, many in the ungoverned lands. That was an Achilles' heel, long recognized by Strong and others. It was the reason for using equipment from different manufacturers all over the world, and for settling for second-class gear in some of the most critical applications. How could they know, *for certain*, that the equipment they bought was not booby-trapped or bugged? There was historical precedent: The outcome of the Bobble War had been due in large part to Tinker meddling with the old Peace Authority's reconnaissance system.

Strong recognized the stretch of road they were coming up on: A few hundred meters beyond the lead tank lay an irregular blackened area and the twisted metal that had once been a helicopter.

A puff of smoke appeared by the lead tank, followed by the faint crack of an explosion. Bill Alvarez's voice came on an instant after that. "Under fire. Light mortar." The tank was moving again, but in a large circle, toward the ditch. Guns and sensors on the other armor swung north. "The enemy was lucky, or that was a smart round. We've got radar backtrack. The round came from beyond the other side of the farm we're passing. Looks like a tunnel entrance to the old Fort Riley— Wait, we got enemy radio traffic just before it happened."

His voice was replaced by the crackling of high amplification. The new voice was female, but barely understandable. "General van Steen to forces [unintelligible]. You may fire when ready." There was a screaking sound and other voices.

Strong saw Swensen's jaw sag in surprise, or horror. "*General van Steen?*"

Colonel Alvarez's voice came back. "There were replies from several points farther north. The original launch site has fired two more rounds." As he spoke, black smoke appeared near the treads of two more tanks. Neither was destroyed, but neither could continue.

"Mr. President, Mr. Strong, all rounds are coming from the same location. These are barely more than fireworks—except that they're smart. I'll wager 'General van Steen' is some local gangster putting up a brave front. We'll see in a minute." On the holomap, two blips drew away from the other support aircraft and began a low level dash across the miniature Kansas landscape.

The President nodded, but addressed another unseen observer. "General Crick?"

"I concur, sir." Crick's voice was as loud and clear as Alvarez's, though the general was 50 kilometers to the east, at the head of the column en route to Topeka. "But we've seen an armored vehicle in the intermediate farmland, haven't we, Bill?"

"Yes," said Alvarez. "It's been there for months. Looks like a hulk. We'll take it out, too."

Strong noticed the northerners tense. Swensen seemed on the verge of screaming something. *What do they know?*

The attack planes, twin engine green-and-gray jobs, were on the main view now. They were only 20 or 30 meters up, well below the camera viewpoint, and probably not visible from the enemy launch site. The lead craft angled slightly to the east, and spewed rockets at an unmoving silhouette that was almost hidden by the hills and the corn. A second later, the target disappeared in a satisfying geyser of flame and dirt.

And a second after *that*, hell on earth erupted from the peaceful fields: beams of pale light flashed from unseen projectors, and the assault aircraft became falling, swelling balls of fire. As automatic fire control brought the tanks' guns to bear on the source of the destruction, rocket and laser fire came from other locations immediately north of the roadway. Four of the tanks exploded immediately, and most of the rest were on fire. Tiny figures struggled from their machines, and ran from the flames.

North of the farm, Strong thought he saw explosions at the source of the original mortar attack. Something was firing in that direction too!

Then the camera chopper took a hit, and the picture swung round and round, descending into the fire storm that stretched along the roadway. The view went dark. Strong's carefully planned presentation was rapidly degenerating into chaos. Alvarez was shouting over other voices, demanding the reserves that still hung along Old70 directly south of Manhattan, and he could hear Crick working to divert portions of his air cover to the fight that was developing.

It wasn't till much later that Strong made sense of the conversation that passed between the northerners just then:

"Kiki, how could you!" Swensen slumped over the holomap, shaking his head in despair (shame?).

Brierson eyed the displays with no visible emotion. "What she did is certainly legal, Al."

"Sure it is. And immoral as hell. Poor Jake Schwartz. Poor Jake."

The view of the battle scene reappeared. The picture was almost the same perspective as before but grainier and faintly wavering—probably from a camera aboard some recon craft far south of the fighting. The holomap flickered as major updates came in. The locals had been thorough and successful. There were no effective New Mexican forces within five kilometers of the original flareup. The force dug in to the farmland was firing rockets southward, taking an increasing toll of the armored reinforcements that were moving north from Old70.

"Crick here, Mr. President." The general's voice was brisk, professional. Any recriminations with Intelligence would come later. "The enemy is localized, but incredibly well dug in. If he's isolated, we *might* be able to bypass him, but neither Alvarez nor I want something like that left on our flank. We're going to soften him up, then move our armor right in on top."

Strong nodded to himself. In any case, they had to take this strong point just to find out what the enemy really had. In the air over the holomap, dozens of lights moved toward the enemy fortress. Some flew free ballistic arcs, while others struck close to the ground, out of the enemy's direct fire. Across the table, the holo lit the northerners' faces: Swensen's seemingly more pale than before, Brierson's dark and stolid. There was a faint stench of sweat in the air now, barely perceptible against the stronger smells of metal and fresh plastic.

Damn. Those three had been surprised by the ambush, but Strong was sure that they understood what was behind the attack, and whence the next such would come. Given time and Special Service drugs, he could have the answers. He leaned across the table and addressed the MSP officer. "So. You aren't entirely bluff. But unless you have many more such traps, you won't do more than slow us up, and kill a lot of people on both sides."

Swensen was about to answer, then looked at Brierson and was silent. The black seemed to be deliberating just what or how much to say; finally, he shrugged. "I won't lie to you. The attack had nothing to do with MSP forces."

"Some other gang then?"

"No. You just happened to run into a farmer who defends his property."

"Bull." Ed Strong had spent his time in the military in combat along the Colorado. He knew how to read the intelligence displays and manage tactics. But he also knew what it was like to be on the ground where the reality was bullets and shrapnel. He knew what it took to set up a defense like the one they had just seen. "Mr. Brierson, you're telling me one man could afford to buy the sort of equipment we saw and to dig it in so deep that even now we don't have a clear picture of his setup? You're telling me that one man could afford an MHD source for those lasers?"

"Sure. That family has probably been working at this for years, spending every spare gAu on the project, building the system up little by little. Even so," he sighed, "they should be out of rockets and juice soon. You could lay off."

The rain of rocket-borne and artillery high explosives was beginning to fall upon the target. Flashes and color sparkled across the screen, more an abstract pattern than a landscape now. There was no human life, no equipment visible. The bombers were standing off and lobbing their cargo in. Until the enemy's defenses were broken, any other course was needless waste. After a couple minutes, the airborne debris obscured all but the largest detonations. Napalm flared within, and the whole cloud glowed beautiful yellow. For a few seconds, the enemy lasers still flashed, spectacular and ineffective in all the dirt. Even after the lasers died, the holomap showed isolated missiles emerging from the target area to hunt for the bombers. Then even those stopped coming.

Still the barrage continued, raising the darkness and light high over the Kansas fields. There was no sound from this display, but the *thudthudding* of the attack came barely muffled through the hull of the C&C van. They were, after all, less than 7,000 meters from the scene. It was mildly surprising that the enemy had not tried to take them out. Perhaps Brierson was more important, and more knowledgeable, than he admitted.

Minutes passed, and they all—President and gangsters alike—watched the barrage end and the wind push the haze away from the devastation that modern war can make. North and east, fires spread through the fields. The tanks—and final, physical possession of the disputed territory—were only minutes away.

The destruction was not uniform. New Mexican fire had focused on the projectors and rocket launchers, and there the ground was pulverized, ripped first by proximity-fused high explosives, then by digger bombs and napalm. As they watched, recon craft swooped low over the landscape, their multiscanners searching for any enemy weapons that might be held in reserve. When the tanks and personnel carriers arrived, a more thorough search would be made on foot.

Finally, Strong returned to Brierson's fantastic claim. "And you say it's just coincidence that this one farmer who spends all his money on weapons happens to be on our line of march."

"Coincidence and a little help from General van Steen."

President Martinez raised his eyes from the displays at his end. His voice was level, but Strong recognized the tension there. "Mr., uh, Brierson. Just how many of these miniforts are there?"

The other sat back. His words might have seemed insolent, but there was no sarcasm in his voice. "I have no idea, Mr. Martinez. As long as they don't bother our customers, they are of no interest to MSP. Many aren't as well hidden as Schwartz's, but you can't count on that. As long as you stay off their property, most of them won't touch you."

"You're saying that if we detect and avoid them, they are no threat to our plans?"

"Yes."

The main screen showed the tank forces now. They were a few hundred meters from the burning fields. The viewpoint rotated and Strong saw that Crick had not stinted: at least 100 tanks—most of the reserve force—were advancing on a 5,000-meter front. Following were even more personnel carriers. Tactical air support was heavy. Any fire from the ground ahead would be met by immediate destruction. The camera rotated back to show the desolation they were moving into. Strong doubted that anything living, much less anything hostile, still existed in that moonscape.

The President didn't seem interested in the display. All his attention was on the northerner. "So we can avoid these stationary gunmen till we find it convenient to deal with them. You are a great puzzle, Mr. Brierson. You claim strengths and weaknesses for your people that are equally incredible. And I get the feeling you don't really expect us to believe you, but that somehow *you* believe everything you're saying."

"You're very perceptive. I've thought of trying to bluff you. In fact, I did try earlier today. From the looks of your equipment"—he waved his hand at the Command and Control consoles, a faintly mocking smile on his face—"we might even be able to bluff you back where you belong. *This once*. But when you saw what we had done, you'd be back again—next year, next decade—and we'd have to do it all over again without the bluffs. So, Mr. Martinez, I think it best you learn what you're up against the first time out. People like Schwartz are just the beginning. Even if you can rub out them and services like MSP, you'll end up with a guerrilla war like you've never fought—one that can actually turn your own people against you. You do practice conscription, don't you?"

The President's face hardened, and Strong knew that the northerner had gone too far. "We do, as has every free nation in history—or at least every nation that was determined to stay free. If you're implying that our people would desert under fire or because of propaganda, you are contradicting my personal experience." He turned away, dismissing Brierson from his attention.

"They've arrived, sir." As the tanks rolled into position on the smoking hillsides, the personnel carriers began disgorging infantry. The tiny figures moved quickly, dragging gear toward the open tears in the earth. Strong could hear an occasional popping sound: Misfiring engines? Remnant ammo?

Tactical aircraft swept back and forth overhead, their rockets and guns ready to support the troopers on the ground. The techs' reports trickled in.

"Three video hard points detected," small arms fire chattered. "Two destroyed, one recovered. Sonoprobes show lots of tunnels. Electrical activity at—" The men in the picture looked up, at something out of view.

Nothing else changed on the picture, but the radars saw the intrusion, and the holomap showed the composite analysis: a mote of light rose leisurely out of the map—500 meters, 600. It moved straight up, slowed. The support aircraft swooped down upon it and—

A purple flash, bright yet soundless, seemed to go off *inside* Strong's head. The holomap and the displays winked down to nothing, then came back. The President's image reappeared, but there was no sound, and it was clear he was not receiving.

Along the length of the van, clerks and analysts came out of that stunned moment to work frantically with their equipment. Acrid smoke drifted into the conference area. The safe, crisp displays had been replaced by immediate, deadly reality.

"High flux nuke." The voice was calm, almost mechanical.

High flux nuke. Radiation bomb. Strong came to his feet, rage and horror burning inside him. Except for bombs in lapsed bobbles, no nuclear weapon had exploded in North America in nearly a century. Even during the bitterest years of the Water Wars, both Aztlán and New Mexico had seen the suicide implicit in nuclear solutions. But here, in a rich land, without warning and for no real reason—

"You *animals!*" he spat down upon the seated northerners.

Swensen lunged forward. "God damn it! Schwartz isn't one of my customers!"

Then the shock wave hit. Strong was thrown across the map, his face buried in the glowing terrain. Just as suddenly he was thrown back. The prisoners' guard had been knocked into the far wall; now he stumbled forward through Martinez's unseeing image, his stun gun flying from his hand.

From the moment of the detonation, Brierson had sat hunched, his arms extended under the table. Now he moved, lunging across the table to sweep up the gun between his manacled hands. The muzzle sparkled and Strong's face went numb. He watched in horror as the other twisted and raked the length of the van with stunfire. The men back there had themselves been knocked about. Several were just coming up off their knees. Most didn't know what hit them when they collapsed back to the floor. At the far end of the van, one man had kept his head. One man had been as ready as Brierson.

Bill Alvarez popped up from behind an array processor, a five millimeter slug-gun in his hand, flashing fire as he moved.

Then the numbness seemed to squeeze in on Strong's mind, and everything went gray.

*   *   *

Wil looked down the dim corridor that ran the length of the command van. No one was moving, though a couple of men were snoring. The officer with the handgun had collapsed, his hands hanging limp, just a few centimeters from his pistol. Blue sky showing through the wall above Wil's head was evidence of the fellow's determination. If the other had been a hair faster . . .

Wil handed the stun gun to Big Al. "Let Jim go down and pick up the slug gun. Give an extra dose to anyone who looks suspicious."

Al nodded, but there was still a dazed look in his eyes. In the last hour, his world had been turned upside down. How many of his customers—the people who paid for his protection—had been killed? Wil tried not to think about that; indirectly, those same people had been depending on MSP. Almost tripping on his fetters, he stepped over the fallen guard and sat down on the nearest technician's saddle. For all New Mexico being a foreign land, the controls were familiar. It wasn't too surprising. The New Mexicans used a lot of Tinker electronics, though they didn't seem to trust it: much of the equipment's performance was downgraded where they had replaced suspicious components with their own devices. Ah, the price of paranoia.

Brierson picked up a command mike, made a simple request, and watched the answer parade across the console. "Hey, Al, we stopped transmitting right at the detonation!" Brierson quickly entered commands that cleared Martinez's image and blocked any future transmissions. Then he asked for status.

The air conditioning was down, but internal power could keep the gear going for a time. The van's intelligence unit estimated the nuke had been a three kiloton equivalent with a 70 percent radiance. Brierson felt his stomach flip-flop. He knew about nukes—perhaps more than the New Mexicans. There was no legal service that allowed them and it was open season on armadillos who advertised having them, but every so often MSP got a case involving such weapons. Everyone within 2,000 meters of that blast would already be dead. Schwartz's private war had wiped out a significant part of the invading forces.

The people in the van had received a sizable dose from the Schwartz nuke, though it wouldn't be life-threatening if they got medical treatment soon. In the division command area immediately around the van, the exposure was somewhat higher. How long would it be before those troops came nosing around the silent command vehicle? If he could get a phone call out—

But then there was Fate's personal vendetta against W. W. Brierson: Loud pounding sounded at the forward door. Wil waved Jim and Al to be quiet. Awkwardly, he got off the saddle and moved to look through the old-fashioned viewplate mounted next to the door. In the distance he could see men carrying stretchers from an ambulance; some of the burn cases would be really bad. Five troopers were standing right at the doorway, close enough that he could see blistered skin and burned clothing. But their weapons looked fine, and the wiry noncom pounding on the door was alert and energetic. "Hey, open up in there!"

Wil thought fast. What was the name of that VIP civilian? Then he shouted back (doing his best to imitate the clipped New Mexican accent), "Sorry, Mr. Strong doesn't want to breach internal atmosphere." *Pray they don't see the bullet holes just around the corner.*

He saw the sergeant turn away from the door. Wil lip-read the word *shit*. He could almost read the noncom's mind: The men outside had come near to being french-fried, and here some silkshirt supervisor was worried about so-far-nonexistent fallout.

The noncom turned back to the van and shouted, "How about casualties?"

"Outside of rad exposure, just some bloody noses and loose teeth. Main power is down and we can't transmit," Wil replied.

"Yes, sir. Your node has been dropped from the network. We've patched backward to Oklahoma Leader and forward to div mobile. Oklahoma Leader wants to talk to Mr. Strong. Div mobile wants to talk to Colonel Alvarez. How long will it be till you're back on the air?"

How long can I ask for? How long do I need? "Give us fifteen minutes," he shouted, after a moment.

"Yes, sir. We'll get back to you." Having innocently delivered this threat, the sergeant and his troopers moved off.

Brierson hopped back to the console. "Keep your eyes on the sleepers, Al. If I'm lucky, fifteen minutes should be enough time."

"To do what? Call MSP?"

"Something better. Something I should have done this morning." He searched through the command menus for satellite pickups. The New Mexican military was apparently leery of using subscription services, but there should be some facility for it. Ah, there it was. Brierson phased the transmitter for the synchronous satellite the Hainan commune had hung over Brazil. With narrow beam, he might be able to talk through it without the New Mexicans realizing he was transmitting. He tapped in a credit number, then a destination code.

The display showed the call had reached Whidbey Island. Seconds passed. Outside, he could hear choppers moving into the camp. More ambulances? *Damn you, Rober. Be home.*

The conference area filled with bluish haze, then became a sunlit porch overlooking a wooded bay. Sounds of laughter and splashing came faintly from the water. Old Roberto Richardson never used less than full holo. But the scene was pale, almost ghostly—the best the van's internal power supply could do. A heavyset man with apparent age around 30 came up the steps onto the porch and sat down; it was Richardson. He peered out at them. "Wil? Is that you?"

If it weren't for the stale air and the dimness of the vision, Wil could almost believe he'd been transported halfway across the continent. Richardson lived on an estate that covered the whole of Whidbey Island. In the Pacific time zone it was still morning, and shadows swept across lawn-like spaces that stretched away to his manicured forests. Not for the first time, Wil was reminded of the faerie landscapes of Maxfield Parrish. Roberto Richardson was one of the richest men in the world; he sold a line of products that many people cannot resist. He was rich enough to live in whatever fantasy world he chose.

Brierson turned on the pickup that watched the conference table.

"*Dios*. It *is* you, Wil! I thought you were dead or captured."

"Neither, just yet. You're following this ruckus?"

"*Por cierto*. And most news services are covering it. I wager they're spending more money than your blessed Michigan State Police on this war. Unless that nuke was one of yours? Wili, my boy, that was spectacular. You took out twenty percent of their armor."

"It wasn't one of ours, Rober."

"Ah. Just as well. Midwest Jurisprudence would withdraw service for something like that."

Time was short, but Wil couldn't resist asking, "What is MSP up to?"

Richardson sighed. "About what I'd expect. They've finally brought some aircraft in. They're buzzing around the tip of Dave Crick's salient. The Springfield Cyborg Club has gone after the New Mexican supply lines. They ware causing some damage. A cyborg is a bit hard to kill, and Norcross Security is supplying them with transports and weapons. The New Mexicans have Wáchendon suppressors down to battalion level, so there's no bobbling. The fighting looks quite 20th century.

"You've got a lot of public opinion behind you— even in the Republic, I think—but not much firepower.

"You know, Wil, you fellows should have bought more from me. You saved a few million, maybe, passing up those aerial torpedoes and assault craft, and the tanks. But look where you are now. If—"

"Jesus, that's Robber Richardson!" It was Big Al; he had been watching the holo with growing wonder.

Richardson squinted at his display. "I can hardly see anything on this, Wil. Where in perdition are you calling from? And to you, Unseen Sir, it's *Roberto* Richardson."

Big Al walked toward the sunlit porch. He got within an apparent two meters of Richardson before he banged into the conference table. "You're the sort of scum who's responsible for this! You sold the New Mexicans everything they couldn't build themselves: the high-performance aircraft, the military electronics." Al waved at the cabinets in the darkened van. What he claimed was largely true. Wil had noticed the equipment stenciled with Richardson's logo, "USAF Inc—Sellers of Fine Weapon Systems for More than Twenty Years"; the New Mexicans hadn't even bothered to paint it out. Roberto had started out as a minor Aztlán nobleman. He'd been in just the right place at the time of the Bobble War, and had ended up controlling the huge munition dumps left by the old Peace Authority. That had been the beginning of his fortune. Since then, he had moved into the ungoverned lands, and begun manufacturing much of his own equipment. The heavy industry he had brought to Bellevue was almost on the scale of the 20th century—or of modern New Mexico.

Richardson came half out of his chair and chopped at the air in front of him. "See here. I have to take enough such insults from my niece and her grandchildren. I don't have to take them from a stranger." He stood, tossed his display flat on the chair, and walked to the steps that led down to his shaded river.

"Wait, Rober!" shouted Brierson. He waved Big Al back to the depths of the van. "I didn't call to pass on insults. You wondered where I'm calling from. Well, let me tell you—"

By the time he finished, the old gunrunner had returned to his seat. He started to laugh. "I should have guessed you'd end up talking right out of the lion's mouth." His laughter halted abruptly. "But you're trapped, aren't you? No last minute Brierson tricks to get out of this one? I'm sorry, Wil, I really am. If there were anything I could do, I would. I don't forget my debts."

Those were the words Wil had been hoping to hear. "There's nothing you can do for me, Rober. Our bluff in this van is good for just a few minutes, but we could all use a little charity just now."

The other looked nonplussed.

"Look, I'll bet you have plenty of aircraft and armor going through final checkout at the Bellevue plant. And I know you have ammunition stocks. Between MSP and Justice, Inc. and a few other police services, we have enough war buffs to man them. At least we have enough to make these New Mexicans think twice."

But Richardson was shaking his head. "I'm a charitable man, Wil. If I had such things to loan, MSP could have some for the asking. But you see, we've all been a bit outsmarted here. The New Mexicans—and people I now think are fronting for them—have options on the next four months of my production. You see what I mean? It's one thing to help people I like and another to break a contract—especially when reliability has always been one of my most important selling points."

Wil nodded. So much for that brilliant idea.

"And it may turn out for the best, Wil," Richardson continued quietly. "I know your loudmouth friend won't believe this, coming from me, but I think the Midwest might now be best off not to fight. We both know the invasion can't stick, not in the long run. It's just a question of how many lives and how much property is going to be destroyed in the meantime, and how much ill feeling is going to be stored up for the future. Those New Mexicans deserve to get nuked and all the rest, but that could steel them for a holy war, like they've been fighting along the Colorado for so long. On the other hand, if you let them come in and take a whack at 'governing'—why, in twenty years, you'll have them converted into happy anarchists."

Wil smiled in spite of himself. Richardson was certainly the prime example of what he was talking about. Wil knew the old autocrat had originally been an agent of Aztlán, sent to prepare the Northwest for invasion. "Okay, Rober. I'll think about it. Thanks for talking."

Richardson seemed to have guessed Wil's phantom position on his porch. His dark eyes stared intensely into Wil's. "Take care of yourself, Wili."

The cool, northern playground wavered for a second, like a dream of paradise, then vanished, replaced by the hard reality of dark plastic, glimmering displays, and unconscious New Mexicans. *What now, Lieutenant?* Calling Rober had been his only real idea. He could call MSP, but he had nothing helpful to tell them. He leaned on the console, his hands sliding slickly across his sweating face. Why not just do as Rober suggested? Give up and let the force of history take care of things.

No.

First of all, there's no such thing as "the force of history," except as it existed in the determination and imagination of individuals. Government had been a human institution for thousands of years; there was no reason to believe the New Mexicans would fall apart without some application of physical force. Their actions had to be shown to be impractically expensive.

And there was another, more personal reason. Richardson talked as though this invasion were something special, something that transcended commerce and courts and contracts. That was wrong. Except for their power and their self-righteousness, the New Mexicans were no different from some chopper gang marauding MSP customers. And if he and MSP let them take over, it would be just as much a default. As with Rober, reliability was one of MSP's strongest selling points.

So MSP had to keep fighting. The only question was, what could he and Al and Jim do now?

Wil twisted around to look at the exterior view mounted by the hatch. It was a typically crass design flaw that the view was independent of the van's computers and couldn't be displayed except at the doorway.

There wasn't much to see. The division HQ was dispersed, and the van itself sat in the bottom of a ravine. The predominant impression was of smoking foliage and yellow limestone. He heard the keening of light turbines. *Oh boy*. Three overland cars were coming their way. He recognized the sergeant he had talked to a few minutes earlier. If there was anything left to do, he'd better do it now.

He glanced around the van. Strong was a high presidential advisor. Was that worth anything? Wil tried to remember. In Aztlán, with its feudal setup, such a man might be very important. The safety of just a few leaders was the whole purpose of that government. The New Mexicans were different. Their rulers were elected; there were reasonable laws of succession, and people like Strong were probably expendable. Still, there was an idea here: Such a state was something like an enormous corporation, with the citizens as stockholders. The analogy wasn't perfect—no corporation could use the coercion these people practiced on their own. And there were other differences. But still. If the top people in such an enormous organization were threatened, it would be enormously more effective than if, say, the board of directors of MSP were hassled. There were at least 10 police services as powerful as MSP in the ungoverned lands, and many of them subcontracted to smaller firms.

The question, then, was how to get their hands on someone like Hastings Martinez or this General Crick. He punched up an aerial view from somewhere south of the combat area. A train of clouds had spread southeast from the Schwartz farm. Otherwise, the air was faintly hazy. Thunderheads hung at the northern horizon. The sky had that familiar feel to it. Topeka Met Service confirmed the feeling: This was tornado weather.

Brierson grimaced. He had known that all day. And somewhere in the back of his mind, there had been the wild hope that the tornados would pick the right people to land on. Which was absurd: Modern science could kill tornadoes, but no one could direct them. *Modern science can kill tornadoes*. He swallowed. There *was* something he could do—if there was time. One call to headquarters was all he needed.

Outside, there was pounding on the door and shouting. More ominous, he heard a scrabbling noise, and the van swayed slightly on its suspension: someone was climbing onto the roof. Wil ignored the footsteps above him, and asked the satellite link for a connection to MSP. The black and gold Michigan State logo had just appeared when the screen went dead. Wil tapped futilely at emergency codes, then looked at the exterior view again. A hard-faced major was standing next to the van.

Wil turned on the audio and interrupted the other. "We just got sound working here, Major. What's up?"

This stopped the New Mexican, who had been halfway through shouting his message at them. The officer stepped back from the van and continued in more moderate tones. "I was saying there's no fallout problem." Behind him, one of the troopers was quietly barfing into the bushes. There might be no fallout, but unless the major and his men got medical treatment soon, they would be very sick soldiers. "There's no need for you to stay buttoned up."

"Major, we're just about ready to go back on the air. I don't want to take any chances."

"Who am I speaking to?"

"Ed Strong. Special Advisor to the President." Wil spoke the words with the same ponderous importance the real Ed Strong might have used.

"Yes, sir. May I speak with Colonel Alvarez?"

"Alvarez?" Now that was a man the major must know. "Sorry, he got the corner of an equipment cabinet in the head. He hasn't come to yet."

The officer turned and gave the sergeant a sidelong look. The noncom shook his head slightly. "I see." And Wil was afraid that he really did. The major's mouth settled into a thin line. He said something to the noncom, then walked back to the cars.

Wil turned back to the other displays. It was a matter of seconds now. That major was more than suspicious. And without the satellite transmitter, Brierson didn't have a chance of reaching East Lansing or even using the loudmouth channels. The only comm links he had that didn't go through enemy nodes were the local phone bands. He could just reach Topeka Met. They would understand what he was talking about. Even if they wouldn't cooperate, they would surely pass the message back to headquarters. He ran the local directory. A second passed and he was looking at a narrowband black-and-white image. A young, good-looking male sat behind an executive-sized desk. He smiled dazzlingly and said, "Topeka Meteorological Service, Customer Relations. May I help you?"

"I sure hope so. My name's Brierson, Michigan State Police." Wil found the words tumbling out, as if he had been rehearsing this little speech for hours. The idea was simple, but there were some details. When he finished, he noticed the major coming back toward the van. One of his men carried comm gear.

The receptionist at Topeka Met frowned delicately. "Are you one of our customers, sir?"

"No, damn it. Don't you watch the news? You got four hundred tanks coming down Old70 toward Topeka. You're being invaded, man—as in *going out of business!*"

The young man shrugged in a way that indicated he never bothered with the news. "A gang invading Topeka? Sir, we are a *city*, not some farm community. In any case, what you want us to do with our tornado killers is clearly improper. It would be—"

"Listen," Wil interrupted, his voice placating, almost frightened. "At least send this message on to the Michigan State Police. Okay?"

The other smiled the same dazzling, friendly smile that had opened the conversation. "Certainly, sir." And Wil realized he had lost. He was talking to a moron or a low-grade personality simulator; it didn't matter much which. Topeka Met was like a lot of companies—it operated with just enough efficiency to stay in business. Damn the luck.

The voices from the exterior pickup were faint but clear, "—whoever they are, they're transmitting over the local phone bands, sir." It was an enlisted man talking to the New Mexican major. The major nodded and stepped toward the van.

This was it. No time left to think. Wil stabbed blindly at the directory. The Topeka Met Customer Relations "expert" disappeared and the screen began blinking a ring pattern.

"All right, Mr. Strong," the major was shouting again, loudly enough so that he could be heard through the hull of the van as well as over the pickup. The officer held a communications headset. "The President is on this line, sir. He wishes to speak with you—right now." There was a grim smile on the New Mexican's face.

Wil's fingers flick across the control board; the van's exterior mike gave a loud squawk and was silent. With one part of his mind, he heard the enlisted man say, "They're still transmitting, Major."

And then the ring pattern vanished from the phone display. Last chance. Even an auto answerer might be enough. The screen lit up, and Wil found himself staring at a 5-year-old girl.

"Trask residence." She looked a little intimidated by Wil's hulking, scowling image. But she spoke clearly, as one who has been coached in the proper response to strangers. Those serious brown eyes reminded Brierson of his own sister. Bounded by what she knew and what she understood, she would try to do what was right.

It took a great effort to relax his face and smile at the girl. "Hello. Do you know how to record my call, Miss?"

She nodded.

"Would you do that and show it to your parents, please?"

"Okay." She reached offscreen. The recording telltale gleamed at the corner of the flat, and Wil began talking. Fast.

The major's voice came over the external pickup: "Open it up, Sergeant." There were quick footsteps and something slapped against the hatch.

"Wil!" Big Al grabbed his shoulder. "Get down. Away from the hatch. Those are slug-guns they have out there!"

But Brierson couldn't stop now. He pushed Al away, waved for him to get down among the fallen New Mexicans.

The explosion was a sharp cracking sound that rocked the van sideways. The phone connection held, and Wil kept talking. Then the door fell, or was pulled outward, and daylight splashed across him.

"Get away from that phone!"

On the display, the little girl seemed to look past Wil. Her eyes widened. She was the last thing W. W. Brierson saw.

There were dreams. In some he could only see. In others, he was blind, yet hearing and smell were present, all mixed together. And some were pure pain, winding up and up while all around him torturers twisted screws and needles to squeeze the last bit of hurt from his shredded flesh. But he also sensed his parents and sister Beth, quiet and near. And sometimes when he could see and the pain was gone, there were flowers—almost a jungle of them—dipping near his eyes, smelling of violin music.

Snow. Smooth, pristine, as far as his eyes could see. Trees glazed in ice that sparkled against cloudless blue sky. Wil raised his hand to rub his eyes and felt faint surprise to see the hand obey, to feel hand touch face as he willed it.

"Wili, Wili! You're really back!" Someone warm and dark rushed in from the side. Tiny arms laced around his neck. "We knew you'd come back. But it's been so *long*." His 5-year-old sister snuggled her face against him.

As he lowered his arm to pat her head, a technician came around from behind him. "Wait a minute, honey. Just because his eyes are open doesn't mean he's back. We've gotten that far before." Then he saw the grin on Wil's face, and *his* eyes widened a bit. "L-Lieutenant Brierson! Can you understand me?" Wil nodded, and the tech glanced over his head—probably at some diagnostic display. Then he smiled, too. "You do understand me! Just a minute, I'm going to get my supervisor. Don't touch anything." He rushed out of the room, his last words more an unbelieving mumbling to himself than anything else: "I was beginning to wonder if we'd ever get past protocol rejection."

Beth Brierson looked up at her brother. "Are you okay, now, Wili?"

Wil wiggled his toes, and *felt* them wiggle. He certainly felt okay. He nodded. Beth stepped back from the bed. "I want to go get Mom and Dad."

Wil smiled again. "I'll be right here waiting."

Then she was gone, too. Brierson glanced around the room and recognized the locale of several of his nightmares. But it was an ordinary hospital room, perhaps a little heavy on electronics, and still, he was not alone in it. Alvin Swensen, dressed as offensively as ever, sat in the shadows next to the window. Now he stood up and crossed the room to shake hands.

Wil grunted. "My own parents aren't here to greet me, yet Big Al *is*."

"Your bad luck. If you'd had the courtesy to come around the first time they tried to bring you back, you would have had your family and half MSP waiting for you. You were a hero."

"Were?"

"Oh, you still are, Wil. But it's been a while, you know." There was a crooked smile on his face.

Brierson looked through the window at the bright winter's day. The land was familiar. He was back in Michigan, probably at Okemos Central Medical. But Beth didn't look much older. "Around six months, I'd guess."

Big Al nodded. "And, no, I haven't been sitting here every day watching your face for some sign of life. I happened to be in East Lansing today. My Protection Racket still has some insurance claims against your company. MSP paid off all the big items quick, but some of the little things—bullet holes in outbuildings, stuff like that—they're dragging their heels on. Anyway, I thought I'd drop by and see how you're doing."

"Hmm. So you're not saluting the New Mexican flag down there in Manhattan?"

"What? Hell no, we're not!" Then Al seemed to remember who he was talking to. "Look, Wil, in a few minutes you're gonna have the medical staff in here patting themselves on the back for pulling off another medical miracle, and your family will be right on top of that. And after *that*, your Colonel Potts will fill you in again on everything that's happened. Do you really want Al Swensen's Three Minute History of the Great Plains War?"

Wil nodded.

"Okay." Big Al moved his chair close to the bed.

"The New Mexicans pulled back from the ungoverned lands less than three days after they grabbed you and me and Jim Turner. The official Republic view was that the Great Plains Action was a victory for the decisive and restrained use of military force. The 'roving gangster bands' of the ungoverned wastes had been punished for their abuse of New Mexican settlers, and one W. W. Brierson, the ringleader of the northern criminals, had been killed."

"I'm dead?" said Wil.

"Dead enough for their purposes." Big Al seemed momentarily uneasy. "I don't know whether I should tell a sick man how much sicker he once was, but you got hit in the back of the head with a five-millimeter exploder. The Newmex didn't hurt me or Jim, so I don't think it was vengeance. But when they blew in the door, there you were, doing something with their command equipment. They were already hurting, and they didn't have any stun guns, I guess."

A five-millimeter exploder. Wil knew what they could do. He *should* be dead. If it hit near the neck, there might be some forebrain tissue left, but the front of his face would have been blown out. He touched his nose wonderingly.

Al saw the motion. "Don't worry. You're as beautiful as ever. But at the time, you looked *very* dead—even to their best medics. They popped you into stasis. The three of us spent nearly a month in detention in Oklahoma. When we were 'repatriated,' the people at Okemos Central didn't have any trouble growing back the front of your face. Maybe even the New Mexicans could do that. The problem is, you're missing a big chunk of brain. He patted the back of his head. "*That* they couldn't grow back. So they replaced it with processing equipment, and tried to interface that with what was left."

Wil experienced a sudden, chilling moment of in-

trospection. He really should be dead. Could this all
be in the imagination of some damned prosthesis
program?

Al saw his face, and looked stricken. "Honest, Wil,
it wasn't *that* large a piece. Just big enough to fool
those dumbass New Mexicans."

The moment passed and Brierson almost chuckled. If self-awareness were suspect, there could
scarcely be certainty of anything. And in fact, it was
years before that particular terror resurfaced.

"Okay. So the New Mexican incursion was a great
success. Now tell me why they *really* left. Was it
simply the Schwartz bomb?"

"I think that was part of it." Even with the nuke,
the casualties had not been high. Only the troops
and tankers within three or four thousand meters of
the blast were killed—perhaps 2,000 men. This was
enormous by the standards Wil was used to, but not
by the measure of the Water Wars. Overall, the New
Mexicans could claim that it had been an "inexpensive" action.

But the evidence of casual acceptance of nuclear
warfare, all the way down to the level of an ordinary
farmer, was terrifying to the New Mexican brass.
Annexing the Midwest would be like running a grade
school where the kids carried slug guns. They probably didn't realize that Schwartz would have been
lynched the first time he stepped off his property if
his neighbors had realized beforehand that he was
nuke-armed.

"But I think your little phone call was just as
important."

"About using the tornado killers?"

"Yeah. It's one thing to step on a rattlesnake, and
another to suddenly realize you're up to your ankles
in 'em. I bet the weather services have equipped
hundreds of farms with killers—all the way from
Okemos to Greeley." And, as Wil had realized on

that summer day when last he was truly conscious, a tornado killer is essentially an aerial torpedo. Their use was coordinated by the meteorological companies, which paid individual farmers to house them. During severe weather alerts, coordinating processors at a met service headquarters monitored remote sensors, and launched killers from appropriate points in the countryside. Normally, they would be airborne for minutes, but they could loiter for hours. When remote sensing found a twister, the killers came in at the top of the funnel, generated a 50-meter bobble, and destabilized the vortex.

Take that loiter capability, make trivial changes in the flight software, and you have a weapon capable of flying hundreds of kilometers and delivering a one tonne payload with pinpoint accuracy. "Even without nukes they're pretty fearsome. Especially if used like you suggested."

Wil shrugged. Actually, the target he had suggested was the usual one when dealing with marauding gangs. Only the scale was different.

"You know the Trasks—that family you called right at the end? Bill Trask's brother rents space for three killers to Topeka Met. They stole one of them and did just like you said. The news services had spotted Martinez's location; the Trasks flew the killer right into the roof of the mansion he and his staff were using down in Oklahoma. We got satellite pics of what happened. Those New Mexican big shots came storming out of there like ants in a meth fire." Even now, months later, the memory made Big Al laugh. "Bill Trask told me he painted something like 'Hey, hey Hastings, the *next* one is for real!' on the fuselage. I bet even yet, their top people are living under concrete, wondering whether to keep their bobble suppressors up or down.

"But they got the message. Inside of twelve hours, their troops were moving back south and they were starting to talk about their statesmanship and the lesson they had taught us."

Wil started to laugh, too. The room shimmered colorfully in time with his laughter. It was not painful, but it was disconcerting enough to make him stop. "Good. So we didn't need those bums from Topeka Met."

"Right. Fact is, they had me arrest the Trasks for theft. But when they finally got their corporate head out of the dirt, they dropped charges and tried to pretend it had been their idea all along. Now they're modifying their killers and selling the emergency control rights."

Far away (he remembered the long hallways at Okemos Central), he heard voices. And none familiar. *Damn.* The medics were going to get to him before his family. Big Al heard the commotion, too. He stuck his head out the door, then said to Wil, "Well, Lieutenant, this is where I desert. You know the short version, anyway." He walked across the room to pick up his data set.

Wil followed him with his eyes. "So it all ended for the best, except—" *Except for all those poor New Mexican souls caught under a light brighter than any Kansas sun, except for—*"Kiki and Schwartz. I wish they could know how things turned out."

Big Al stopped halfway to the door, a surprised look on his face. "Kiki and Jake? One is too smart to die and the other is too mean! She knew Jake would thump her for bringing the New Mexicans across his land. She and my boys were way underground long before he wiped off. And Jake was dug in even deeper.

"Hell, Wil, they're even bigger celebrities than you are! Old Jake has become the Midwest's pop armadillo. None of us ever guessed, least of all him: he *enjoys* being a public person. He and Kiki have buried the hatchet. Now they're talking about a world-wide club for armadillos. They figure if one can stop an entire nation state, what can a bunch of them do? You know: 'Make the world safe for the ungoverned.' "

Then he was gone. Wil had just a moment to chew on the problems van Steen and Schwartz would cause the Michigan State Police before the triumphant med techs crowded into his room.

How serious am I about the anarcho-capitalism in "The Ungoverned"? It is something I think could really work. In fact, it's the endpoint of many good trends of the last five hundred years. Unlike some, I don't think it could work without a high degree of individual understanding (awareness of where one's long-term self-interest lies), and a generally tranquil atmosphere; events such as those in the story better be the exception. If you are interested in a detailed nonfiction analysis of such ideas, I strongly recommend David Friedman's The Machinery of Freedom. *If you'd like to see my future history before and after the time of "The Ungoverned", there is a prequel novel,* The Peace War, *and a sequel,* Marooned in Realtime—*both available from Baen Books.*

The point I make about nuclear weapons in "The Ungoverned" is more controversial (and hopefully irrelevant). Since 1945, we have lived in fear of proliferation and put what trust we have in nuclear monopolies. The trouble with nuclear monopolies is that while they may prevent nuclear war, if it does happen it will involve the use of thousands of weapons. Heaven forbid that we have such a war, but if it comes, I suspect future historians will not wonder what caused it so much as how it was avoided for so long, in the presence of massive weapon stockpiles and interlocking defense treaties. The most likely postwar scenario is one in which nukes are occasionally used, but never in large numbers—basically because large power blocs are not tolerated by their smaller neighbors. Such a world would be a moderately dangerous place (especially for bullies), but it might be safer than our world. (Henry Kuttner made some of these points in his novel, Mutant. Of all the pre-Hiroshima nuclear sf, his story may be the least remembered—and the most prophetic.) In the long run, of course, even individuals will have enormous destructive power—just another reason why one planet is too small a place for a race to live safely.

By itself, it seems unlikely that war could destroy the race, or even bring a permanent halt to our slide into the Singularity. Yet the universe itself can be a rough place; we have plenty of evidence of mass extinctions. If we had a technology-smashing war plus an extended natural catastrophe, we could join the dinosaurs. And of course, there are natural cataclysms that could destroy not just life, but entire planets. Fortunately, the most extreme stellar catastrophes—supernovas—are impossible for a star like our sun. What about smaller events, burps in the life of otherwise placid stars? We have no surety that our sun is safe from these. What would we do if—in the next fifteen years—we discovered that our sun was about to enter an extended period of increased luminance, frying the surfaces of the inner planets? Given a decade, could we establish a self-sustaining colony in the outer solar system? If not, could we find Earth-like planets elsewhere? At present, sending even the smallest probe to the nearest star is just beyond our ability. Not a single living person could be saved. Whatever we tried would indeed be a—

LONG SHOT

They named her Ilse, and of all Earth's creatures, she was to be the longest lived—and perhaps the last. A prudent tortoise might survive three hundred years and a bristle-cone pine six thousand, but Ilse's designed span exceeded one hundred centuries. And though her brain was iron and germanium doped with arsenic, and her heart was a tiny cloud of hydrogen plasma, Ilse *was*—in the beginning—one of Earth's creatures: she could feel, she could question, and—as she discovered during the dark centuries before her fiery end—she could also forget.

Ilse's earliest memory was a fragment, amounting to less than fifteen seconds. Someone, perhaps inadvertently, brought her to consciousness as she sat atop her S-5N booster. It was night, but their launch was imminent and the booster stood white and silver in the light of a dozen spotlights. Ilse's sharp eye scanned rapidly around the horizon, untroubled by the glare from below. Stretching away from her to the north was a line of thirty launch pads. Several had their own boosters, though none were lit up as Ilse's was. Three thousand meters to the west were

257

more lights, and the occasional sparkle of an automatic rifle. To the east, surf marched in phosphorescent ranks against the Merritt Island shore.

There the fragment ended: she was not conscious during the launch. But that scene remained forever her most vivid and incomprehensible memory.

When next she woke, Ilse was in low Earth orbit. Her single eye had been fitted to a one hundred and fifty centimeter reflecting telescope so that now she could distinguish stars set less than a tenth of a second apart, or, if she looked straight down, count the birds in a flock of geese two hundred kilometers below. For more than a year Ilse remained in this same orbit. She was not idle. Her makers had allotted this period for testing. A small manned station orbited with her, and from it came an endless sequence of radioed instructions and exercises.

Most of the problems were ballistic: hyperbolic encounters, transfer ellipses, and the like. But it was often required that Ilse use her own telescope and spectrometer to discover the parameters of the problems. A typical exercise: determine the orbits of Venus and Mercury; compute a minimum energy flyby of both planets. Another: determine the orbit of Mars; analyze its atmosphere; plan a hyperbolic entry subject to constraints. Many observational problems dealt with Earth: determine atmospheric pressure and composition; perform multispectrum analysis of vegetation. Usually she was required to solve organic analysis problems in less than thirty seconds. And in these last problems, the rules were often changed even while the game was played. Her orientation jets would be caused to malfunction. Critical portions of her mind and senses would be degraded.

One of the first things Ilse learned was that in addition to her private memories, she had a programmed memory, a "library" of procedures and facts. As with most libraries, the programmed memory was not as accessible as Ilse's own recollections, but the information contained there was much more complete and precise. The solution program for almost any ballistic, or chemical, problem could be lifted from this "library," used for seconds, or hours, as an integral part of Ilse's mind, and then returned to the "library." The real trick was to select the proper program on the basis of incomplete information, and then to modify that program to meet various combinations of power and equipment failure. Though she did poorly at first, Ilse eventually surpassed her design specifications. At this point her training stopped and for the first—but not the last—time, Ilse was left to her own devices.

Though she had yet to wonder on her ultimate purpose, still she wanted to see as much of her world as possible. She spent most of each daylight pass looking straight down, trying to see some order in the jumble of blue and green and white. She could easily follow the supply rockets as they climbed up from Merritt Island and Baikonur to rendezvous with her. In the end, more than a hundred of the rockets were floating about her. As the weeks passed, the squat white cylinders were fitted together on a spidery frame.

Now her ten-meter-long body was lost in the webwork of cylinders and girders that stretched out two hundred meters behind her. Her programmed memory told her that the entire assembly massed 22,563.901 tons—more than most ocean-going ships—and a little experimenting with her attitude control jets convinced her that this figure was correct.

Soon her makers connected Ilse's senses to the mammoth's control mechanisms. It was as if she had been given a new body, for she could feel, and see, and use each of the hundred propellant tanks and each of the fifteen fusion reactors that made up the assembly. She realized that now she had the power to perform some of the maneuvers she had planned during her training.

Finally the great moment arrived. Course directions came over the maser link with the manned satellite. Ilse quickly computed the trajectory that would result from these directions. The answer she obtained was correct, but it revealed only the smallest part of what was in store for her.

In her orbit two hundred kilometers up, Ilse coasted smoothly toward high noon over the Pacific. Her eye was pointed forward, so that on the fuzzy blue horizon she could see the edge of the North American continent. Nearer, the granulated cloud cover obscured the ocean itself. The command to begin the burn came from the manned satellite, but Ilse was following the clock herself, and she had determined to take over the launch if any mistakes were made. Two hundred meters behind her, deep in the maze of tanks and beryllium girders, Ilse felt magnetic fields establish themselves, felt hydrogen plasma form, felt fusion commence. Another signal from the station, and propellant flowed around each of ten reactors.

Ilse and her twenty-thousand-ton booster were on their way.

Acceleration rose smoothly to one gravity. Behind her, vidicons on the booster's superstructure showed the Earth shrinking. For half an hour the burn continued, monitored by Ilse, and the manned station now fallen far behind. Then Ilse was alone with her booster, coasting away from Earth and her creators at better than twenty kilometers a second.

So Ilse began her fall toward the sun. For eleven weeks she fell. During this time, there was little to do: monitor the propellants, keep the booster's sunshade properly oriented, relay data to Earth. Compared to much of her later life, however, it was a time of hectic activity.

A fall of eleven weeks toward a body as massive as the sun can result in only one thing: speed. In those last hours, Ilse hurtled downwards at better than two hundred and fifty kilometers per second—an Earth to Moon distance every half hour. Forty-five minutes before her closest approach to the sun—perihelion— Ilse jettisoned the empty first stage and its sunshade. Now she was left with the two-thousand-ton second stage, whose insulation consisted of a bright coat of white paint. She felt the pressure in the propellant tanks begin to rise.

Though her telescope was pointed directly away from the sun, the vidicons on the second stage gave her an awesome view of the solar fireball. She was moving so fast now that the sun's incandescent prominences changed perspective even as she watched.

Seventeen minutes to perihelion. From somewhere beyond the flames, Ilse got the expected maser communication. She pitched herself and her booster over so that she looked along the line of her trajectory. Now her own body was exposed to the direct glare of the sun. Through her telescope she could see luminous tracery within the solar corona. The booster's fuel tanks were perilously close to bursting, and Ilse was having trouble keeping her own body at its proper temperature.

Fifteen minutes to perihelion. The command came from Earth to begin the burn. Ilse considered her own trajectory data, and concluded that the command was thirteen seconds premature. Consultation with Earth would cost at least sixteen minutes, and her decision must be made in the next four seconds. Any of Man's earlier, less sophisticated creations would have accepted the error and taken the mission on to catastrophe, but independence was the essence of Ilse's nature: she overrode the maser command, and delayed ignition till the instant she thought correct.

*   *   *

The sun's northern hemisphere passed below her, less than three solar diameters away.

Ignition, and Ilse was accelerated at nearly two gravities. As she swung toward what was to have been perihelion, her booster lifted her out of elliptic orbit and into a hyperbolic one. Half an hour later she shot out from the sun into the spaces south of the ecliptic at three hundred and twenty kilometers per second—about one solar diameter every hour. The booster's now empty propellant tanks were between her and the sun, and her body slowly cooled.

Shortly after burnout, Earth off-handedly acknowledged the navigation error. This is not to say that Ilse's makers were without contrition for their mistake, or without praise for Ilse. In fact, several men lost what little there remained to confiscate for jeopardizing this mission, and Man's last hope. It was simply that Ilse's makers did not believe that she could appreciate apologies or praise.

Now Ilse fled up out of the solar gravity well. It had taken her eleven weeks to fall from Earth to Sol, but in less than two weeks she had regained this altitude, and still she plunged outwards at more than one hundred kilometers per second. That velocity remained her inheritance from the sun. Without the gravity well maneuver, her booster would have had to be five hundred times as large, or her voyage three times as long. It had been the very best that men could do for her, considering the time remaining to them.

So began the voyage of one hundred centuries. Ilse parted with the empty booster and floated on alone: a squat cylinder, twelve meters wide, five meters long, with a large telescope sticking from one end. Four light-years below her in the well of the night she saw Alpha Centauri, her destination. To the naked human eye, it appears a single bright star, but with her telescope Ilse could clearly see two stars, one slightly fainter and redder than the other. She carefully measured their position and her own, and concluded that her aim had been so perfect that a midcourse correction would not be necessary for a thousand years.

For many months, Earth maintained maser contact—to pose problems and ask after her health. It was almost pathetic, for if anything went wrong now, or in the centuries to follow, there was very little Earth could do to help. The problems were interesting, though. Ilse was asked to chart the nonluminous bodies in the Solar System. She became quite skilled at this and eventually discovered all nine planets, most of their moons, and several asteroids and comets.

In less than two years, Ilse was farther from the sun than any known planet, than any previous terrestrial probe. The sun itself was no more than a very bright star behind her, and Ilse had no trouble keeping her frigid innards at their proper temperature. But now it took sixteen hours to ask a question of Earth and obtain an answer.

A strange thing happened. Over a period of three weeks, the sun became steadily brighter until it gleamed ten times as luminously as before. The change was not really a great one. It was far short of what Earth's astronomers would have called a nova. Nevertheless, Ilse puzzled over the event, in her own way, for many months, since it was at this time that she lost maser contact with Earth. That contact was never regained.

Now Ilse changed herself to meet the empty centuries. As her designers had planned, she split her mind into three coequal entities. Theoretically each of these minds could handle the entire mission alone, but for any important decision, Ilse required the agreement of at least two of the minds. In this fractionated state, Ilse was neither as bright nor as quick-thinking as she had been at launch. But scarcely anything happened in interstellar space, the chief danger being senile decay. Her three minds spent as much time checking each other as they did overseeing the various subsystems.

The one thing they did not regularly check was the programmed memory, since Ilse's designers had—mistakenly—judged that such checks were a greater danger to the memories than the passage of time.

Even with her mentality diminished, and in spite of the caretaker tasks assigned her, Ilse spent much of her time contemplating the universe that spread out forever around her. She discovered binary star systems, then watched the tiny lights swing back and forth around each other as the decades and centuries passed. To her the universe became a moving, almost a living, thing. Several of the nearer stars drifted almost a degree every century, while the great galaxy in Andromeda shifted less than a second of arc in a thousand years.

Occasionally, she turned about to look at Sol. Even ten centuries out she could still distinguish Jupiter and Saturn. These were auspicious observations.

Finally it was time for the mid-course correction. She had spent the preceding century refining her alignment and her navigational observations. The burn was to be only one hundred meters per second, so accurate had been her perihelion impulse. Nevertheless, without that correction she would miss the Centauran system entirely. When the second arrived and her alignment was perfect, Ilse lit her tiny rocket—and discovered that she could obtain at most only three quarters of the rated thrust. She had to make two burns before she was satisfied with the new course.

For the next fifty years, Ilse studied the problem. She tested the rocket's electrical system hundreds of times, and even fired the rocket in microsecond bursts. She never discovered how the centuries had robbed

her, but extrapolating from her observations, Ilse
realized that by the time she entered the Centauran
system, she would have only a thousand meters per
second left in her rocket—less than half its designed
capability. Even so it was possible that, without further complications, she would be able to survey the
planets of both stars in the system.

But before she finished her study of the propulsion
problem, Ilse discovered another breakdown—the
most serious she was to face:

She had forgotten her mission. Over the centuries
the pattern of magnetic fields on her programmed
memory had slowly disappeared—the least used
programs going first. When Ilse recalled those programs to discover how her reduced maneuverability
affected the mission, she discovered that she no longer
had any record of her ultimate purpose. The memories ended with badly faded programs for biochemical reconnaissance and planetary entry, and Ilse guessed
that there was something crucial left to do after a
successful landing on a suitable planet.

Ilse was a patient sort—especially in her cruise
configuration—and she didn't worry about her ultimate purpose, so far away in the future. But she did
do her best to preserve what programs were left. She
played each program into her own memory and then
back to the programmed memory. If the process were
repeated every seventy years, she found that she
could keep the programmed memories from fading.
On the other hand, she had no way of knowing how
many errors this endless repetition was introducing.
For this reason she had each of her subminds perform the process separately, and she frequently
checked the ballistic and astronomical programs by
doing problems with them.

Ilse went further: she studied her own body for
clues as to its purpose. Much of her body was filled
with a substance she must keep within a few degrees

of absolute zero. Several leads disappeared into this mass. Except for her thermometers, however, she had no feeling in this part of her body. Now she raised the temperature in this section a few thousandths of a degree, a change well within design specifications, but large enough for her to sense. Comparing her observations and the section's mass with her chemical analysis programs, Ilse concluded that the mysterious area was a relatively homogeneous body of frozen water, doped with various impurities. It was interesting information, but no matter how she compared it with her memories she could not see any significance to it.

Ilse floated on—and on. The period of time between the midcourse maneuver and the next important event on her schedule was longer than Man's experience with agriculture had been on Earth.

As the centuries passed, the two closely set stars that were her destination became brighter until, a thousand years from Alpha Centauri, she decided to begin her search for planets in the system. Ilse turned her telescope on the brighter of the two stars . . . call it Able. She was still thirty-five thousand times as far from Able—and the smaller star . . . call it Baker—as Earth is from Sol. Even to her sharp eye, Able didn't show as a disk but rather as a diffraction pattern: a round blob of light—many times larger than the star's true disk—surrounded by a ring of light. The faint gleam of any planets would be lost in that diffraction pattern. For five years Ilse watched the pattern, analyzed it with one of her most subtle programs. Occasionally she slid occulting plates into the telescope and studied the resulting, distorted, pattern. After five years she had found suggestive anomalies in the diffraction pattern, but no definite signs of planets.

No matter. Patient Ilse turned her telescope a tiny fraction of a degree, and during the next five years she watched Baker. Then she switched back to Able. Fifteen times Ilse repeated this cycle. While she watched, Baker completed two revolutions about Able, and the stars' maximum mutual separation increased to nearly a tenth of a degree. Finally Ilse was certain: she had discovered a planet orbiting Baker, and perhaps another orbiting Able. Most likely they were both gas giants. No matter: she knew that any small, inner planets would still be lost in the glare of Able and Baker.

There remained less than nine hundred years before she coasted through the Centauran system.

Ilse persisted in her observations. Eventually she could see the gas giants as tiny spots of light—not merely as statistical correlations in her carefully collected diffraction data. Four hundred years out, she decided that the remaining anomalies in Able's diffraction pattern must be another planet, this one at about the same distance from Able as Earth is from Sol. Fifteen years later she made a similar discovery for Baker.

If she were to investigate both of these planets she would have to plan very carefully. According to her design specifications, she had scarcely the maneuvering capability left to investigate one system. But Ilse's navigation system had survived the centuries better than expected, and she estimated that a survey of both planets might still be possible.

Three hundred and fifty years out, Ilse made a relatively large course correction, better than two hundred meters per second. This change was essentially a matter of pacing: it would delay her arrival by four months. Thus she would pass near the planet she wished to investigate and, if no landing were attempted, her path would be precisely bent by Able's gravitational field and she would be cast into Baker's planetary system.

Now Ilse had less than eight hundred meters per

second left in her rocket—less than one percent of her velocity relative to Able and Baker. If she could be at the right place at the right time, that would be enough, but otherwise . . .

Ilse plotted the orbits of the bodies she had detected more and more accurately. Eventually she discovered several more planets: a total of three for Able, and four for Baker. But only her two prime candidates—call them Able II and Baker II—were at the proper distance from their suns.

Eighteen months out, Ilse sighted moons around Able II. This was good news. Now she could accurately determine the planet's mass, and so refine her course even more. Ilse was now less than fifty astronomical units from Able, and eighty from Baker. She had no trouble making spectroscopic observations of the planets. Her prime candidates had plenty of oxygen in their atmospheres—though the farther one, Baker II, seemed deficient in water vapor. On the other hand, Able II had complex carbon compounds in its atmosphere, and its net color was blue green. According to Ilse's damaged memory, these last were desirable features.

The centuries had shrunk to decades, then to years, and finally to days. Ilse was within the orbit of Able's gas giant. Ten million kilometers ahead her target swept along a nearly circular path about its sun, Able. Twenty-seven astronomical units beyond Able gleamed Baker.

But Ilse kept her attention on that target, Able II. Now she could make out its gross continental outlines. She selected a landing site, and performed a two hundred meter per second burn. If she chose to land, she would come down in a greenish, beclouded area.

Twelve hours to contact. Ilse checked each of her subminds one last time. She deleted all malfunctioning circuits, and reassembled herself as a single mind out of what remained. Over the centuries, one third of all her electrical components had failed, so that besides her lost memories, she was not nearly as bright as she had been when launched. Nevertheless, with her subminds combined she was much cleverer than she had been during the cruise. She needed this greater alertness, because in the hours and minutes preceding her encounter with Able II, she would do more analysis and make more decisions than ever before.

One hour to contact. Ilse was within the orbit of her target's outer moon. Ahead loomed the tentative destination, a blue and white crescent two degrees across. Her landing area was around the planet's horizon. No matter. The important task for these last moments was a biochemical survey—at least that's what her surviving programs told her. She scanned the crescent, looking for traces of green through the clouds. She found a large island in a Pacific sized ocean, and began the exquisitely complex analysis necessary to determine the orientation of amino acids. Every fifth second, she took one second to re-estimate the atmospheric densities. The problems seemed even more complicated than her training exercises back in Earth orbit.

Five minutes to contact. She was less than forty thousand kilometers out, and the planet's hazy limb filled her sky. In the next ten seconds she must decide whether or not to land on Able II. Her ten-thousand-year mission was at stake here. For once Ilse landed, she knew that she would never fly again. Without the immense booster that had pushed her out along this journey, she was nothing but a brain and an entry shield and a chunk of frozen water. If she decided to bypass Able II, she must now use a large portion of her remaining propellants to accelerate at right angles to her trajectory. This would cause her to miss the upper edge of the planet's atmosphere, and she would go hurtling out of Able's planetary system. Thirteen months later she would arrive in the vicinity of Baker, perhaps with enough left in her rocket to guide herself into Baker II's atmosphere. But, if that planet should be inhospitable, there would be no turning back: she would have to land there, or else coast on into interstellar darkness.

Ilse weighed the matter for three seconds and concluded that Able II satisfied every criterion she could recall, while Baker II seemed a bit too yellow, a bit too dry.

Ilse turned ninety degrees and jettisoned the small rocket that had given her so much trouble. At the same time she ejected the telescope which had served her so well. She floated indivisible, a white biconvex disk, twelve meters in diameter, fifteen tons in mass.

She turned ninety degrees more to look directly back along her trajectory. There was not much to see now that she had lost her scope, but she recognized the point of light that was Earth's sun and wondered again what had been on all those programs that she had forgotten.

Five seconds. Ilse closed her eye and waited.

Contact began as a barely perceptible acceleration. In less than two seconds that acceleration built to two hundred and fifty gravities. This was beyond Ilse's experience, but she was built to take it: her body contained no moving parts and—except for her fusion reactor—no empty spaces. The really difficult thing was to keep her body from turning edgewise and burning up. Though she didn't know it, Ilse was repeating—on a grand scale—the landing technique that men had used so long ago. But Ilse had to dissipate more than eight hundred times the kinetic energy of any returning Apollo capsule. Her maneuver was correspondingly more dangerous, but since her designers could not equip her with a rocket powerful enough to decelerate her, it was the only option.

Now Ilse used her wits and every dyne in her tiny electric thrusters to arc herself about Able II at the proper attitude and altitude. The acceleration rose steadily toward five hundred gravities, or almost five kilometers per second in velocity lost every second. Beyond that Ilse knew that she would lose consciousness. Just centimeters away from her body the air glowed at fifty thousand degrees. The fireball that surrounded her lit the ocean seventy kilometers below as with daylight.

Four hundred and fifty gravities. She felt a cryostat shatter, and one branch of her brain short through. Still Ilse worked patiently and blindly to keep her body properly oriented. If she had calculated correctly, there were less than five seconds to go now.

She came within sixty kilometers of the surface, then rose steadily back into space. But now her velocity was only seven kilometers per second. The acceleration fell to a mere fifteen gravities, then to zero. She coasted back through a long ellipse to plunge, almost gently, into the depths of Able II's atmosphere.

At twenty thousand meters altitude, Ilse opened her eye and scanned the world below. Her lens had been cracked, and several of her gestalt programs damaged, but she saw green and knew her navigation hadn't been too bad.

It would have been a triumphant moment if only she could have remembered what she was supposed to do *after* she landed.

At ten thousand meters, Ilse popped her paraglider from the hull behind her eye. The tough plastic blossomed out above her, and her fall became a shallow glide. Ilse saw that she was flying over a prairie spotted here and there by forest. It was near sunset and the long shadows cast by trees and hills made it easy for her to gauge the topography.

Two thousand meters. With a glide ratio of one to four, she couldn't expect to fly more than another eight kilometers. Ilse looked ahead, saw a tiny forest, and a stream glinting through the trees. Then she saw a glade just inside the forest, and some vagrant memory told her this was an appropriate spot. She pulled in the paraglider's forward lines and slid more steeply downwards. As she passed three or four meters over the trees surrounding the glade, Ilse pulled in the rear lines, stalled her glider, and fell into the deep, moist grass. Her dun and green paraglider collapsed over her charred body so that she might be mistaken for a large black boulder covered with vegetation.

The voyage that had crossed one hundred centuries and four light-years was ended.

Ilse sat in the gathering twilight and listened. Sound was an undreamed of dimension to her: tiny things burrowing in their holes, the stream gurgling nearby, a faint chirping in the distance. Twilight ended and a shallow fog rose in the dark glade. Ilse knew her voyaging was over. She would never move again. No matter. That had been planned, she was sure. She knew that much of her computing machinery—her mind—had been destroyed in the landing. She would not survive as a conscious being for more than another century or two. No matter.

What did matter was that she knew that her mission was not completed, and that the most important part remained, else the immense gamble her makers had undertaken would finally come to nothing. That possibility was the only thing which could frighten Ilse. It was part of her design.

She reviewed all the programmed memories that had survived the centuries and the planetary entry, but discovered nothing new. She investigated the rest of her body, testing her parts in a thorough, almost destructive, way she never would have dared while still centuries from her destination. She discovered nothing new. Finally she came to that load of ice she had carried so far. With one of her cryostats broken, she couldn't keep it at its proper temperature for more than a few years. She recalled the apparently useless leads that disappeared into that mass. There was only one thing left to try.

Ilse turned down her cryostats, and waited as the temperature within her climbed. The ice near her small fusion reactor warmed first. Somewhere in the frozen mass a tiny piece of metal expanded just far enough to complete a circuit, and Ilse discovered that her makers had taken one last precaution to insure her reliability. At the base of the icy hulk, next to the reactor, they had placed an auxiliary memory unit, and now Ilse had access to it. Her designers had realized that no matter what dangers they imagined, there would be others, and so they had decided to leave this back-up cold and inactive till the very end. And the new memory unit was quite different from her old ones, Ilse vaguely realized. It used optical rather than magnetic storage.

Now Ilse knew what she must do. She warmed a cylindrical tank filled with frozen amniotic fluid to thirty-seven degrees centigrade. From the store next to the cylinder, she injected a single microorganism into the tank. In a few minutes she would begin to suffuse blood through the tank.

It was early morning now and the darkness was moist and cool. Ilse tried to probe her new memory further, but was balked. Apparently the instructions were delivered according to some schedule to avoid unnecessary use of the memory. Ilse reviewed what she had learned, and decided that she would know more in another nine months.

"Long Shot" was many things to me. I wanted the apotheosis of all planetary missions that dominated space exploration in the twentieth century. I wanted to describe the smallest (human) colony mission that could ever be attempted. (In fact, my only authorly reason for "blowing up" the sun was to justify such a screwball attempt.)

That part of the adventure I show is certainly a "long shot," but it's not the most desperate part of the mission. At the end of the story, we know that Ilse is bearing human zygotes. Consider her size: she could contain many zygotes, but nowhere near the mass to bring them all to term. And what will she do with the babies? How to feed them, how to teach them? Surely, humanity did not expect that there was an alien civilization at the target. (Hmm, maybe they did! We only know what Ilse remembers. An alien race would be a copout, but it would make writing a sequel more fun.) Hey, I really do have some ideas about Ilse's future (though this is the true "long shot" behind the title). The unwritten sequel would probably take place about ten years later, and a good title might be "Firstborn Son."

Of course, Ilse is far from being the smallest possible interstellar probe. Early in the 20th-century, Svante Arrhenius suggested that micro-organisms might survive interstellar voyages, spreading some forms of life throughout the universe. Even if spread deliberately, such "probes" would be a slow and limited thing. Since writing "Long Shot," I've seen discussions of directed, useful probes much smaller than Ilse: Robert L. Forward has described an interstellar probe missing just a few grams ("Starwisp,"

Hughes Research Labs Research Report 555, June 1983). Mark Zimmermann has combined that idea with AI to suggest sentient probes in the same mass range. Look around you! Similar travelers may be snugged away in that pebble on the driveway, in that thistledown floating across the yard.

It is humbling to have one's great ideas so easily topped. But it's happening over and over—to everyone. We are in a golden age, and science fiction is in a golden age. To us writers this appears in the form of intense competition, in the existence of so many sharp new writers, telling stories so good it makes you want to cry. Yet few call this a golden age. The reason? Such times are not normally recognized except when bad times follow. If we have good luck and no world catastrophe, the future won't remember this as a "golden age." We'll be thought of fondly, for our awkward attempts to recognize the obvious, to create the Singularity.

Here is an excerpt from Vernor Vinge's new novel, Marooned in Realtime, *coming in June 1987 from Baen Books:*

The town nestled in the foothills of the Indonesian Alps, high enough so that equatorial heat and humidity was moderated to an almost uniform pleasantness. Here the Korolevs and their friends had finally assembled the rescued from all the ages. At the moment the population was less than two hundred, every living human being. They needed more; Yelén Korolev knew where to get one hundred more. She was determined to rescue them.

Steven Fraley, President of the Republic of New Mexico, was determined that those hundred remain unrescued. He was still arguing the case when Wil Brierson arrived. ". . . and you don't appreciate the history of our era, madam. The Peacers came near to exterminating the human race. Sure, saving this group will get you a few more warm bodies, but you risk the survival of our whole colony, of the entire human race, in doing so."

Yelén Korolev looked calm, but Wil knew her well enough to recognize the signs of an impending explosion: there were rosy patches on her cheeks, yet her features were otherwise even paler than usual. She ran a hand through her blond hair. "Mr. Fraley, I really do know the history of your era. Remember that almost all of us—no matter what our present age and experience— have our childhoods within a couple hundred years of one another. The Peace Authority"—her lips twitched in a quick smile at the name—"may have started the general war of 1997. They may even be responsible for the terrible plagues of the early twenty-first century. But as governments go, they were relatively benign. This group in Kampuchea"—she waved toward the north— "went into stasis in 2048, when the Peacers were overthrown. That was before decent health care was available. It's entirely possible that none of the original criminals are present."

Fraley opened and closed his mouth, but no words

came. Finally: "Haven't you heard of their 'Renaissance' scheme? In '48 they were ready to kill by the millions again. Those guys under Kampuchea probably got more hell-bombs than a dog has fleas. That base was their secret ace in the hole. If they hadn't screwed up their stasis, they'd've come out in 2100 and blown us away. And you probably wouldn't even have been born—"

Yelén cut into the torrent. "Hell-bombs? Popguns. Even you know that. Mr. Fraley, getting another hundred people into our colony will make our settlement just big enough to survive. Marta and I haven't spent our lives setting this up just to see it die like the undermanned attempts of the past. The only reason we postponed the founding of Korolev till megayear fifty was so we could rescue those Peacers when their bobble bursts."

She turned to her partner. "Is everybody accounted for?"

Marta Korolev had sat through the argument in silence, her dark features relaxed, her eyes closed. Her headband put her in communication with the estate's autonomous devices. No doubt she had managed a half dozen fliers during the last half hour, scouring the countryside for any truant colonists the Korolev satellites had spotted. Now she opened her eyes. "Everybody's accounted for and safe. In fact"—she caught sight of Wil standing at the back of the amphitheater and grinned—"almost everyone is here on the castle grounds. I think we can provide you people with quite a show this afternoon." She either hadn't followed or—more likely—had chosen to ignore the dispute between Yelén and Fraley.

"Okay, let's get started." A rustle of anticipation passed through the audience. Many were from the twenty-first century, like Wil. But they'd seen enough of the advanced travelers to know that such a statement was more than enough signal for spectacular events to happen.

From his place at the top of the amphitheater, Wil

had a good view to the north. The forests of the higher elevations fell away to a gray-green blur that was the equatorial jungle. Beyond that, haze obscured even the existence of the Inland Sea. Even on the rare, clear day when the sea mists lifted, the Kampuchean Alps were hidden beyond the horizon. Nevertheless, the rescue should be visible; he was a bit surprised that the bluish white of the northern horizon was undisturbed.

"Things will get more exciting, I promise." Yelén's voice brought his eyes back to the stage. Two large displays floated behind her.

"As Mr. Fraley says, the Peacer bobble was supposed to be a secret. It was originally underground. It is much further underground now—somebody blundered. What was to be a fifty-year jump became something . . . longer. As near as we can figure, their bobble should burst sometime in the next few thousand years; they've been in stasis fifty million years. During that time, continents drifted and new rifts formed. Parts of Kampuchea slid deep beneath new mountains." The display behind her lit with a multicolored transect of the Kampuchean Alps. The surface crust appeared as blue, shading into yellow and orange at the greater depths. Right at the margin of orange and magma red was a tiny black disk—the Peacer bobble, afloat against the ceiling of hell.

Inside the bobble, time was stopped. Those within were as they'd been at that instant of a near-forgotten war when the losers decided to escape to the future. No force could affect a bobble's contents; no force could affect its duration—not the heart of a star, not the heart of a lover.

But when the bobble burst, when the stasis ended . . . The Peacers were about forty kilometers down. There would be a moment of noise and heat and pain as the magma swallowed them. One hundred men and women would die, and a certain endangered species would move one more step toward final extinction.

The Korolevs proposed to raise the bobble to the

surface, where it would be safe for the few remaining millennia of its duration. Yelén waved at the display. "This was taken just before we started the operation. Here's the ongoing view."

The picture flickered. The red magma boundary had risen thousands of meters above the bobble. Pinheads of white light flashed in the orange and yellow that represented the solid crust. In the place of each of those lights, red blossomed and spread, almost—Wil winced at the thought—like blood from a stab wound. "Each of those sparkles is a hundred-megaton bomb. In the last few seconds, we've released more energy than all mankind's wars put together."

The red spread as the wounds coalesced into a vast hemorrhage in the bosom of Kampuchea. The magma was still twenty kilometers below ground level. The bombs were timed so there was a constant sparkling just above the highest level of red, bringing the melt closer and closer to the surface. At the bottom of the display, the Peacer bobble floated, serene and untouched. On this scale, its motion towards the surface was imperceptible.

Wil pulled his attention from the display and looked beyond the amphitheater. There was no change: the northern horizon was still haze and pale blue. The rescue site was fifteen hundred kilometers away, but even so, he'd expected something spectacular.

The elapsed-time clock on the display showed almost four minutes. The Korolev pattern of bomb bursts was still thousands of meters short of the surface.

President Fraley rose from his seat. "Madame Korolev, please. There is still time to stop this. I know you've rescued all types, cranks, joyriders, criminals, victims. But these are *monsters*." For once, Wil thought he heard sincerity—perhaps even fear—in the New Mexican's voice. *And he might be right.* If the rumors were true, if the Peacers had created the plagues of the early twenty-first century, then they were responsible for the deaths of billions. If they had succeeded with their Renaissance Project, they would have killed most of the survivors.

Yelén Korolev glanced down at Fraley but didn't reply. The New Mexican stiffened, then waved abruptly to his people. One hundred men and women—most in NM fatigues—came quickly to their feet. It was a dramatic gesture, if nothing else: the amphitheater would be almost empty with them gone.

"Mr. President, I suggest you and the others sit back down." It was Marta Korolev. Her tone was as pleasant as ever, but the insult in the words brought a flush to Steve Fraley's face. He gestured angrily and turned to the stone steps that led from the theater.

The ground shock arrived an instant later.

320 pp. • 65647-3 • $3.50

To order any Baen Book by mail, send the cover price plus 75 cents for first-class postage and handling to: Baen Books, Dept. B, 260 Fifth Avenue, New York, N.Y. 10001.

HE'S OPINIONATED

HE'S DYNAMIC

HE'S LARGER THAN LIFE

MARTIN CAIDIN

Martin Caidin is a bestselling novelist, pilot *extraordinaire*, and expert on America's space program. *He's also a prophet of technological change.* His ability to predict future trends verges on the psychic, as when he wrote *Cyborg* (the novel which became "The Six Million Dollar Man") and *Marooned* (which precipitated the American-Soviet Apollo-Soyuz linkup mission). His tense, action-filled stories are based on personal experience in fields such as astronautics, aviation, oceanography and the military.

Caidin's characters also know their stuff. And they take on real life, because they're based on real people. Martin Caidin spent a stint as a merchant seaman in Europe and Africa, worked for Air Force Intelligence in the U.S. and Asia, and has flown his own planes to many parts of the world. His adventures can be yours in these novels from Baen Books.

— — — — — — — — — — — — — —

EXIT EARTH—Just as the US and the USSR have finally settled their differences, American scientists discover that the solar system is about to pass through a cloud of cosmic dust that will incite the Sun to a paroxysm of fury. All will die. There can be no escape—except, possibly, for a very few. *This is their story.* 656 pp. • 65630-9 • $4.50 _____

KILLER STATION—Earth's first space station *Pleiades* is a scientific boon—until one brief moment of sabotage changes it into a terrible Sword of Damocles. 55996-6 • 384 pp. • $3.50 _____

THE MESSIAH STONE—"An unusual thriller . . . not only in subject matter, but in the fact that the author claims that the basic idea behind the book is real! [THE MESSIAH STONE] concerns the possession of a stone; the person who controls the stone rules the world. The last such person is rumored to be Adolf Hitler. . . . Harrowing adventure and nonstop action."—*Science Fiction Review.* 65562-0 • 416 pp. • $3.95 _____

ZOBOA—It started with the hijacking of four atomic bombs, and ended with the Space Shuttle atop a pillar of fire. . . . "From the marvelous, cinematic opening pages, Caidin sweeps the reader along in a raucous, exciting thriller."—*Publishers Weekly* 65588-4 • 448 pp. • $3.50 _____

To order these Baen Books, check each title selected and return with a check or money order for the combined cover price. Send to Baen Books, 260 Fifth Avenue, New York, N.Y. 10001.

197
ⁿ   1047

Distributed by Simon & Schuster
1230 Avenue of the Americas • New York, N.Y. 10020